SEVEN
BLESSINGS

SEVEN BLESSINGS

Ruchama King

St. Martin's Press ≈ New York

SEVEN BLESSINGS. Copyright © 2003 by Ruchama King. All rights reserved. Printed in the United States of America. No part of this book may be used or reproduced in any manner whatsoever without written permission except in the case of brief quotations embodied in critical articles or reviews. For information, address St. Martin's Press, 175 Fifth Avenue, New York, N.Y. 10010.

www.stmartins.com

Design by Susan Yang

Library of Congress Cataloging-in-Publication Data

King, Ruchama.
    Seven blessings / Ruchama King.—1st ed.
      p. cm.
    ISBN 0-312-30915-5
    1. Jewish women—Fiction.   2. Triangles (Interpersonal relations)—Fiction.   3. Marriage brokerage—Fiction.   4. Orthodox Judaism—Fiction.   5. Jerusalem—Fiction.   I. Title.

PS3611.I585S49 2003
813'.6—dc21

2003040616

First Edition: August 2003

10   9   8   7   6   5   4   3   2   1

For Yisrael

Acknowledgments

Thanks to Emily Benedek, who helped in countless ways, most importantly, by introducing me to my agent. Thanks to my agent, Ann Rittenberg, who believed in this novel and guided me with wisdom and love through the writing of numerous drafts before submitting it to publishers. Thanks to my editor, Jennifer Weis, for her insight, enthusiasm, and beautiful work, and to the excellent staff at St. Martin's. Thanks to the talented and generous writers in our three-year writing group—Joyce, Charlotte, Sarah, Susan, Karen, Patsy, Alice, and Cynthia. Thanks to my friends, whose goodness, deep intelligence, and spiritual strivings have made life more fun and meaningful, and an extra thanks to Yitta Mandelbaum, a true writing cheerleader. Many thanks to the Feuermans, the Kings, and the Brans, my loving family, and to Yisrael Feuerman, my husband and co-creator in many good projects, particularly this last one. Todah to my parents, Bert and Lily, for sending me to Jewish schools and to Israel, and to the gifted Torah teachers and writing teachers I met along the way.

A special thanks to Sherri Mandell for allowing me the use of her poem "Secrets Rachel Gave." May the memory of her son, Kobi—brutally murdered in his thirteenth year by Arab terrorists while out hiking—be a blessing to her and all of klal Yisrael.

Whoever cannot see the hand of God in finding their mate, will never see the hand of God in anything.

—JEWISH PROVERB

PART I

Chapter One

TSIPPI KRAUTHAMMER NOTICED THINGS ABOUT HER CUSTOMERS, but the American woman caught her interest more than the others for a simple reason: Tsippi made matches, arranged blind dates with all kinds of people, and here might be an opportunity to make a shidduch. She gravitated toward the difficult ones, the ones other matchmakers were reluctant to touch, those who had given up hope: a widow with seven young children, men missing parts of their bodies from the wars, a professor who had twenty-seven rabbits in his living room and wouldn't let a single one go. Between weighing the onions and making a clatter on the cash register, she had pulled off more than fifty marriages. And every marriage better than my own, she joked. A woman of forty-eight told her, "I thought I would marry one day, but never—ever—did I expect to feel this happiness, happy like a bride of eighteen." To bring together disparate souls gladdened her. She didn't get paid for her work, though often she received substantial presents: a rug, a ceiling fan for the store, a fancy juice maker. Others got paid a thousand dollars from each party, but she did it for the sake of the mitzvah and the pleasure it brought her.

What she had first noticed about the American woman was her hair. The hair itself was an anomaly in this street of yarmulka, scarf, wig, and black hat wearers. Either she was not religious, Tsippi surmised, or maybe not as pious as the block's Ashkenazi Orthodox residents, or else she was simply not married and had no reason for covering her hair. This American woman—she had to be an American: Who else would pay three times the price for StarKist Tuna instead of opting for the serviceable Israeli brands? And anyway her accent betrayed her—this American brought her moods to the grocery store. Sometimes she walked down the aisles, poking, turning a cereal box in her hands, groping, squinting, yearning for something Tsippi's shelves couldn't deliver; sometimes she seemed annoyed, scowling at an eggplant, shrugging at a tomato; and sometimes her hands moved with a happy efficiency, like the hands of a regular ba'alabusta whose years of list-making had already been absorbed into her very fingertips.

Tsippi tucked a strand of gray hair under her paisley scarf and busied herself ringing up the items of a customer, a young boy with blond-haired peyos wrapped delicately behind his ears. She cut him a hunk of pumpkin squash for his mother's chicken soup, threw in a free bag of chocolate dreidels (leftovers from her Hanukkah stock), and recorded the entire amount in a shiny green notebook. The boy's family paid at the end of the month, though only the Almighty knew how. They always rushed for the two-day-old bread on sale, the rotten bananas nobody else would buy. Lately, things had gotten worse with the recent cuts in food subsidies. Though when it came time for Mr. Weinshtock to pay the bill, he'd crisply lay out the shekels on the counter as if nothing was amiss. Other customers who had more were always wringing their hands and asking for extensions. Not him. She wondered about his wife and how scraping by had affected their marriage. Then she shook her head. What business did she have thinking about other people's marriages? Better to save her speculations for the unwed.

Now this American woman with her bare head of hair (possibly the only uncovered woman over twenty on the block) intrigued her with her dreamy way of walking and her forlorn, slightly aggrieved air. She looked about thirty-five, educated, attractive—well, attractive enough. Tsippi wondered which street she lived on and why she had only begun to come to the store in the last month. Maybe she had just moved to Kinnor Road. There could also be another reason. Lately, a flock of Moroccans, Iraqis and Yemenites had been making their way to her store, along with other assorted Sephardim, and she had finally figured out why. Her store was not far from a small Sephardic courtyard of houses, Harp Court, which for years had its own Makolet grocery store, but recently it had closed down. Perhaps the American woman had come in on that wave, though it hardly seemed possible that she lived there, in the ramshackle Sephardic area, with people who did not seem to be the educated type, though it was unfair to judge. Tsippi had begun stocking more of the spices the Sephardim liked: the cumin and cardamom and turmeric, the hawajj and hilbe. Gradually she would accommodate the Sephardim. But before she went around rearranging her shelves she wanted to know these customers were here to stay.

As for the American woman, she would have to go through her list more carefully to see if anyone sprang to mind. Her sons (all five of them married, thank God, with children of their own) were always asking about her methods, how she decided to put so and so with that one and not another. How could she explain? She liked to juxtapose two people in her mind, imagine them eating a falafel together, or setting a table. If no sparks flashed, she dropped it cold. Still, the hard part wasn't coming up with a match, but executing it, and there was the real secret of making a shidduch: chutzpah, pure nerve. Because many people could come up with good ideas. It annoyed her the way acquaintances would say, "Oh yes, I thought of Yossi and Miriam, too," and she would always restrain herself from asking, "So why didn't you, then?" She knew why. They were frightened. She, Tsippi, normally on the timid side, for some reason was never upset if the parties were insulted (Me with him? Do I look fifty pounds overweight? Do I?) and abused her with their complaints, their How-could-you's, their wounded expressions. She brushed them off and did her work. She had conceived this idea, that she would make matches, after she had been liberated from the camps, at Treblinka. All around her, Jews—the few that remained—were stretched out, dying of Red Cross rations consumed too rapidly, their shriveled stomachs unable to bear the onslaught of nutrition, and a great murderous rage rose up inside her. She would get even with Hitler. She would make matches, shidduchs. Every couple she brought together—saliva in Hitler's stupefied face. Every child born—more dirt and worms on his grave. The best revenge in the world. This was how she had started long ago. And God had blessed her with the chutzpah to make matches that others might only dream of, in a land that had been dreamed into existence less than four decades ago.

"Tzippalah, Tzippalah, whatever are you thinking?"

"Shlomo," she said, almost reproachfully. Her husband had emerged from the little room in the back and had caught her unaware. He knew how to move quietly for a large man. She stared at the reddish tips of his white beard and offered him a small oval plum from a wicker basket on the counter.

"Any new deliveries?" Shlomo asked. He muttered a blessing and ate the plum whole.

Tsippi pointed to the bins in the back of the store. He took out a pen and paper and a small coin, and began to make calculations, sorting through the potatoes and yams and leeks and kumquats, measuring, removing a portion for the poor and other groups. All fresh produce that arrived went through the same tithing ritual. Then he returned to the little room where his chevrutah study partner sat waiting for him in front of an open Talmud. They had been learning

6

together now, almost every day, for over ten years. Before this, Shlomo had been a kosher slaughterer, a shochet, but as he got older he no longer had the stamina for the bloody work, and so she'd opened this Makolet grocery store. In this way, she had enabled Shlomo to study— not just a few hours, but full-time, like a regular yeshiva student.

Throughout the day little bursts of Aramaic pierced the grocery— *ein haki nami, l'afookay, ma chazis dedamach sumak tfey?*—sounds that settled over the fruits and vegetables and canned goods like some exotic spice. She didn't understand a word of Aramaic, but the men's Talmud study nourished her. What they were doing back there was important, and so she felt important and holy, too, even while involved in mundane matters like cleaning out the freezer or balancing the books. She was lucky, luckier than most. Others had far less. Why should she complain?

※ ※ ※

"Can't you stay longer, Bet?" said Zahava, pronouncing her name minus the "th," like most Israelis.

Beth shook her head and saw the young woman's features visibly sag. "Sorry, Zahava. Shabbat's coming and I have to go." She shrugged guiltily toward the sun. Actually, it was a fat three hours until sunset, and she could've spared an extra twenty minutes, but she didn't feel up to it. The psychiatric ward, with its cloying over-medicated smell, gave her a headache where once the place had charmed. She had been volunteering for a year now at the psychiatric ward of Healer of the Broken Souls Institute. At first she'd been entranced by the magical-schizophrenic utterances of Zahava, the disturbed woman she regularly visited. The first time she met a patient who thought she was a Biblical prophetess, Beth couldn't get enough details. But the place was filled with such characters. Eventually the Deborahs and Miriams, the Ezekiel wannabes, all lost their shock and entertainment value (for unwittingly, she acknowledged, she had

7

turned the patients into entertainment) and became just everyday emotionally-disturbed persons in need of care. And she did care, particularly about Zahava. But she had to pace herself or she'd sap out completely. Beth slung her batik knapsack across her shoulders and began the walk home.

The stretch along Kveesh Darom extended for three miles and should've been considered the most morbid in Jerusalem. At the farthest end was a prison buried in the trees of the Jerusalem Forest, then a rifle range, followed by the geriatric-psychiatric institution where she volunteered, and then as the road curved closer to the residential blocks, a tombstone factory. But Beth paid no attention to these grim landmarks. Her walk home took fifteen minutes and she enjoyed every moment of it. Few cars came this way and even fewer buses. The sky, even now in the post-Hanukkah rainy season, had its days of vivid, optimistic blue. When the day gave forth clouds, they piled on dramatically in gigantic swirls. Olive and acacia and fig and carob trees grew on one side of the winding road, giving way to a downward sloping hill dotted with occasional boulders.

Down below, the Jerusalem Forest stretched on, an endless wave of evergreens. Israel was strange that way. In the summertime trees drooped, and now in the winter they came to life, helped on, no doubt, by the five months of rain. On the other side of the road, a hill rose sharply and became a more sedate, manicured forest, its prickly eucalyptus trees steepling into the sky.

Just past the tombstone factory, Beth wound her way down a thin dirt path and settled under her favorite tree. She pulled out an Egozi chocolate candy bar, her reward for her good deed at Broken Souls, and drank a can of mango soda, also a treat, resting the items on a flat-topped boulder. Good ole Jerusalem Forest. She could always count on the forest to restore her and, lately, she was in sore need of it. The past year she'd been undergoing a crisis of faith. Not enough to abandon the

8

mitzvahs or her way of life, but enough so that she'd stopped attending Torah classes at a women's yeshiva where she'd been a part-time student. A skepticism had seized her. Verses and sections that had made sense now mystified or even outraged her—animal sacrifices, the laws about Canaanite slaves, that disturbing verse: "an eye for an eye, a tooth for a tooth." It got to be she couldn't pick up a Bible. She might've asked a rabbi or teacher to help her interpret these verses, but she never could bring herself to approach anyone. It was like sharing her mess, opening up the fridge for the world to see the spilled juice, the rotting, moldy food. So she had settled into a chronic religious anxiety while staying connected by whatever means—more meticulous observance of the laws, increased prayer—until, she hoped, she would feel differently. Prayer had always been something of a struggle for her, but here in the Jerusalem Forest, talking to God came more easily. The Hassidic masters said a person should pray to God like a child pestering his mother or father. The forest was the place she pestered God—for clarity, for direction, for some Divine attention.

The forest was also mildly dangerous. Sometimes a boulder from the tombstone factory came lurching down the mountain. Sometimes strange men wandered through. Once, on Lag B'Omer National Picnic Day, she'd settled herself into an isolated campsite with lunch and a booklet, *Outpouring of the Soul*. In the distance she saw a small truck full of Arab workers coming at her, screaming, rakes and axes jutting out through the open windows. They'll pass by, she thought, clutching her booklet, they're headed somewhere else, but the truck came to a dusty screech ten feet away from her. Still screaming and shouting, they took their rakes and stamped out a still-smoking fire that had been left by the previous picnickers. Just as quickly, they piled back into the truck and left. Beth still hadn't moved from her spot. It occurred to her then that the Arab workers had saved her life and prevented a massive forest fire. But what if the truck had carried a bunch of rapists or escaped convicts or terrorists? She was defenseless in the forest. Anything could happen. She continued to come anyway, but sometimes she'd carry a big rock she happened to find along the way as protection.

She crumpled her candy bar wrapper into her purse, wiped her fingers and recited a Psalm, "I Lift My Eyes Unto the Mountains." She couldn't linger, though. The sun had dropped lower. Shabbat was coming.

She entered Kinnor Road, the black-hat rigorously Orthodox block consisting mostly of Jews of Eastern European Ashkenazi origin, and then made a sharp right up the hill on Levites Street. Another right into Harp Court, with its red-tiled slanting roofs, the Sephardic enclave—home to Jews from Iraq and Morocco and Yemen and Algeria. On the other side of Levites Street loomed "Beit Morris," the huge American apartment complex built of Jerusalem stone, named after a philanthropist from Florida who'd donated money for the playground. That's what she liked about Israel. She'd only walked three blocks, and here she was, traversing civilizations. She was the lone American who lived in Harp Court, which was fine with her. She hadn't traveled six thousand miles from Pittsburgh just to be with Americans. Still, she liked having her compatriots fairly close by, on the other side of Levites Street.

At home—the upper floor of a three-story cement building—she lit two candles on the small round table she'd covered with lace just as the Shabbat alarm sounded through the streets, wailing like an air raid siren. She recited the blessing, and then climbed down the stairs to the ground floor. All around her, men and women were emerging from cement houses surrounded by low stone walls or chicken wire fences laced with grapevines and ivy, everyone walking toward the tiny synagogue.

"Shabbat Shalom, Bet," a woman called out to her. Beth turned to see her neighbor, Estrella Abutbul, waving from her overgrown front yard, sunflower plants mounted and splayed out on wood posts like exhausted scarecrows. Estrella was plump and Moroccan, in her mid-thirties, with a kerchief on her head and ten thin gold bracelets on either arm. "You'll come tonight?" she asked as she opened a metal gate and walked toward her.

Beth shook her head with an air of regret and pointed across the street at Beit Morris. "I'm eating at the Bartosky's."

"Weelie, weelie." Estrella shook her arm and the bracelets made a pleasant jingle. Beth had learned that "weelie weelie" was the Sephardic equivalent of "oy vey." "Why do you always go to those vooz-voozim?"

Beth shrugged. "I'm a vooz-vooz, too, you know." Her grandparents came from Poland, so technically she was an Ashkenazi.

"Yes, but you're different. You have a neshama, a soul. Those Ashkenazim walk around"—Estrella pressed her knees together and took a few penguin-like steps, side-stepping a cranky, arthritic rooster that had escaped someone's yard—"they walk like they're constipated. They don't know how to sing, not like we do."

Beth looked skyward, squinting slightly, unsure how to respond. She knew the Sephardim hardly considered her one of them, but were complimented by her living and praying with them. Still, she didn't eat with them. She would have liked to, but she didn't know who kept kosher—who *really* kept kosher, because they all professed to. Beth believed them, but what if someone was making a chicken soup and lifted the pot cover and steam drops fell into a cup of hot chocolate? Would the cook recognize that it was a problem, know that it was necessary to ask a rabbi? And what about the families with less religious grown sons and daughters who brought all kinds of food into the home from their own kitchens? These questions were delicate, ones she wouldn't dream of asking for fear of offending. So sometimes she'd accept an invitation for tea and cake on obscure fast days, and then once she arrived she'd clop the side of her head and say, "Oh dear. It's the Fast of Gedaliah." Actually, Estrella herself kept a high kosher standard, more meticulous than most people in the courtyard, but it wouldn't do to start going to anyone's house too often. It was sure to be noticed. Jealousy would be aroused.

Beth kissed the ceramic mezuzah on the doorpost as she entered the synagogue. Inside, maroon and burnt sienna carpets hung from the walls, and a large window faced a grassy cliff that looked out on the Judean hills. A gauzy curtain fluttered between the men's and women's sections. Instead of chairs, a gold velvet cushioned seat curved around the small, rectangular room for women. There was enough space for everyone, but the arrangement meant that the women faced each other while they prayed and so could not avoid looking and being looked at, a slightly uncomfortable sensation for Beth. She made herself stare at a small picture of a hamsa hand just above one of the women's heads, the hand that warded off the evil eye. Each finger was crammed full of Kabbalistic lore written in Aramaic. She didn't believe in the evil eye, certainly not like the Sephardim, but the drawing compelled her.

Someone on the men's side took up the first chapter in Song of Songs. "I am to my beloved, and my beloved is mine." The man recited one verse, and everyone responded with the second verse in a singing, pounding chant. The instant the man finished his chapter, another voice took over the following chapter: "I am the rose of Sharon, and the lily of the valleys." A second's lull, and a young Bar Mitzvah boy's voice seized the next chapter: "By night on my bed I sought him whom my soul loveth: I sought him but I found him not." Then came a gravelly older voice. Beth wondered how they knew who would say which chapter when. Was it prearranged by the rabbi? Was it like an auction with secret signals? No one pointed or said, "It's my turn," but the beautiful verses of Song of Songs went on without missing a beat, sweeping the congregants up in its rhythm. Beth imagined this was what it was like in the original temple, the Beit Hamikdash, where prayer was tuneful, truly communal, visceral, sung from the feet and not just the head.

Then Rabbi Bar-Chaim, a short, dark, thick-necked man, ushered everyone outside to the grassy plain on the edge of the cliff. The men stood on one side of a pomegranate tree dressed in their army-issue parkas and open white shirts and gold necklaces, the women on the other side with their bangles and kerchiefs and braided hair hanging down their backs. The pomegranate tree only partly obscured a small junkyard which had recently sprung up. There were a few such impromptu junkyards in Harp Court, where wild cats roamed and children tinkered, but on Shabbat Beth trained her eye to look past, to notice only the good. The singing began: "Come, my beloved Queen, *Lecha Dodi Likrat Kalla.*" With their heads bowed, the people looked intently into siddurs even though they knew the words by heart. The sun was going down in orange clouds and Beth's eyes stung at the corners, as they always did when she reached the Lecha Dodi part. Her father, may he rest in peace, used to say, "A good Lecha Dodi makes my week," and that was why Beth came here to pray. This was how the holy Arizal, the Kabbalist, used to greet the Shabbat, outside in the darkening fields, not like an uptight Ashkenazi locked up inside a shul. She knew, as she stood there, curtsying to the Shabbat Queen, welcoming the extra soul that was descending and entering her that very moment, that the Sephardim had something pure and joyous that their Ashkenazi counterparts would never have.

After the services, Rabbi Bar-Chaim began to speak and Beth closed her eyes. "And the children died in the bus accident . . . Do you know why? Because their parents were Shabbat desecraters, going to the movies on Friday night. Right next to the movie theater, that's where it happened. But the 'free ones,' do you think they will see God's hand?" He paused, heavily, and threw his arms up. "The truth, they refuse to accept." She peered at her fellow worshipers, wondering why his words failed to outrage them, given that many of their own sons and daughters went to the movies on Shabbat if they could, and certainly to the beach. Some of the parents went, too. They listened, some gravely, some raptly, nodding vigorously, others with their heads tilted backward from a certain philosophic distance. But no one's attitude reflected offense at the rabbi's moral crudeness. She found herself in this position often—wincing, cringing at the remarks of rabbis, particularly those in public positions. Why was it that back in Pittsburgh she hardly ever found herself embarrassed by the doings and sayings of rabbis, but here so many in the Rabbinate came across as buffoons? Well, this was the way of the land. After years spent polishing their phrases and explaining their religion so that the foreign powers would tolerate their presence, the religious Jews had tired of living apologetically. Now in their own land, they reveled in "telling it like it is," with no sense of how their words might be received or even how accurate they were. Beth liked the absence of the "observing eye," that what-will-the-goyim-think that accompanied a Jew everywhere in exile, but she also missed some of the discretion and good sense that came with exile.

As she walked toward the Bartosky's she tried to recapture the prayerful glow of the Lecha Dodi. She hummed a stanza, clasped her leatherbound siddur to her heart and walked slowly toward Harp Court.

On Levites Street, three dark-skinned men stood leaning against a bus shelter eating pumpkin seeds. One held a brown bottle in his hand. The second violently spat a stream of chewed up shells to the sidewalk.

The third, thin-lipped, with a long jaw, gave Beth a mocking smile, his eyes darkening. He placed himself directly in her path. "If only you and I could pray together"—he dropped his voice to a sultry whisper—"just the two of us!"

She walked by, putting on her grow-up-will-you look, the one she used on her boss when he was being particularly obnoxious and juvenile. Still, she couldn't help thinking what a holy country it was. Even the pick-up lines reflected God.

⸙　⸙　⸙

"More kugel, Beth?" Judy Bartosky gestured toward the tea cart, indicating the side dishes, condiments and drinks.

"Yes, thanks." Beth unloosened a hefty wedge of apple cinnamon kugel onto her plate. Judy watched her eat with faint dismay. When she'd met Beth five years ago at the bus stop on Levites Street, she had thought her slim and good-looking, even though she dressed indifferently. She was still a nice-looking woman, but Judy couldn't help noticing that her hips had expanded with the years, growing broader and more practical. And, unfortunately, Beth had adopted the Israeli "zarook" style, the thrown-together look, with shirts never tucked into skirts, flat, horsey comfort shoes, and hair caught up in a ponytail or thrown to the side. Judy had tried once or twice to make suggestions about her appearance and had even offered to lend her a dress for some of the dates she'd tried to arrange, but Beth had reacted with a surprising vehemence. The subject was just too touchy and Judy left it alone.

"Some people may be dropping by for coffee and cake," Judy said to Beth at the end of the meal. "Remember that artist I mentioned to you that lives in the complex—Binyamin Harris? He's not your type but he's fun to talk to, always has lots of tricks up his sleeve. Why don't you stay?"

"Can't, Judy. I promised a neighbor—" she motioned vaguely toward the street. "Another time."

Later in bed, Judy mentally reviewed the meal, trying to find the source of her vague dissatisfaction. Her children had behaved themselves, and knew the answers on the Torah sheet their father quizzed them on; the food had turned out well, and her conversation with Beth had been engaging. As usual Beth had played the role of the drawer-outer, the elicitor of old memories, and had Judy and her husband talking about the old days when he had been the rabbi in Minneapolis and she the Rebbetzin. She had been a well-known town figure in those days, and people came to her with their questions, their histories, their deference. She was busy, truly useful, and had more than enough status. Everyone had wanted a piece of her then. Later, when they had emigrated to Israel and her husband had taken a job fumigating cockroaches—which he'd developed into a fairly successful extermination business—she had lost her official title of Rebbetzin. Some people still called her Rebbetzin—mostly the people she set up on dates, but she'd correct them—Mrs. Bartosky is just fine, she told the young men. As for the women, she didn't mind a little first-name familiarity. "Call me Judy." How long could she wear a title that no longer fit?

Here in Jerusalem, she was just a regular nice lady from the Beit Morris complex who made matches in her spare time. She didn't stand out at all. But Jerusalem offered other compensations: children. The first time she'd visited Israel on her junior year abroad, that's what she had noticed. Jerusalem children had a certain wholesome quality. The children played outside, constantly, in droves. They hiked. Boys and girls alike, they knew the names of plants, shrubs, trees and especially flowers. It was a national thing. She'd watch them playing "Levaya," bellowing out upcoming funerals from their tricycles just as they'd heard the Chevra Kadisha burial society call out on megaphones from their cars. She'd seen four-year-olds talk politics to storekeepers with more assurance than her seventeen-year-old niece had. These children walked tall with their Jewishness, blessings said loudly, not mumbled under the breath at the library or masked with a hand over the mouth, no embarrassed explanation to the neighbors about why they were dressed up as clowns and princesses in March for Purim instead of Halloween. She had wanted that pride and naturalness for her own future children, and when she had met Dovid in her last year of college, part of her attraction to him was that he wanted Israel, too.

She turned to Dovid, who had not yet recited the bedtime Shma prayer, which meant conversation was still an option. "Does Beth look all right to you?"

"She looks fine." Dovid scratched the armpit of his whale-print pajamas and yawned. She'd bought him the pajamas on a lark and he loved wearing them, though he did look a bit foolish.

"Doesn't she seem to be gaining weight?"

"Not that I noticed. It's possible. Women tend to spread after a while, you know." He shot his wife a sidelong glance. "Look at you," he said, a mocking gleam in his eye. His hand swept the length of her body.

"Hah." The jibe didn't even merit a response. Her body had held up nicely through the years and the child-bearing. Not that she didn't work at it. Judy lapsed into thought for a moment, then said, "I wish she'd try harder. Just how many years of child-bearing does she think she has left? She mentioned once that her father died when she was thirty. And she told me just the other day that the last time she'd even been touched by a man was nine years ago, by her father. That makes her thirty-nine." She shuddered. "How awful."

Dovid leaned on an elbow. "What's awful, her age or not being touched?"

"Both!" She sat up in bed, pulling her knees close. "Can you imagine, a virgin at thirty-nine? Sometimes I just want to shake her."

Dovid's head hit the pillow with a whoosh. "Leave Beth alone, already. Everyone has their own destiny. She'll find her way, trust me."

"I feel bad for her. She's an orphan. Her mother's dead, too, you know."

"Come on, Judy. She doesn't need you to feel sorry for her. Think of something better to do with your time."

Judy frowned, and suddenly realized what had been missing from the table, the source of her irritation. "By the way, you didn't say a dvar Torah tonight," she told her husband. Actually, now that she thought about it, he hadn't offered an inspiring Torah thought for the past few Shabbats. It always left her flat when he failed to say one at the Shabbat table. A dvar Torah lifted up a meal to a higher status, conferring a glow of rabbinic royalty, not only on the one who spoke it but on the ones who listened, on the food, the silverware and dishes. Just because Dovid was no longer a rabbi in name didn't mean they had to backslide.

"I forgot," he said shortly.

This was a sore point, she knew. He hardly had the time he once had to devote to Torah study. At one point he'd fallen into a small depression over it, until he'd been able to adjust his expectations. "Why don't you come up with the dvar Torah tomorrow?" Dovid said sleepily from his bed.

"Me?" She was startled. "What could I have to say?"

"Something . . . I hope," she heard from under his quilt.

Judy glared at him as she reached for the plastic-coated Shma prayer on her night table, but his head was already submerged.

Chapter Two

TSIPPI WAS GOING OVER THE MONTH'S STOCK WHEN A SEPHARDIC gentleman came into the Makolet. As she rang up his pack of Europa, he commented on the orderly way she stocked her shelves. Then he said, "Do you know, whenever I walk in, I notice the good smell here. As soon as I walk in"—his eyes closed and he inhaled deeply—"I can smell the bread smell, and the cheese and the olives and the milk smell." His fingers fluttered under his nose, his eyes still shut, brows cast upward in an attitude of ecstasy. "And the fruit, too," he said, his eyes opening.

Yes, there was a good Makolet smell here, she thought, and per-haps that was why she was always glad to enter and do her work, this, despite the Makolet being dark, practically a dug-out, and not exactly spacious. "Do you smell the spices?" she asked, just to be sociable. "I've been stocking cardamom, hilbe and hawajj, and some others."

"You like those spices?" A look of delight seized his face. "Then let me tell you my mother's recipe for Iraqi chameen." He immediately launched into long, complicated instructions ("first make pockets out of the chicken, and don't forget a needle and thread after you stuff it"), while she sat on a stool, looking at his hands. They moved up, down, sideways, carving jagged lines and figure-eights in the air, opening and shutting, insinuating multiple shades of feeling. And all this for an Iraqi cholent recipe! As she discreetly moved aside a glass candy jar on the counter that he almost knocked over, it dawned on her that the man was bantering with her. Some might even say flirting. Yes, flirting! And she almost seventy years old, with a dynasty of grandchildren. She hardly knew what to say, that's how disturbed she felt. Such talk wasn't proper or modest and she wanted no part of it. And yet it wasn't inconceivable that he should speak this way to her, was it? She looked well, she knew: her spine was straight, her eyes clear with none of the milkiness of age, and her neck didn't hang in folds or jiggle when she shook her head. It wasn't so outrageous, then. Still, it never would've occurred to her husband to flirt with her. Her sisters envied the quiet sweetness of her life with Shlomo. People were amazed how they never fought. But privately there was a dryness between them. The first year of her marriage, she had prayed for her husband to be more romantic. She supposed God had answered her, "No, it wasn't meant to be. Accept this." And so she had. And she went on to have a very good life with him. As she sat at the register, listening and smiling, pretending to file away the information for a future cholent, she became conscious of voices from the back of the store, her husband's pleasantly even-pitched, mingling with his chevrutah's voice, his study partner's lower and harder, like stones knocking against each other. The sounds, even though she understood nothing, helped her remember herself and her place. She was a wife enabling her husband to study Torah. She did not engage in banter with men. She stood. "Here's your change," she told the Sephardic customer. "Have a nice day." Her no-nonsense look effectively dismissed him. She had work to do.

She was reviewing the overdue accounts in her green notebook when the American woman walked in. Today the American seemed to know what she wanted and selected her vegetables, yeast and yogurts without much deliberation. Then she brought them up and pointed to the eggs behind the counter.

"Why so little food?" Tsippi said conversationally as she gathered the items.

The woman held out her palms. "It's just me." She added, "I'm not married."

"Ah." Tsippi gazed meditatively at her hairline. Unwedded, uncovered, just like she had thought. Tsippi placed six beige speckled eggs into the woman's open egg tray and snapped the tray shut. "Why not?"

"Why not?" The woman moistened her lips. "I never really thought about it."

Oh, of course. Tsippi rolled her eyes. Never thought about it. She packed the groceries into the woman's crocheted shopping bag. Something homespun about the bag made her stop and warm a certain idea in her thoughts. "And what if I were to suggest someone to you?"

The woman blinked. "Well I—" She shrugged. "I hardly know you." She twiddled with the zipper of her sweater jacket, gray and unraveled at the elbows and cuffs.

"What's your name?" Tsippi asked quickly.

"Beth. Beth Wilner."

"Bet?"

The woman nodded.

"Bet," she repeated. "Bet means a house in Hebrew, you know. A home. Everyone should have one. A good sign. Well, now." She folded her arms and looked intently at her. "Would you like to hear about him?"

"Thanks for your interest, but," she cleared her throat, "forgive me, you know nothing about me except the food I buy."

Tsippi propped her elbows on the counter. "Ah, but that's plenty. I see you buy simple, healthy foods, okay," she acceded, "maybe only now and then a candy bar. You choose with care. You don't push in

21

lines. You don't start up with the others, but I like how you have a pleasant thing to say if someone talks first to you. You are kind, you have restraint, dignity. These are good qualities." She leaned her head toward Beth's. "The man I am thinking of, he has these qualities, too."

"I'm a virtual stranger," she said.

"So what? I am a shadchan, an experienced matchmaker. That makes me no stranger. Lots of people use a matchmaker in Jerusalem. And not just the religious. Why, even in Tel-Aviv some of the secular will go to a matchmaker. How long are you in this country?"

"Five years."

"So you should know. The Sages said, 'What is God doing all day? Making shidduchs.' "

"Certainly that's not meant literally, that God's making matches all day?" The American gave her a quizzical look. "Anyway, you couldn't possibly know what I need."

"Ah, but you are making a very big mistake." Tsippi pushed up her sleeves, now in full chutzpah gear. "You think coming up with a shidduch is a logical matter—a person decides with her own head, this one goes with that one—but you are wrong. Is this shidduch really coming from me, a simple grocer woman? No—it's from God, and I am just the agent that brings it about. Now, how can you say no to what God has in mind for you?"

Beth picked up a pencil and tapped it against the counter. "Okay, okay. So who is he already?"

His name was Akiva. He was forty-one. A ba'al teshuva, a relative newcomer to Torah practices. He studied Talmud in a yeshiva academy for men and worked as a house painter part-time. He had lived in Scotland for a few years. He had a twitch. He was originally from Canada. He went to—

"A twitch?" Beth said. "Do you mean an eye tic?" She had been doodling on a scrap of paper, drawing a picture of a globe twirling on a fingertip, and she stopped.

"No, it's not an eye tic," Tsippi said slowly. "It's hard to describe."

The American was silent. She looked at her fingernails, then down at her shoes. Tsippi saw her lips moving slightly as she mulled it over. Tsippi felt for her. How was this woman to know if it was a worthwhile venture or a hoax, a waste of time? How much stock to put in a stranger's words (for that's what she was in the end)? How much was an older single woman supposed to lead her life based on a string of This-Could-Be-the-Ones, and You-Never-Can-Tells, when years of experience let her know it never was the one, and most often, you definitely could tell. Tsippi shut her eyes and beamed a command in the woman's direction: Say Yes.

Suddenly a staccato of Aramaic burst from the back of the store—*tav lemeisiv tan du maylemeisiv armaloo.* Tsippi's hand jumped, and the candy jar almost toppled. There they were again, discussing, disagreeing, arguing, again and again. She suddenly wondered what it might be like to be in a passionate argument with her husband.

Finally Beth raised her head. She said slowly, "Once I went out with a guy who supposedly had a limp, and I hardly noticed."

"This you'll notice," said Tsippi in a sobering voice. She didn't believe in being unnecessarily explicit. Nor did she believe in misrepresentation.

Beth's face became shot with alarm. Then her face relaxed and resigned itself to some inner decision. "All right," she said. "I'll meet him." She held her bag of food close to her chest. "But I believe in reciprocity. I'd like to introduce you to someone, if I may."

Now Tsippi took a step back. She touched her collarbone. "Me? I'm married."

Beth shook her head. "There's a blind woman I just heard about from my work. She's—"

"Excuse me, where do you work?"

"At the Hebrew Institute for the Prevention of Blindness. I'm a bookkeeper," she added, probably sensing the question was soon forthcoming. "This woman, she's just a few minutes away at the geriatric institute farther down the road. She needs someone to come in and read the Bible to her. It's the one thing she loves to do, studying the Torah. She has no one, apparently. Would you do it?"

Would she? Well, she had always enjoyed studying the Five Books of the Torah. When her sons were younger she had helped them with their Bible studies, and they had done very well under her instruction. She had a knack for it. But then the boys had graduated to studying Mishna and Talmud, and hardly ever looked back at the Bible. She pondered this as she watched Yehudah, the chevrutah, emerge from the back to make a phone call. He was always there—a fact on the ground, that's what she called him. He spent more time with Shlomo than she, even coming regularly to their home after dinner to study together. One night she had shooed Yehudah from the apartment an hour early, so as to have time alone with Shlomo. But what was the point when he'd just spent the evening reading a book? And speaking of time, did she really have extra hours to help this old woman?

"Let me think about it," Tsippi began to say out loud, but the steely look in Beth's eyes made her stammer and say, "Well, why not? It's a good deed, a mitzvah, I suppose."

Goodness! Tsippi thought as she heard the door shut behind the American woman. Apparently she was not the only woman in the world blessed with chutzpah.

⁂ ⁂ ⁂

From his plush maroon chair in the King Solomon Hotel lobby, Binyamin Harris watched another drop of water fall from the ceiling into a plastic bucket. The hotel's swimming pool, one floor above, had sprung a tiny leak, or so a waiter had told him the last time Binyamin had brought a blind date to that lobby. It had been ages since he'd last gone to this hotel lobby, and still the hole hadn't been fixed. Hotel lobbies were not his favorite place to meet, but that's how it was done in Jerusalem yeshiva-type circles, the waiters and waitresses substituting as discreet chaperons. Tonight another prospect sat before him, a woman the matchmaker had promised he wouldn't regret meeting—those were Mrs. Bartosky's actual words, and she was almost always to be taken at her word.

The first time Binyamin had been brought over to the matchmaker's home for an interview, he had expected a caricature—a double-chinned bubbe surrounded by immense pots of chicken soup, gurgling with homey advice and horrific dates, but Mrs. Bartosky had surprised him. She was a beautiful woman, even with every hair piously covered. He spent many Shabbats at the Bartosky home which she ran efficiently and gracefully. He had assumed there would be other religious women like herself in Jerusalem, but had been frustrated time and again. Still, he wasn't complaining. Jerusalem had been good to him on many counts, from the moment he had decided to make Israel his home three years ago. First he had discovered Judaism and become Torah observant, which had enhanced his life immeasurably. Then he'd found a cheap studio apartment just a block away from a little Sephardic enclave, Harp Court, where he was surrounded by the lushest trees and mountains and Biblical vistas an artist could hope for. Then, amazingly, his work had taken off as it never had before, his earnings surpassing what he'd ever made in New Jersey or New York. True, it was hard to find a woman that appealed to him—to all of his senses. But with God's help, it would happen, hopefully soon. Binyamin turned his eyes to his date of the evening.

Talya sat across from him, her navy blue skirt hooped out like a beach umbrella. She was interesting and nice-looking, just like Mrs. Bartosky had said. But he wasn't exactly bowled over. She wasn't beautiful. No one would ever say, "Where did you *find* her? She's a knock-out!" Mrs. Bartosky would ask him, "Why not?" And truthfully, he couldn't pinpoint why. Her shoulders hunched upward, squirrel-like, and her chin was a trifle large, but was that enough of a reason to disqualify a woman? Call him shallow, call him superficial, but yes, it did bother him. A rabbi at the yeshiva where he studied once told him, "Marry the person it's easy for you to love, easy for you to give to," and Binyamin knew a less than beautiful woman would make him mean, begrudging. Right now she was plucking at the laminated dessert menu. Hadn't he already bought her the Frozen Yogurt a la Dizengoff? He wished he could give her tips on how to present herself just a little more appealingly.

That had never been his problem. At forty-two, dark-bearded, tall, trim, personable, a part-time yeshiva student and now a successful artist to boot, he had his pick of the English-speaking women of Jerusalem. And people thought he was younger, even with all the gray in his beard, which opened up the selection even more. True, some women preferred not to date a ba'al teshuva newcomer, and Binyamin had entered the fold only three years ago. He would never become an accomplished Talmudic scholar: He had simply started too late. This bothered many women (not to mention himself), but on meeting him reservations melted away. He was one in a thousand—a Torah observant, creative man *and* he made a good living.

Talya was leaning toward him, smiling. "I saw one of your paintings at a friend's—the one with the hazy mountains and the letter Aleph in the corner." She jerked a thumb upward. "Really nice, and the Aleph was a cool, kabbalistic touch." She ducked her head. "Though I was wondering what exactly you had in mind when you put it there."

Binyamin frowned slightly, carefully crossing his legs to avoid banging them against the coffee table. Actually, no particular idea had seized him when he had placed the Aleph on the canvas except the thought that the painting would probably sell better. A misty, pastel mountain hardly grabbed anyone's attention, but a misty mountain with a Jewish symbol was a different matter. Tourists went crazy for those symbols, especially Torah scrolls and Hanukkah menorahs. (Stars of David were on the wane.)

Years ago he had painted purely, not caring if his paintings sold. He would whirl around in his studio like a dervish before he set paintbrush to canvas, whirl and turn, the ground moving under him, and when he stopped and the world continued to rush by, knocking him, disorienting him in a way that he craved, that's when he ran to the canvas. This was how he had created. A few of his old paintings still buoyed him with pride and amazement—precious children that had sprung impossibly from his own loins, children he could hardly account for. But all his purity and devotion and work had gotten him nowhere, just a small obscure following that had never even led to a private show. So what if he stuck a menorah on a painting to help it sell? He had earned the right.

"Truthfully, Talya, I wouldn't advise entering too deeply inside an artist's head. It's a murky, incomprehensible place." With eyes half-closed (but still peering at her to see how his words had registered) he languidly stroked the base of a filigreed lamp. Her forehead was bunching up rather unattractively, he thought, and then his chest gave a prick of remorse. He had just learned in that morning's Ethics of the Fathers class how important it was to judge the whole of a person, yet here he was, dissecting the poor woman. Enough already. Was it her fault she had been set up with him? No, it was Mrs. Bartosky's fault. He'd have to set her straight. A beauty, dammit, that's what he wanted. Attractive wouldn't do. Maybe the matchmaker was holding out on him, reserving the beauties for the Torah scholars. But she liked him, this Mrs. Bartosky. She was on his side.

"I like murky, strange places," Talya said. "And I'd love to be clued in to," her fingers lifted and curled, making quotation marks in the air, "the artistic process."

"The process is untranslatable," he declared. "Goethe said, 'Artist—create; do not talk.' " He gave a sagelike nod. "That's what he said."

Talya's mouth formed a small O. "I see," she said. She folded her arms and looked away. Binyamin yawned and glanced around the lobby, at the over-size paintings (Chagall imitations, all of them) that sprawled across the hotel's walls and at the other blind dates that were unfolding around him in various corners of the place. His eyes finally rested on the bucket in the center of the floor; soon the water would spill if they didn't watch out. Drip, drip. He imagined it dripping for eternity. Some hotel worker would always be there ready to refill that pool, as surely as there would always be some matchmaker ready—no, eager—to introduce him to another woman, even with his lack of Talmudic expertise. All he had to do was make the call.

Binyamin glanced at Talya, at her fingers, which she had caged together in her lap. Her hands were pretty, he saw, but her fingernails were all different lengths, and slightly ragged. His mother had never bothered much with her nails, either. She kept them clean but unfiled, like a row of mountains with sharp crags and peaks. To have a manicure never would've occurred to her. Her toenails were in even worse shape, yellowed spades.

A Talmudic saying came to him: A beautiful wife expands a man's outlook. Whenever the matchmakers harangued him for not being satisfied with a woman's appearance, he made sure to quote it. People could talk as much as they wanted about a person's goodness or inner charm, but there was no question: A beautiful woman offered compensation. A beautiful woman cast a protective glow on whoever was lucky enough to sit under the shade of her good looks. With a beauty—a real beauty—at his side, even the learned rabbis would be forced to look up to him.

Binyamin squelched another yawn, wondering how he could kill another half hour before making a respectable exit. He could ask Talya if she'd ever gone to a tzaddik or a rebbe or a holy man for a blessing, and then regale her with his own sagas. Women were always intrigued to learn he had a mystical aspect. Still, he'd had that conversation so many times before that all the life was sucked out of it. He turned to Talya. "I've got an idea. Take this pen, write down a few words here"—he unfolded a large white paper napkin—"just write anything, it doesn't matter what."

She tipped her head and for a second her extravagant brown hair floated about her face. "Hey, are you going to analyze my handwriting?"

"Actually, yes. Do you mind?"

"No, I'd be flattered," she said, as Binyamin had known she would. Women loved to have their characters analyzed, for good or for bad. Whenever he pulled his handwriting stunt they sat up straight, a flush fell on their cheeks, and they clamped their knees tightly together.

She leaned against the coffee table, pen pressed to napkin, and regarded him. "Should I write in Hebrew or English?"

Show-off, he thought, wincing. Mrs. Bartosky had told him Talya worked as a speech therapist and spoke a fluent Hebrew, but he, after living in Jerusalem three years, still struggled to order pizza with Hebraic aplomb. "English," he muttered.

While Talya filled her napkin with forward-sprawling letters, avoiding the hotel's gold crown insignia in the middle, Binyamin glanced at a couple taking a space close by. Both were dressed in black. The woman was tall, her dark hair parted dramatically to the left, and she wore a black moire dress. The fellow's black yeshiva-style fedora was slanted at a rakish angle. He wore a Hassidic overcoat and black scruffy jeans, and his blond corkscrew side curls swung as he slouched into the leather sofa. Binyamin watched him, a little smile of scorn curling his lips. The fellow was all mixed up: today a Hassid, tomorrow a yeshiva student, Thursday a plumber, and yesterday a college boy. He was obviously new to the scene, the kind of ba'al teshuva who said his Amens too loudly. But the woman! With her elegant arms and her dark river of hair, she was exquisite. She'd probably look beautiful even with all her hair covered.

29

"Hello?" Talya was dangling her napkin before his face. "Yoo hoo?"

Binyamin blinked and bent his head low to pore over her scribblings. He had to admit that at first glance her handwriting impressed him. The lower, middle, and upper zones functioned in smooth balance. The rightward slant stood for extroversion; the pleasing roundness of the letters showed warmth and femininity; and the gamma style of her letter "g" meant she was a cultured person. He was about to tell her these things when the woman in black moire let out a laugh so light and loose it stung him. He tried to catch snatches of their conversation but she didn't speak much. Her date was monopolizing it, taking advantage of her good manners.

He turned back to Talya's napkin. "Do you perceive yourself as second best, always getting the leftovers of life?"

Talya was stacking packets of sugar on the coffee table. She glanced up. "Not really."

Binyamin held up the napkin to the lamp light and squinted. "Oh, now I understand. You're the second child in your family, am I right?"

"Right!" She smiled, making a thumbs-up sign. Her little house of sugar packets collapsed.

He dove back into the napkin. "I see here"—he jabbed a finger at her personal pronoun "I"—"this indicates a neurotic independence from your parents, your entire family, in fact." He stared at her soberly. "You have no connection with them."

"Thank God!" She fanned her neck with the dessert menu. "They're one big mess."

What was wrong with her? he wondered. By now she should have had that hangdog, worshipful look in her eye. He felt a distant vibration—of curiosity? interest?—in his heart. Her spunky attitude, which seemed to have sprung out of nowhere, was stirring him up, intriguing him despite himself. There was a certain quirky gladness about her that teased him into wanting to know more. Why not just give in and like her? Before he could ponder this further, Talya, with a toss of her head, rose from the armchair. "Excuse me a minute, will you?" Her skirt slapped from side to side as she strode toward the rest rooms.

Binyamin glanced to his left. The woman in black moire was gone. But the college-boy-nouveau-Hassid, his sneakered feet lodged on the coffee table, appeared unconcerned. She also must have gone to the bathroom, Binyamin concluded. Why was it no one had ever introduced *them*? That should've been him sitting across from her making light, witty conversation. And come to think of it, it should've been his paintings hanging in the lobby here instead of those pathetic Chagall spin-offs plastered on the walls.

"Did you hear anything interesting?"

Binyamin swiveled in his seat. From the leather sofa, two eyes were fixed on him. He felt his ears and the back of his neck flushing and he gave the nouveau Hassid a feeble smile. "Uh, what do you mean?"

"I mean you've been eavesdropping on our conversation for the last half hour. Did you hear anything interesting?" He said this mildly, picking at some skin at the side of his fingernail.

Outrage smoldered in Binyamin's stomach. Why should this upstart get this woman and not he? There was only a fixed amount of happiness in the world, no matter what the rabbis said.

"You're mistaken. I didn't hear a word," Binyamin told him coldly.

A laugh erupted, rippling through the lobby. The woman in moire was walking alongside Talya. She glided like a wave, while Talya stepped jauntily along in her A-line skirt. He stared at one, then the other. Funny, Talya made the prettier woman seem slightly overdone, and the woman in black gave Talya a horsey air. A man behind the desk, a hotel management person, was also watching them, and Binyamin could see him making comparisons, too, with Talya on the losing side. Some instinct made him want to rush up to her, remove his jacket, and shield her from the man's critical eye. Talya didn't deserve that. She was fun and good-looking, too. But of course, not beautiful.

Meanwhile Talya neatly side-stepped the bucket and stood before Binyamin at the coffee table. Her lips gleamed with pale, newly applied lipstick. She pointed to the napkin. "Do you have anything else to say?"

His nose itched, and without thinking he reached for the napkin and sneezed wetly into it. A moment later he peered up at Talya. "Oops."

By the time they stood to leave the hotel, the water in the bucket had brimmed over.

⋇   ⋇   ⋇

Judy sat across the table from Naomi Safran, the dean of Beit Shifra Yeshiva for Women, who was dressed, strikingly, in a teal dress that flowed to the ground and all around her. The dean's headscarf was festive and sparkly, tied in a knot just above her right ear, making her look rakish and pious at the same time. But she looked stern now, or perhaps just extremely focused, her gray eyes trained on Judy like she was a religious text that needed decoding. Now she was saying in an accent still tinged with Chicago, "We try to create a serious atmosphere of learning here. Our students sign up for the full-time program or the half-day program. We're not really interested in women drifting in for a class now and then to sit back and be entertained."

Judy's face retained a Rebbetzin-like neutrality, even as she suppressed a rueful twinge of recognition. That was exactly what had prompted her to check out the school, which was just a neighborhood away from her own. She was hoping to grab a bit of inspiration from a Torah class now that her youngest child was in a nursery school. But was that so awful? She felt rebuked. She fought down an impulse to casually mention how her husband had been the rabbi in Minneapolis and she the Rebbetzin. But she doubted that this fact would impress

Naomi unless she had been the kind of Rebbetzin who taught, gave Torah classes; in fact, what Judy had mostly done was work out the knots between spouses, visit the sick, make matches, and so on. The only class she'd ever given was on how to bake challahs. She said, "A friend of mine, Beth Wilner, told me about this school. She didn't mention how rigorous it was."

"Beth Wilner! You know her?" Naomi half stood. "She used to be a real regular here. Quite an able student, you should know. She was even getting a scholar's stipend. And then she disappeared, just like that!" Her fingers shot outward, like a star. "I thought she went back to America." Her eyes clouded a moment, and she tugged on the tail end of her scarf. "Tell her we really want to see her."

"I definitely will." Judy tapped her temple, making a mental note. She gazed at a sign hanging on the wall behind Naomi: "A tzaddik, a righteous one doesn't rant against evil, but adds goodness, doesn't attack falsehood but adds truth" and something else, but Naomi's head blocked the other words. "So, what exactly is your school interested in accomplishing?"

Naomi Safran reached across the table toward a stack of books: a Bible, a maroon volume of Midrash Rabbah, a Mishna Brura, a ragged copy of Rambam's *Introduction to Perek Helek*, Rabbi Chaim Volozhin's *Soul of Life*. "I want my students to progress to the point that they don't need me—or any teacher—eventually, so that they have direct access to these books, the key, the skills to study them on their own." She thumbed expertly through the pages of the Bible. "Independence."

"Why is that so important?" Judy asked.

"Why?" A thick eyebrow arched. "I'll tell you why. Torah is a vast sea. It's easy to drown in other people's opinions masquerading as scholarship. A teacher's personal predilection for strict rulings is disguised as the plain law. A student falls sway to a certain brand of Judaism only to discover it was the charismatic personality of a teacher he or she was drawn to, and not the teaching itself. When my students ask, 'But doesn't Judaism say—' I never let them finish. 'Judaism says?' I never heard of that book. I tell them, 'Show me where it's written.' "

Judy smiled wryly. "I'm probably just the dilettante you're trying to avoid having here. I like to be religiously informed, but I'm fairly content to let others do the studying." She looked at Naomi, as if expecting to be interrupted. "My husband once said the difference between an intellectual and a pseudo-intellectual is that the intellectual tries to get his questions answered; the pseudo-intellectual also has questions, but feels satisfied knowing someone else is trying to figure them out."

Naomi threw her head back and let out a bark of laughter. Her sparkly scarf flashed little sequins of light, and Judy regarded her with faint alarm. Naomi recovered quickly, though. "I like that," she said. "Mind if I write it down?" Judy shook her head. Naomi scribbled something on a piece of paper. Then she picked up a thin beige volume and absently rubbed the edge against her jaw. She said, "The truth is, Torah study is not just about achieving intellectual independence. The truth is," here her gray eyes shone and protruded slightly, "a woman who doesn't engage in Torah learning dooms herself to spiritual stagnation, to non-movement."

Strong words, Judy thought. She tried to remember the last time she had truly devoted herself to Torah study or to any serious intellectual inquiry. She was no fool. In school she had always done well enough to make her parents and teachers happy but she had never been the kind of girl who enjoyed study for its own sake or got a thrill from applying her mind. People held her interest far more. She had just started to develop an interest in social work when she had married Dovid in her last year of college and had never quite finished her bachelors. That was fine with her; her hands-on work as a Rebbetzin was the ultimate social worker's degree. Yet looking back on her years as a child-bearer and a Rebbetzin, she saw she'd never really set aside a space for her mind. She'd never given herself a real chance. She said out loud, "I'd like to try out your morning program, if I may."

Naomi stood. "Try it out. See if it's for you. You're under no obligation to continue, of course." She gathered up the books on the table like they were stuffed toys, beaten, pawed over, held close, favored through the years. "By the way," she turned and faced Judy, "I was wondering if you happen to know anyone for Beth."

Ah, this was familiar territory, Judy thought. "Believe me, I'm working on it all the time," she said. Then she added, "I think she may be busy right now."

Naomi's hands came together. "Oh good! And please tell her we want her back here already."

Chapter Three

ETH WAS WAITING IN THE YEMIN MOSHE COURTYARD FOR HER
date, the Canadian house painter, to appear, feeling the cool but
not biting December evening air, tapping the cobblestone
ground with her foot. Yemin Moshe, with its artists' quarters, turn-of-
the-century windmill, view of the Old City of Jerusalem, and little
benches tucked away in alcoves, provided all the right ingredients for
the launching of a shidduch. She was grateful that the grocery lady,
Tsippi, had the sense to choose a private place instead of a more public hotel lobby. Who knew what this man's twitch would look like?
Anyway, she couldn't stand hotel lobbies. She always imagined the
secular waiters and waitresses snickering and winking among themselves at the modestly attired blind dates attempting to connect over
cups of tea, an ocean of a coffee table separating them.

It had been four months now since her last date. It used to be she
had dates all the time, the entire city always plotting to marry her off,
even strangers—both secular and religious—seized with an urgency to
hook her up with a man, as if her single status was a blight on the
Jerusalem family landscape, conveying something profoundly wrong

with her—a lung missing perhaps, or a pancreas or some other vital organ. Nowadays set-ups came along more randomly. She knew why. She was getting to That Age. Less and less marriage-worthy, less procreation-worthy with every passing year. She didn't know whether to feel relieved at being spared awful blind dates, or heartbroken that she no longer even merited an evening with a loser. She was tired of hoping, of praying. Both made a fool of her. When people came up to her at weddings and said, "Soon by you," she just looked at them and stared them down until they backed away.

She drank from a water fountain made of stone. The moon hung low and white in the sky. She thought of her father suddenly, his hunched shoulders and the brown battered hat he wore to work at Wonder Falls Massage Company. He sold vibrating massage furniture for people with back pains, all kinds of body pains. The concept never completely took off, and they had a few pieces around the house. He liked to sit in the beige chair best and tell stories to her at the end of the day. She especially loved how he used to place his hand on her head, spreading out his fingers like a blessing. "Beth, you have the softest hair," he'd say. When she felt bad about not having a head covering, like the married women, she'd remember his hand.

Beth looked around the courtyard, scanning for her date. There were a few possibilities: a man in a black hat who wore his trench coat cape-like around his shoulders, probably from the Chofetz Chaim Yeshiva judging from the little feather in his hat; another man, in a huge knitted yarmulka and a Theodor Hertzl–style beard, who was standing in a halo of orange light reading from a plaque about the philanthropist Sir Moses Montefiore. That one had to be from the Rav Kook camp, an ultra-Zionist, she surmised.

A shadow moved under an olive tree. A man stumbled forward, a thin-limbed Hassid with sad, sloping eyebrows.

"Rachel," he said in a low, accusing voice.

"Ah, no!" She whirled around. A young woman was leaning

against the windmill, partly concealed by the shadow of its arm. Beth pointed into the courtyard. "That could be her."

He raised his hands, turned and walked toward a woman with a huge scarf draped around her coat. She stared at the retreating Hassid. Her date could easily have been him or the Yeshiva guy or the Rav Kooknik. It could've been any of them. She'd certainly dated each of their types before. Why not? She had reached a point where she had eaten in the homes, formed attachments to families and dated men from almost every faction religious Judaism had to offer. She knew the specific rabbis and customs each chose to follow, their methods of learning Torah, the philosophies behind each of their systems, why they considered themselves to be the true center of Judaism, the ones that the Messiah, when he came at the end of days—the group that the Messiah himself would turn to and nod and say, "Yes, the others had their purpose, but you are what God intended all along, the most authentic articulator of His will." The sad thing was that hearing the factions talk and speculate, it was obvious they were clueless about each other. They seized on clichés and acquired their information from newspaper depictions of fringe types or from comments they'd overheard while waiting in line at the bank.

And here was the source of Beth's pride. By dint of her "single" experiences, her extended exile, her invitations to a multitude of people's homes, the endless dating with the various factions, she was in a position to see the entire picture. This had made her easy to set up, because each faction assumed she belonged to them when, in fact, she belonged to no one brand in particular. She liked and hated them all. She wanted someone religiously passionate like she was, but being passionate to only one brand of Judaism felt too babyish for her. When she had tried to explain these things to the matchmakers, they looked at her like she was crazy. So she had stopped.

She stared at a tall man standing near the windmill, partly obscured by its giant shadow. He wore a cap pulled low on his forehead, and he stood with his hands thrust into the pockets of his toggle coat, a leather satchel at his feet. It most probably was Akiva, though she wondered at his informal clothes. Tsippi had told her he went to a very religious black-hat hareidi yeshiva, yet from the look of him he seemed two steps removed from that world. He looked about six feet, at least half a foot taller than she was, big-boned, thick-necked, nicely pulled together, perhaps a little on the chunky side. She noted his beard—luxuriant, dark, and full, but as he came toward her she saw with a shock that he was blond-haired, his beard a mixture of blond and red lights. The shadows of the windmill had fooled her.

He lifted his eyebrows as he walked toward her, the satchel slung across his back, and a little smile passed his mouth. She thought: Maybe he likes broad-hipped women. A few yards away, he placed his hands on the rim of the stone water fountain and crouched, playfully ducking behind it. Then he straightened and laughed. She knew he was just clowning around but she couldn't help wondering if that was the twitch.

"Just protecting myself," he said.

Beth shook her head as if she didn't understand, but she did, all too well. Even before the date began, he saw himself in the down position, the one with the problem that needed overlooking, and she with all the cards, with the likelihood of a relationship entirely in her hands. She was used to the reverse. Normally, it was the man consenting to go out, despite her age.

"You're late," he said, and pulled a yellow leaf from a low-hanging kumquat tree.

"Am I?" Beth asked, startled. She held up her arms as an afterthought. "Bare wrists," she said. He eyed her wonderingly. "No watch," she explained, and he chuckled.

They walked toward two stone benches with a view of King David's Citadel and the Greek Orthodox Monastery lit in yellow lights. He sat facing her, his arm along the back of the bench. His hands looked knuckly and hard-worked, like her father's. No paint-splattered fingers, she noticed with satisfaction. But through his coat one shoulder hunched a bit higher than the other. Was that the twitch?

They got onto the topic of religion. "I was thirty-one and I was hiking in the Grand Canyon," he said, explaining how he had become a ba'al teshuva. "Two bats flew out of a cave, I was on LSD, and just at that moment, it clicked."

Beth's head jerked. "Really?" She leaned forward.

"Actually, no." He looked down at his knuckles and smiled.

She tipped her head back and laughed. Her laughter sounded new and witty to her, and made a light and pretty sound. Was it possible that she'd enjoy herself? Then she bit down harshly on her lip: the violence of hope.

"Is something wrong?"

She looked up at him and shook her head. Akiva was no longer smiling but his hazel eyes looked with an open-hearted gaze into her brown ones. This man was terribly nice, she decided, even taking into account that most people seemed nice the first half hour you met them. But where was his twitch? She couldn't relax till she saw it.

He caught her staring at his shoulders. "Tsippi told me you eat health food," she said, glancing away. "Are you what they call 'macrobiotic?' "

"Something like that. Everyone in yeshiva makes fun of my rabbit food." He stopped. "That reminds me." He bent down, opened his satchel and spread a blue napkin on the bench, which he covered with some gnarled, misshapen cookies.

"You made these?" She suddenly felt cloistered in her jacket and shrugged her way out of it, draping it around her shoulders.

He nodded.

The cookies were tasty but tough to chew, made out of some coarse grain. "They're good," she said.

They settled down into regular, rambling talk: music tastes, family, hometowns, hobbies, religious background. He'd grown up with little bits and pieces like lighting Hanukkah candles, having a Passover Seder, eating out in treife restaurants with his family but leaving the cheese off the hamburgers because they were Jewish. The strange thing was, at age thirteen when he rebelled and refused to ever attend another Seder, he hadn't a clue what he was rebelling against. In college he became something of a seeker. He began spending a lot of time on the road, checking out spiritual communities wherever he could find them, settling in if there was something that attracted him. He'd been living in Scotland for two years, doing his paint jobs and occasional fix-it work on Scottish country ground, living alongside peaceful people. On one of his supply trips to Edinburgh, he'd met up with a Jewish family that was involved in living a religious life, keeping the laws and traditions. They weren't especially unusual people, but they moved him. They kept urging him to visit Israel, and one day he bought a ticket and went. How could he explain what he'd experienced as he traveled through Tiberias, Hebron, Safed and Jerusalem? It was pure longing, a longing that intensified with every step he took.

His voice soothed and stimulated her at the same time. She found herself talking about her favorite books, her volunteer work at Broken Souls and then she drifted into memories of her childhood and related an incident that happened on a Shabbat day in Pittsburgh, just after shul let out. They all were crossing the street at a major intersection, the men in their striped prayer shawls, the throngs of children, the women in their veils and hats. A teenager in a Jaguar raced his engine as they all walked by. He leaned out his window and yelled: "Here come the Jews crossing the Red Sea!" She never knew how uncomfortable she was in America until she came to Israel.

Akiva sat, chin wedged into fist, listening with an attention so complete it almost distracted her. Usually she never bothered revealing anything personal or new on a date. She had her repertoire, her amusing stories, she even had the more private confidences lined up for the following date that would suggest a deepening connection. For instance, she might tell someone on a third meeting how she had taken a break from Torah study because she wanted to devote more time to prayer, to develop a relationship with God more from the heart, less from the head. This was true, but only the thinnest layer of truth.

Her mind jumped back to a year ago, when she'd been a student at the Beit Shifra Yeshiva. She had been preparing for a class when she noticed Naomi Safran, the school's dean, walking in her direction. All the students seemed to have an easy, bantering way with the down-to-earth dean. Not Beth. She was too much in awe of Naomi's knowledge, her religious commitment, her togetherness, and kept her distance. But that day she saw Naomi with her bulging pregnant belly making her way toward her, squeezing between the tables until she came to Beth's little spot by the hot water urn. Naomi said, "You like it here?" 'Like' was hardly the word. She treasured the place, she wished she could afford to be a full-time student. Beth nodded. "And we like having you here," Naomi finished. Beth stared up warily, waiting for the inevitable But. Naomi said, "We'd like you to consider teaching one of the Torah classes here next semester." Beth's body instantly became suffused with heat. They wanted her—her! She gazed up at Naomi as at a fairy godmother. "I'd be honored," she managed to choke out. This was one of the great moments of her life, to be acknowledged so, to be received and appreciated. Yet later, at home, she wondered how she could have consented. How could she stand in front of a class? How much did she really know? And what did she believe, truly, in her heart of hearts? Maybe she had enough faith to sustain herself, but enough to inspire students, to publicly make sense of God's word? The responsibility terrified her.

Suddenly, she was harassed by doubts, by questions she'd thought she'd struggled with and overcome years ago: rabbinic interpretations that were a whitewash, textual redundancies, anachronisms, primitive-sounding verses and laws. She longed to discuss her difficulties with the staff at Beit Shifra, yet she sensed they would think less of her even as they might reassure her that such questions were normal. Somehow the teaching position would never be brought up again. She was torn. In the end she left Beit Shifra, and decided that she wasn't taking a single step further in the intellectual realm of study until she had first developed her heart (her heart!). And searching her heart had taken her to pray in the Jerusalem Forest. She'd be foolish to discuss this on a date. She never had. Perhaps that was why she was always bored on these dates, because she bored herself, never saying anything new.

Right now, Akiva was asking why she hadn't married yet.

She blinked and said, as if it had just occurred to her, "Because the desirable is unobtainable, and the obtainable is undesirable." This was a line she used often.

He let out a snort of laughter, gave her a wary look, then laughed again, shaking his head.

Her shoulders lifted slightly in a sigh only perceptible to herself. Sometimes she'd feared she had nothing new left to say, even to herself. That's why she liked going to the Jerusalem Forest. Hidden by the trees, sitting on her favorite boulder under a pine tree, she forgot she was a thirty-nine-year-old bookkeeper; an unmarried woman in the land of marrieds; a woman of no unusual talent, brains, beauty or even great kindness; an American who, while speaking the Hebrew language fluently, would always be on the outside of things. She forgot all that in the forest. There, she sobbed, loud and uninhibited. Where did her tears come from and what did they mean? The sniffling, the wet, smeared cheeks, the nose-blowing—all this repelled her, yet she kept returning to the forest, drawn into the canopy of trees, curious and amazed at what the forest could pull out of her each time. Afterward she felt vivid to herself. Touchable. Her sobs were proof; she wasn't as prim and composed and invulnerable as they imagined her to be. She had a wild, beautiful core. Maybe being married—to the right man—

would be like being in the forest. There, in the trees, she was hidden, and that helped her reveal something of who she was. Maybe with a scarf on her head she'd be able to reveal herself—a kind of covering up for the sake of uncovering.

How odd that now she was truly enjoying herself, and enjoying Akiva, too: the attentive way he looked at his fig before he offered the blessing and ate it, the way he gave travel directions three times to a French tourist couple in the same even tone, the crazy way he lifted his eyebrows when he explained a Hassidic concept; his eyes looked skyward and he was gone for a second. Something in his blend of sincerity and irony was affecting her. Was it possible that the twitch story was a bluff? An excuse to not marry?

They walked down stone-floored alleys, wandered into a lighted art gallery, got into a discussion on art aesthetics which neither of them knew much about, pathetically laying the bit of knowledge they had about Impressionism at each other's feet before they sheepishly turned to each other in the same instant and laughed at their attempts at sophistication.

Sitting outside again on wooden benches, Akiva dipped his head toward hers. "Tell me, do you have any Indian blood? You have such high cheekbones."

She raised her hand to her cheek. It was hot. "My grandparents are Polish," she said in a faltering voice.

"Really, Polish? Wilner—Vilna. Maybe that explains your last name. Do you have a Hebrew first name?"

She ducked her head. "My parents gave me a strange name, which I don't use."

"What is it?" he asked, with such direct warmth that she lowered her eyes and answered him. "Yenta Shprinzer." She waited to hear his reaction. Very few people knew her Hebrew name. "It isn't my parents' fault," she went on quickly. "My grandparents wanted them to name me after somebody in the family. I've been looking for another Hebrew name, but none of the B's satisfy me."

"Hm." He gave her a long stare. "What about Batya?"

"Batya," she sounded it aloud. "Batya. That *is* nice. Daughter of God. I like it." Then she sighed.

"What is it?"

"My black-hat yeshivish friends, they'll use the Ashkenazic pronunciation. They'll call me Bassy."

He shook his head. "I see what you mean. Too unlyrical. That's not for you."

This man spoke as if he knew her. Her hands were in her lap and she stared down at them. They seemed delicate, poignant and feminine, not the usual doughy, square-tipped impression they gave her.

"Do you have any other ideas for names?"

"It depends on what happens with us," he said. "You can't expect me to give everything away."

Beth breathed in and shut her eyes. Her stomach fluttered. This was too much, too fast, and she liked it.

When she opened her eyes he had turned his head away from her and she saw the cords of his neck strain tautly from the jaw to the base of his neck.

She stared. "Is everything all right—"

Suddenly his arms flung into the air. A convulsed sound came from his throat, a tortured hiccup. His head fell forward as if it were no longer attached. It jerked up and rapidly twisted back and forth. His arms and shoulders quivered as if he were being shaken violently by another person.

She gripped her arms with her hands. Her mouth fell open.

Then his body went slack and boneless. He sank back into the bench, his legs sprawled. He clasped his fingers behind his neck and shook his head. He bent to pick up his satchel, which had fallen to the ground. Akiva gave her a rueful smile. His face assumed the same honest, quietly amused expression she had begun to grow accustomed to.

"Yes, so there it was. You saw it," he said.

She let out her breath. Her hands still gripped her arms, and she unclenched them. "Yes, I—I was wondering when it would come."

He tilted his head. "Did it frighten you?"

Her heart turned over. He had undergone the ordeal, yet he was thinking of her. After a moment, she said, "A bit. Mostly because I didn't know when it was coming. Does it happen often?"

"Sometimes two hours'll pass and there's nothing. Then again, it can happen three times in half an hour." He shrugged and spread out his hands. "I never know."

She would never know either. If she dated him, she'd always be on edge. Could she trust him to drive a car? Hold a baby? How would he act in shul? Those terrible hiccups. "Does it hurt you?"

"It shakes me up a lot but it doesn't hurt." He patted himself. "I'm okay."

"Could you tell me what causes—" She stopped, blushing in confusion. "I'm sorry. Please forgive me for all these intrusive questions, I'll just be quiet."

"No," he said. "I prefer you to ask me instead of just ignoring it. Most women do that, they pretend that nothing's happened, but I can tell from their faces that they're not interested anymore. And from the way they've handled it, neither am I." He looked ahead, but his eyes were turned inward. "It's a metabolic derangement in my body and it gets aggravated by all kinds of tension. My muscles kind of contract like a pretzel and, well, you saw what happened. Asperclonus Type Syndrome—that's the name they gave it. Which means they don't really know what it is. I started having spasms in junior high school and it hasn't gone away since. I tried some drug called pamphaldamine, but the side-effects were pretty awful. The doctors really can't do anything, though one suggested this macrobiotic diet to help reduce the intensity of the attacks." He shrugged. "At least it's not hereditary. Sometimes—I wonder if it'll disappear when I marry."

She heard the strains of "Smoke Gets In Your Eyes" playing in an art gallery, or perhaps in someone's home. A dog barked. The Hassid from the olive tree walked by with his date, both staring off in different directions. A teenager swung a tennis racket in the air as he climbed some steps. She buried her head in her hands.

Akiva was making an offering of some kind and she had to decide. She felt a momentary shot of anger toward Tsippi for not having better prepared her. This is what she called a twitch? But she was glad Tsippi hadn't been more specific. Who knew if she even would have agreed to see him at all? And she did want to see him again. Often, a small thing could turn her off: a pronounced Adam's apple, an overuse of certain adjectives, chewing too loudly. But here she was, attracted, with his twitch and all. That had to mean something. Still, she imagined people saying all sorts of crazy things: Poor desperate Beth. She never was much good at attracting normal men. True, her real friends would never think in such crude terms. But she pictured even Judy Bartosky, who wanted to see her married at all costs, saying, "You have to feel proud walking down the street with your man." A person should feel happy when she's walking down that street. Shouldn't that be enough?

Akiva's arms and legs were shaking faintly. He smacked his lips. It was just a mild spasm compared to before, but she had to avert her eyes. Everything was on the outside. It was too much, all those crazy physical inklings of what was going on in his soul. She felt a queasy dread, outweighed only by a queasy joy gnawing inside her. She felt a pull toward him in the low pit of her stomach.

She said loudly, "Why should your spasm disappear? What are you talking about? Why should it disappear?"

Akiva's eyes shot wide open. Then he smiled in the tenderest way and she bowed her head.

It was 1 A.M., and the buses in Jerusalem stopped running at twelve. Instead of hailing a taxi, they walked home, their strides falling into the same rhythm. She kept looking at him, his friendly, even teeth, his blond hair slightly lifted by a breeze and newly parted to the other side. She was full of wonder to be walking next to such a handsome man. As they got closer to home, they both instinctively drew deep, strong breaths, taking in the warm moist bread smell coming from Yussel's Bakery, even at this late hour, a scent that hung over the entire neighborhood. That's what she liked most about living in her area: She always smelled bread, except on Shabbat when the establishment was closed. Akiva bought her a cinnamon roll, and for himself whole wheat challah.

Outside her apartment door, they made plans to get together. He lived fairly close by, on Shofar Avenue, just two bus stops past Levites Street. There was a little awkward pause just after they exchanged goodnights, the pause that opened the door for some physical gesture between them and in the same instant shut it. Some part of her wanted to graze the side of his face, the skin just above his beard, with her pinky. Of course, she would never do that. The laws of the Torah were unequivocal on that subject. They were wise, protective laws, said the rabbis. Truth to tell, what did she know of such things? Men might as well have been living on another planet, that's how few opportunities she'd had. Maybe that was because she'd become more religious in her teens, when everyone else was rebelling. Her family had kept the basics, Shabbat and kosher, but she'd grown up watching television, wearing pants and less modest clothing, appearing to the outsider's eye like a regular American who was immersed in the culture. But soon after her mother had died, she and her father had become involved with families more religious than her own, had taken to going to Torah classes, had met a few inspiring rabbis and somehow she had drifted into piety—praying twice a day, wearing only modest skirts and dresses, keeping the fine points of Torah law and eventually attending a college exclusively for religious Jewish women. She had definitely been sequestered, and by her own choice. Well, she couldn't even claim to have been sorely tempted, since the men who'd come her way had hardly been appealing.

Before going to sleep, she stared at herself in the full-length mirror and at the little chart taped to its side. Good Daily Habits, etched in pencil because she was forever changing them. This month it read: Limit gossip, do thigh exercises (she half-heartedly raised her leg), use hand cream, say Psalm 20 for the soldiers, make bed on rising. She gave the mirror a last look, then she recited the Shma prayers and went to sleep.

⁂ ⁂ ⁂

Mediterranean sunlight slanted into the bedroom of his apartment. Binyamin rubbed his forehead and yawned, his eyes going to a pastel abstract that hung to the right of his bed. It was one of his old-style paintings (he'd named it "The Ten Commandments or Letters of Pure Consciousness"), but it had not sold, probably because he hadn't put any symbol on it anywhere. A Torah scroll or Jewish star would have done the trick, but he couldn't bring himself to kitschify the painting. As he stared at it, last night's date came back to him in waves, with each surge releasing a piece of the evening: A ceiling with a drip. Talya, the speech therapist. Talya fanning her neck with a menu. Talya stacking her sugar packets. He felt his lips forming a smile. Then he recalled the college-boy Hassid and his classy date. The woman in black moire. He sat up in bed. She, now *she* was worth remembering.

Binyamin dressed quickly and caught a bus to town, then took another to Jaffa Gate. He hurried to his prayers, rushing down the stone alleys, past the archeological digs and Roman pillars and pizza shops, past the soldiers who stood guard at the Western Wall who didn't bother to check his bag for bombs because he was a regular, past the old Yemenite who gave out black beanies to the bareheaded, until he found his spot in the leftmost corner against the wall of the Kotel. There he prayed, feeling a sense of belonging, as he always did in Jerusalem. In New Jersey he had never walked down the streets, breathed in the grimy air and thought: Mine. This belongs to me. But that's how he felt in Jerusalem, and more: He belonged to it, or her. Under the wing of this holy city. Protected. In New Jersey, in public school, they called the Jewish kids bagels and matza balls. Not in Jerusalem.

He touched the stone's crevices. When he came as a tourist to Jerusalem, at first he'd hardly noticed the scenery, so consumed was he by a drop-dead gorgeous Norwegian he'd hooked up with. They hung out in youth hostels and toured bars. One morning an old, trampy-looking man had approached them while they sat drinking a cappuccino on Ben Yehudah Street. "Do you want some peace?" the man asked. "Sure, I'll take some," Binyamin (aka Barry) had said with a smirk. The old man reached out his hands and blessed him in part Hebrew, Yiddish and English. And when the old man took away his canopy of fingers, peace whacked Binyamin on the head like a block of cement. He looked around, stunned, at one with himself in a way he'd never experienced, relaxed and hungry for more. The old man was gone. "Where is he, who is he?" he muttered out loud while his girl-friend was drumming her fingers on the table. (Her voice was permanently devoid of inflection. It was like talking to a Frigidaire. They split soon after.) A waiter passing by with white arcs of glacee told him, "Ben-Something. You can find him in the yellow pages of saints and mystics." Binyamin got hold of the saint directory and began going down the list in search of the old man: Ben Azzai, Ben Chaim, Ben Dovid. His search led him to other saints, rebbes, mystics and holy folk: the Rebbe who had told him to buy a lottery ticket from a certain booth at a certain street corner, and he had done exactly that and won third prize, the equivalent of five thousand dollars, only to spend it all on expensive dental surgery the following week; a stocky old woman who had given him a red string to tie around his wrist, and detailed instructions on where his future wife was at that very moment, instructions he couldn't recall to save his life; the white-bearded octogenarian who had shouted "Impure!" after looking at him for a few seconds, and had violently gestured for him to leave the room at once. By the time he had reached the end of the list, Binyamin had forgotten about the trampy old man. Instead, he had become curious about these outlandish Jews, so different from the upwardly mobile New Jersey kind he'd known, and that curiosity had led him to a place he wouldn't have believed possible for himself.

Now Binyamin heard a soft clucking and glanced upward. Two doves pecked at the paper notes, petitions to God wedged in the stone's cracks. He had never again felt that intense peace as he had that day on Ben Yehudah Street. A deep closeness to God had eluded him, too, even with all the commandments he performed. Still, his life was better. He had people to talk to, people he could trust, not like the back-stabbers it had been his misfortune to know in the art world. The women here weren't as beautiful, but at least they could take care of themselves. His last girlfriend had the looks of a runway model, but she couldn't drive, she didn't have a checkbook, she would cook the same sesame chicken dish over and over. The sad thing was, she was crazy. Here, the women felt saner, focused. Better potential wives, not to mention mothers. Basically, he liked the whole Torah life package. Here he had purpose, belonging, dignity, and if he didn't have outright fulfillment, he had the hope of fulfillment that a wife and family of his own making would surely bring.

As for the family he had been born into, he still maintained a connection. He sent them a filagree mezuzah cover, a wooden Hanukkah dreidel, Hassidic rock tapes for his niece—Jerusalem care packages. He visited home once a year. He tried hard to fulfill the dictum of honoring his parents, yet he couldn't help feeling offended by his father's off-color jokes, and oppressed by the sight of his mother's enormous thighs in her ridiculous summer shorts. He trekked out to visit his sister, pretty Amanda, tucked away in a Connecticut suburb, her husband a doctor. These beautiful women, he thought, they lived in a different world from the rest of us, excused from the drudgery of earning a living, earning affection. Privileged characters. When he first told her of his plan to remain in Jerusalem and study in yeshiva, Amanda had said, "Religion is only for people who are already good." With that statement she exempted herself. "Yeah, but haven't you ever thought of these things, God, the Ten Commandments, the afterlife?" She said, "Barry, I've got my hands full with two kids and Mark's practice. I just don't have time for . . ."

"God."

"Yes, if you put it that way." But who could blame her? Religion was an elective in life, not binding. It was the American way.

And truthfully, there, at his parents' house, a spiritual malaise crept over him. He didn't *feel* like praying, he didn't *feel* like getting up and reciting Kiddush Friday nights with *Bonanza* reruns blaring in the background. Instead he just wanted to join them in front of the TV, slouching with a beer in his hand and a bowl of cream of mushroom soup in his lap, the kind that didn't have the OU kosher symbol on it. Suddenly, at his parents' home, religion had become a chore and a bore, all that he had dreaded in his Sunday School classes. No, he couldn't entirely blame his parents for his malaise. He missed Jerusalem. There he could count on a richly hued sunset throwing a toasty light on the apartment walls, making the individual stones look like whole wheat bread baking. Jerusalem gave significance and glamour to the smallest petty Jewish law, like saying the After-Bathroom blessing, or checking eggs for blood spots. Sure, Torah was the Truth and the Right Thing To Do, but keeping the mitzvahs outside of Israel—in New Jersey, for instance—felt like doing laps in a bathtub. It lacked context. As with his art, the setting was everything.

Binyamin unwrapped the phylacteries from his arm and head, and slowly retreated, walking backward as if taking leave of a king. One didn't turn one's back to this most sacred of walls. He passed under the arch of the Jewish Quarter Cafe and made a right onto Jews Street, finally reaching his yeshiva. He spotted his chevrutah study partner at the far end of a large sunny room comprised almost entirely of small tables, chairs, lecterns and bookshelves. Tuvia, fourteen years his junior and recently engaged, sat at a square green formica table, a Jastrow Aramaic Dictionary at his side. "We only have half an hour," Tuvia told Binyamin as he slid into a chair facing him. All around them men jabbered at each other in pairs, getting ready for a lecture a rabbi would give. Binyamin felt his shoulders hunch. He always felt them tense up before he went into yeshiva. This surprised him, because he felt more at home here than anywhere else. Yet he could already feel an ache in his muscles.

He opened an unwieldy volume of the Talmud, scrambling among the pages, until his finger arrived at Brachos, page 17, side two, middle of the page. "Okay, I'm ready." They both read to themselves, translating as best they could.

Binyamin was stuck on the word 'Mutal.' As he shuffled through the dictionary, his fingers twitched in frustration. He couldn't even find the word. " 'Mutal,' what does 'Mutal' mean?" he muttered.

"Dew, I think," said Tuvia.

Binyamin hunched his shoulders and plunged back into the Talmud. He pressed his fingers on the bones just under his eyebrows. "I don't have a clue what it's talking about." He looked mistrustfully at the tiny print. "I think we're translating this wrong."

They stared at each other. They'd been working on this sentence for the past ten minutes. Someone was passing through the labyrinth of chairs and tables, and Binyamin stuck out his arm, seizing the student's wrist. "What's 'Mutal' mean here?"

The yeshiva student obediently brought his head low to the open Talmud. He read to himself, his lips moving faintly as if they itched.

" 'Mutal' here means 'laying before,' as in, 'If someone whose near relative lays dead before him, he is exempt from reciting the Shma, and prayer and putting on tefillin.' "

Binyamin gave the student a pat on the back, effectively thanking him and dismissing him. Then he groaned and clapped a hand to his forehead. "Oh, did we mess up. The Mishna is discussing the obligations of the mourner."

Tuvia tugged on his beard—a patchy, see-through affair which he'd begun to sprout to please his fiancé. "Gosh. Think how bad we would've sounded in class." Then he laughed.

"I don't need to imagine it. It's right here." Binyamin ran his finger across his Adam's apple then fell back limply in his chair, with the relief of one narrowly avoiding a humiliation. He felt pathetic and insignificant, a puny drop of water in a bottomless sea. Well, he'd recently sold a painting for twenty-six-hundred dollars. That was worth something, he told himself. He let out a snort. In the eyes of the world, maybe, but not here in yeshiva, not where unraveling strands of Talmudic logic were what counted most. That's what killed him. Even if the whole section were to be laboriously translated for him, he'd probably not understand. Well, the rabbis kept telling him it would get easier. He sure to God hoped so.

"What's with you, Binyamin?" Tuvia asked.

He lifted his eyes from the Gemara, taking in Tuvia's cheerful, fuzzy face. And that was another thing, he thought. Why him with the fiancé? Why him and not me? I get the Talyas, the Almosts, and he gets The One. "I don't understand it," he said out loud. "I lead a pious life, pray, eat kosher, don't fool around. I play by the rules, right? So why should God make it so difficult to find someone I want to be with?"

"So that's what's eating you?" Tuvia reached across the table and put a hand on his upper arm. "She's out there—I promise. You just have to keep looking for her. 'If you initiate, God will consummate.' Don't give up."

"Yeah?" Binyamin looked at him through half-closed eyes, crocodile-like. Since becoming engaged, Tuvia had acquired the depressing habit of dispensing truisms. Suddenly, he was wise not only for himself but for everyone, had figured out the formula that led to marriage, knew something the others didn't know—when all he'd been was plain lucky.

"Sure! Keep on plugging! Keep calling those matchmakers." Tuvia leaned his chair back, his hands on the edge of the formica table. " *Lfoom tzara agra*'—according to the effort is the reward. Maybe God has some really incredible woman lined up for you but He just wants you to sweat a little before He makes it happen."

Binyamin's lip curled. "Now why would God want me to sweat? Doesn't He have more important things to do than torture me? I don't buy into this Make 'Em Sweat theology." He glanced down at the Mishna, at the two lines they'd been struggling over for the past fifteen minutes. "I sweat enough. Anyway, why should I run after the matchmakers when they're always running after me?"

"No, wait. Maybe that's exactly the point. Humble yourself. Put out some energy." Tuvia made fists like a wrestler and gave a one-two sock into the air. "Maybe God thinks you don't really want to get married. By humbling yourself and taking the initiative and calling, you're saying, 'God, I'm serious!' " He settled back in his chair, rather pleased with his take. "The early bird catches the worm, you know."

Binyamin stood up to buy a Coke. He gave Tuvia an absent tap on the shoulder. "Thanks, buddy, for that invaluable piece of advice. Couldn't live without it." As he fished for some coins, he gave his head a weary shake. That was the worst part about being an older single. Being forced to absorb canned wisdoms from little pishers like Tuvia, simply because they'd lucked into marriage. He put some coins into the machine and listened to the satisfying sound of a Coke can chugging through the slot. Twenty-six-hundred dollars, he thought, recalling his painting. It was not insignificant. No one could say that.

55

There was a phone booth opposite the Coke machine, and he remembered that he hadn't yet spoken to Mrs. Bartosky about last night's date. Once he'd been two days late in getting back to her and she'd chewed his head off. It didn't pay to mess with her. He slipped an asimone phone token into the slot and dialed.

"So how did it go?" Mrs. Bartosky began.

"I liked her," he found himself saying. "She's sweet and kind of spunky. But she's too"—Binyamin's hand groped the air, searching for a word, was it dorky?—"unpolished," he ended, still dissatisfied. He squinted at a white cat that lay curled on top of the Coke machine. He hadn't noticed it before.

She heaved a sigh and called out something to a child in the background. He tensed, waiting for her onslaught. Sometimes she was a tidal wave it made no sense opposing. In her own way, she was something of a bully. A feminine bully.

"You weren't attracted to her?"

"I'm not sure." He leaned against the booth. He didn't have an uncontrollable urge to touch her, but there had been a certain buzz there between them—he couldn't lie. "Well, I guess you could say I was somewhat attracted," he ventured.

"And you liked her company."

Talya's tilted head and dark amused eyes appeared before him. She had a rather winning manner, an attitude which seemed to say *I know your game but I like you anyway.* "Uh huh."

"So what's the problem?"

"What can I tell you?" He held out a hand. "She just doesn't do it for me."

"Do it for you," Mrs. Bartosky repeated.

Binyamin punched the air. Wrong phrase. A reminder of his coarse past, his pre-religious days. Strobe-like images of bars and foxy babes buzzed across the screen of his mind. He bowed his head.

"Oh, I know. She wasn't beautiful enough."

He recalled her ragged nails, the way her hand sliced the air as she made a certain point. He shook his head. "Actually, no," he said. The phone was silent. Then, "All right."

He stared at the Bezek phone logo in the booth. He had to admit, he enjoyed the after-date analyses with the matchmaker, and now he was feeling shortchanged. Also, a part of him was still murky and unsettled about the question of Talya. Maybe another date was in order, just to be on the safe side? There was a girl he had dated in college, an average-looking art student who had captivated him with her audacious paintings and whimsical manner. ("An angel with spice"— that's how he remembered her.) When it was just the two of them he couldn't have been happier. But at the cafeteria, on the campus grounds, he kept imagining his friends snickering at him for the pudgy coed he had fallen for. In the end, he had to give her up. Talya reminded him of her—a little. "Well, uh, was she interested in me?"

A snort crackled in the receiver. "What difference does it make?" A child cried bitterly and he heard her make soothing noises. "Look, I have some things I have to do so if you don't mind—"

"Wait, Mrs. Bartosky, I was wondering about someone else you might have come across. She was at the King Solomon last night. Very stylish and dramatic, tall, extremely good-looking, dark, parts her hair to the side. A bit of silver in it. You'd remember her. In her early thirties, I think—"

He heard a ball bouncing and the matchmaker call out, "Levi, not in the living room." Then, "I think I know who you mean. Did you see her with a man in Hassidic clothes wearing sneakers?"

The coughing fit that overtook him was so loud and abrupt that the cat on the Coke machine awoke, blinking and arching its back. "Yes, yes, that's the one." He wiped the corners of his mouth. "How in the world did you know?"

"They made plans to meet at the King Solomon, too." She paused. "I set them up." She added, "She's not for you."

He tried to calm his erratic breathing. "Why not?" He mopped his neck.

"Rita happens to want a Talmudic scholar, also someone spiritual."

Binyamin winced. Mrs. Bartosky knew he wasn't particularly skilled with a page of Gemara. Did she have to grind his nose in that? He was trying as hard as he could. Anyway, if he wasn't so learned, didn't he at least get credit for being spiritual? What the hell was he doing all those mitzvahs for? "Maybe she'd change her mind if she met me," he offered. "She didn't strike me as so rigid."

"Binyamin, I see no reason such a situation would work between the two of you. I'm sorry, but I really must go. Now isn't the best time." She said good-bye and hung up.

Binyamin replaced the receiver, crestfallen. And he'd been hoping she was going to invite him for a Shabbat meal, too. Well, maybe she was annoyed at him. Maybe the matchmaker had hoped that after all her attempts, Talya would finally be the one. Lately he was finding that these matchmakers took his rejections way too personally, as if he had, in fact, rejected *them*.

So it was back to square one, he thought. Too bad Mrs. Bartosky had refused to set them up. But at least he had her first name: Rita. Jerusalem was small. Jerusalem had a way of surrendering her secrets, of guiding him through corridors, bringing him to the place he needed to be. Here, he felt surrounded by God's will, enveloped in it. Things happened, bizarre coincidences, strange pairings, twists of fate, things that had never happened to him before, only in this city. Jerusalem would show him the way.

※　※　※

"Well?" said Rochel Leah Moskowitz. The old lady sat up in a wood-framed bed, a boxy, mannish hat on her head, both hands knotted in her lap like rolls of white bread.

Tsippi propped a thick blue volume of the Book of Genesis on her knees. " 'Avraham lifted his eyes and he saw three strangers standing a short distance from him,' " she read aloud from the eighteenth chapter. She could think of twenty other places she would rather be than at a geriatric ward reading the Bible to a cantankerous spinster. But how could she refuse? After her first visit, the social worker from the geriatric ward had cornered her and pitched the old woman's plight— eighty-five, no children or family to take her in, and her one love, studying the Bible, now impossible since her vision had deteriorated. How could she say no when the Institute was only a fifteen-minute walk away? Also, she had promised Beth.

"Go on," said Rochel Leah. Tsippi gazed at her pink cat's-eye glasses, and behind the glasses, a little pulsing in her creased lids. Maybe her own eyelids would do the same thing when she was old, she thought with a stab. Tsippi shook her head and snorted. She *was* old: Sixty-nine. She put her finger on the verse and read:

" 'Avraham said, Sirs, if you would, do not go on without stopping by me. Let some water be brought, and wash your feet.' " Tsippi moistened her own throat and went on: " 'Rest under the tree. I will get a morsel of bread for you to refresh—' "

"Hah! 'A morsel of bread.' " Rochel Leah aimed a long arthritic finger at the Bible. Then, with a few impatient flicks of the wrist, "Just look, read what he brought out—read the part where he runs out with a tender choice calf, cooked to perfection, and the fat and the butter and the cottage cheese." Her finger jabbed the air at each item. "Morsel of bread. That old fox didn't fool me." She settled back in bed, and her droopy folds of clothing settled with her. "Why don't you read it already?"

"I'm getting there," Tsippi told her. She didn't like being rushed along in fits and starts like a donkey. But the old woman insisted on going backward and forward seeing fresh angles, skipping some points in favor of others, as if she were playing checkers. Tsippi, on the other hand, liked the verses to flow over her like a river, without interruption. That's how she had taught her sons to study. That way she could catch everything. For instance, the humor. The strangers were really angels in disguise, and it had always struck her as funny, a bit sad, too—a harried Avraham running around, preparing a banquet that the angels, being angels, would only pretend to eat. Of course, Tsippi was here at the nursing home to do a good deed for this woman, and not the reverse, but did that mean she had no say in how the verses should be read? She felt annoyed at Beth for having arranged their coming together, then thought: This is how single people must feel all the time. Manipulated into meetings that had little to offer.

Rochel Leah was eating a potato pancake snuck from the dining room. "That's why the Sages wrote, it's good to 'Say little and do much.' And where do you think they derived this notion?" Her silver brows parted on her forehead. "From Avraham's conduct to the three strangers, from this very place!"

Yes, yes, Tsippi thought. Still, it didn't hurt to be reminded of those good words: Say little and do much. As she continued to read she thought of all the times she'd gotten into trouble doing the opposite. As a matchmaker, she found people did not enjoy being promised or offered more than could be delivered. Underselling, or undertalking, had its virtues.

Rochel Leah was now leaning to the side, her hand groping among the old-lady items on the night table, finally resting on a pad of paper. "Please, will you read something for me, tell me if it's legible?" she said in a voice that was both casual and sly. She tore off a sheet and thrust it at Tsippi. "I can write, but I don't know how it looks on paper, you know," she muttered, holding a magnifying glass to her good eye.

Tsippi took the paper. The letters were big and then suddenly turned small, the pressure faint, then strong, most of the letters misshapen and tilting downward, but they made sense, she could read them, and slowly she did, to herself, pausing to absorb her great astonishment: "Beloved, You are my banner. I dream of you when I pray, I dream of you when I rise up and when I lie down, when I read and when I eat, you, you, you, only you. Please, I beg you, just one hair from your holy earlock, put it inside this note, and give it back to the lady, your holy hair to have with me, to cherish. From the one whose love for you cannot be quenched by rivers."

Tsippi stood still, thunderstruck. She dared not—could not—raise her eyes. The old woman was making a play for a man. And Tsippi had thought her a mere spinster, a dried prune, incapable of passion. She let out her breath sharply, and the air around her lips tasted sour. An absurd thing, an old woman head over heels in love. Well, no one would ever accuse herself of losing her head, thank God. She and Shlomo were solid and unshakable, sensible people, all of her friends said. She sighed and glanced at the bedridden old woman who was sitting forward, placidly eating the remains of the potato pancake. "It's legible but it takes time to read," Tsippi said.

Rochel Leah grunted. "Time he has. As for me, it took twenty minutes to write this." She adjusted the ends of her eyeglasses around her ears. "So take this to Reb Isaac Mordechai, Room 808, and tell me what he says when he reads it." She punched her pillow and fell into it.

Tsippi tucked the yellow note into her pocket. Indeed, Rochel Leah was making a pitch for a man and did not care who knew or saw it. Maybe advanced age took away all embarrassment. She, on the other hand, even if she lived till a hundred, would never be able to bare herself. It was a wonder she had gotten married at all. And that had been no small feat. During the war, in the camps, she had crept into the barracks late at night, where they kept the dead, groped among the bodies, groping among the dead, looking for life, and rubbing the chest, the arms, till life got restored, as it happened on occasion. She had found a man's body with an unusual birthmark and had rubbed his body till she had felt a pulse, then dragged him to safer quarters, to her contact, a young woman from her hometown called The Angel who knew how to procure things like potato peels and extra portions of soup and other unheard-of camp luxuries. Then, through circumstances too coincidental to be believed, she had met up with him again after the war at the Karlsbaad healing waters, recognized the mushroom mark on his neck and, after a brief courtship, had married him. Maybe those nights in the barracks had been her own pitch for love, crazy as it had been. But if she had known she had been doing this for love, she never would have had the nerve.

The old woman had lapsed into sleep, snoring so loudly it sounded as though someone were shoveling rocks. Tsippi took the arm that was hanging over the side of the bed and tucked it under the nubbly green bedcovers, emptied a plate of mangled sunflower seeds into the garbage, gathered her purse, umbrella and jacket, and left. She took the stairs instead of the elevator (the doctor said her legs needed the circulation) and when she came to Room 808, she found a sign that said the patient had been moved to Room 708, so she went a further flight down. She knocked on the door. No one answered. She opened it.

"Excuse me," Tsippi called out, sticking her head through the doorway. "I have something—" Her voice fell away. A man with long white earlocks but no beard lay in the bed, black boxes of tefillin strapped to his forehead. His hands were clenched, and his face was stiff as if stuck in a painful memory. His feet flexed in their dark socks. His entire body was riddled with notes, a veritable Western Wall, some near his hand, some on his shoulders and neck, some in the cracks of his armpit, some in the grooves between his legs, one even flecking down there, the place of the covenant. You'd think he'd at least brush that one away, she thought irrelevantly. She stood at her spot in the doorway, not daring to enter. But there was Rochel Leah Moskowitz's command pounding in her: You must give it to him. And so from the doorway she tossed the note. It landed on the fourth button of his pajamas and bounced off his heart to the floor, where a number of other notes lay scattered. Then she fled.

Chapter Four

AKIVA AWOKE BEFORE HIS ROOMMATE, SAUL. HE REACHED under his bed for the bucket that contained a plastic hand-washing cup filled to the brim with water. Leaning over, he poured the water first over his right hand, then the left, back and forth, three times, the water carefully aimed into the bucket: slow, quiet movements, so as not to startle Saul. It was five-fifteen in the morning.

He washed his fingers and the valleys between them, then looked down at his hands. He liked to perform the handwashing ritual—negel vasser, Saul called it. It was the custom of the ancient priests, the cohanim, to wash their hands with a special cup before they began their sacred work in the temple. He—every person—had a sacred mission for the day, and when he poured the tepid water over his hands before he even took four steps on solid ground it was as if he had channeled his hands to do God's will.

It saddened him that Saul just sloshed the water on his wrists and palms with the same business-like air that he flossed his teeth. He never stopped to consider the act. But could he blame him? Saul had been raised in a Torah-observant home, he'd been doing negel vasser since he was a small child, while he, Akiva, had been initiated into this world only six years ago. He wondered how Beth washed her hands. She also was an FFB—frum from birth—but with an appealing sincerity he hadn't quite expected. He shook his head, lightly smacking the side of his jaw. Who was he to sit in judgment of FFBs?

He washed, dressed, drank a cup of Bancha tea, threw some food items into a knapsack and was out the door. The darkness was just beginning to lift and the fresh, sharp air snapped against his face. His shoulders lifted against the cold. A few blocks away in the Egged garage terminal he could hear the buses snorting and shuddering to life. Soon they'd make their rounds. He leaned against the bus shelter, a new one that the government had just installed, replacing all the old rain-battered ones with the corroding green walls. No one was there and his body felt free to let out a spasm that began with a back and forth twist of his neck, shifting down to his shoulders and hands, a gentle morning spasm.

A red-and-white Egged bus whizzed down Shofar Avenue, a number fifteen, and Akiva sprang forward as it passed, waving his arms. After twenty yards, it braked sharply. As he sprinted toward it, Akiva knew which driver it was: the bald, sullen, handsome man everyone called Kojak.

He stepped inside and held out his card. Kojak punched a hole in it the shape of a sickle. "Why do you hide in the bus shelter so I can't see you?" he asked. Akiva understood the real question: What are you doing up at five-thirty in the morning that you force me to stop for just one person? Most Jerusalemites got up six, six-thirty and tried to make it to synagogue by seven, but Akiva liked to pray in Shaarei Hessed which was a few neighborhoods away, and close to his yeshiva.

Akiva shrugged. "Next time I'll stand closer to the street," he said in his Canadian-accented Hebrew, but he knew it wouldn't help. Kojak hated him. His great aim in life was to dart by so quickly Akiva wouldn't notice the bus in time to stop it. This had happened a few times, but now Akiva's early morning senses were so fine-tuned that nothing passed him by.

From the fifth row of the bus, the smell of soap and french fries nipped at his nostrils. He spotted a greasy plastic plate on the dashboard, a lone french fry mangled and drenched in ketchup. He smelled other things, too: a sour, manly odor as Kojak worked the wheel with his short, massive, salami-like arms, the dankness of his rubbery gray sneakers, the crustiness of his jeans, his wants, his frustrations.

Kojak was now staring at him in the front mirror, casting him angry, wary looks. Akiva turned his gaze toward him, till he dropped his eyes. For the life of him he couldn't understand why Kojak hated him. He was friendly to the others.

Other people began to get on, mostly manual laborers and plump Sephardic women holding empty baskets. At Kings of Israel Street, the crowd shifted. The bus was now entering Meah Sh'orrim territory. Black-hatted and befrocked men got on, followed by the women, one who struck Akiva as particularly handsome, old and flaccid-eyed as she was. She was small and held a tiny book of Psalms, and she carried herself with an elegant piety. Akiva stood and gestured toward his seat, in deference to her age. But she had already passed and another woman, young and modestly attired, slid into his place in one thrusting motion. Akiva's head jerked slightly. Was a spasm coming? He didn't think so. Sometimes he could control a spasm or delay it by at least a minute, and other times it sprang on him like a violent sneeze. There was no telling. He must have felt slightly drawn to the young woman, and guilty about it, too, as if he had already pledged himself to Beth and she to him. He let out a small snort. He knew better than to get his hopes up.

He stood near his seat, his hulking six feet filling the aisle. As his eyes roved the bus, the modestly dressed young woman flashed him a look. A strain registered in Akiva's forehead. He gritted his teeth but the strain only increased. He grunted, and his arms, legs and head went limp. Then his right arm jutted out, slicing the air all around him, and his head jerked sharply, again and again. A hiccup erupted from his mouth. His legs shook, a light flashed in his head, and he would have fallen if he hadn't been holding on to the overhead bar with his left hand. At last the spasm ended. He rubbed his neck, which ached, and bent to gather the carrot sticks, whole wheat cookies, and leather-bound prayerbook that had tumbled from his knapsack. When he rose he saw a busload of faces turned on him. He breathed out and a perverse purr of pleasure rumbled through his body, the aftershocks of the spasm.

Kojak, his fists balled into his hips, was advancing toward him. His bald head gleamed. His lower lip hung slightly in a menacing, sensuous pout. "Get off my bus," he flung at Akiva. "Get off, American hippie. Take your drugs back to New York."

Akiva stood still, his eyes dazed, the irony of the situation rooting him to the spot. A grim smile fixed on his lips. Of course, this was why Kojak hated him. It was his twitch, his spasms which made him suspect.

"Get out, hippie!" Kojak barked, ignoring some stray pleading comments from the passengers. The driver was king of the bus. He could do what he wanted. He stood erect, a meaty arm pointed, his eyes bloodshot and righteous.

Akiva considered correcting him, not only his mistaken perception and the fact that he was from Canada, not New York, but the way he pronounced "hippie" (heepee). He also thought of resisting, gripping the pole with ten dogged fingers, but he didn't see the point. He fixed the knapsack across his shoulders and turned toward the rear exit door.

Just before he stepped off, he heard the beautiful old woman with the psalms call out to the driver, "This man's presence on the bus was an honor too great for you. Too great," she repeated loudly. "Go back to your wheel."

The bus skidded and sped off, leaving him on the curb of Ezekiel Street, just off Sabbath Square. He brushed down his pants, shook his right leg, smoothed down his beard. He walked down the street half-humming, half-muttering the words to an Eric Burdon song, "I'm just a soul whose intentions are good."

❉   ❉   ❉

The walls were painted with a whitewash that flecked off onto your clothing in long, pale dusty scabs. So Judy discovered after she had been leaning against the wall at the Beit Shifra Yeshiva, looking at the women's study hall. Here and there she saw a woman her own age, but mostly they were college girls. The room was so cold that any word or sigh hung in the air, frigid little puffs of breath. The students were dressed in layers: turtlenecks, thick sweaters, colorful leggings peeking out from under long skirts, mostly denim material. The students were so scrubbed, their clothes so new, they smelled of America. Every girl had something in her hair: a rainbow clip, a scrunchy, a headband. Apparently, since her move to Israel, hair accessories had become de rigueur in the States.

Her eyes settled on a woman in a beret. Ah, there was Naomi Safran. She spotted her moving between the tables, going over to the bookshelf, bent over, looking for some volume, answering the questions that the students asked her as she passed by, serving as a floating reference board.

Judy went up to her. "I see there's a few levels here. Where do you suggest I go?"

Naomi was wearing a rather severe blue beret, but her manner was sprightly and welcoming. "You came! Well now." She glanced at the schedule of classes. "You can read Hebrew, right?"

A young woman in a long swishy skirt and Birkenstocks was calling out from a doorway, "Anybody see Mindy Bramson? She's got a call from Toronto!" The students lifted their heads and tittered as a petite girl with a striking short haircut jumped up, scuttled between the tables and darted out the door. One or two cast envious looks.

"It's her fiancé," Naomi explained wryly. "Third time he's called today. So, can you translate?"

Judy nodded. "More or less." She looked at all the young women, some of them quite lovely—young fruit getting snatched off the vine. And yet they'd come to a women's yeshiva to study Torah for a year or two, maybe even three. In her college days, when she had been young and pretty, would she have devoted a year to Torah study? Then she had mostly thought about finding a man who was devoted to Torah study. She wondered if she had done the right thing in coming here, now.

"Level Two," Naomi said decisively. "You'll be taking the class on Genesis, Chapter II." She pointed to the sources Judy would need to look up. "Try to hook up with a chevrutah partner if you can."

She sat down at the corner of a long table where two women, young ones, were arguing over a text, learning together, b'chevrutah. With a Styrofoam cup of coffee at her side, she sat trying to translate the story of the creation of Eve.

What am I doing here with these children? she thought. She should be helping them get married, if anything. Though lately she'd been feeling overwhelmed by the number of calls coming her way. And some of the people were so hopeless, particularly the men. She felt bad for the women. Who were they supposed to marry? How long could she say, 'Yes, the good men are all taken, because after they're taken, they get good'? True, but only to a degree. Maybe marriage might improve someone like a Binyamin Harris, but getting him to marry in the first place would take a miracle or a trick or two she wasn't beyond pulling. He was a narcissist, charming but impossible.

One of the women at her table suddenly clopped her hand down, making Judy startle and cough up some coffee. In a moment or two the young woman was standing next to Judy, apologizing and offering her a napkin.

"Sorry. I get carried away sometimes." She gave a rueful smile. Judy stared at her as she took the napkin and dabbed at her mouth. She was very pretty, with high cheekbones and a barrette clipped over one ear, holding her silky, shoulder-length blond hair in place. Even her Stern College lumpy sweatshirt managed to look elegant on her. She bent over Judy's book. "Looks like you're preparing for the same class. Why don't you join us?"

"Certainly." Judy slid her chair over, somewhat gracelessly, without getting up from her seat.

"My name's Lauren, by the way. And you're—" Her index finger shot out questioningly.

"Judy," she said, flinching slightly. *Rebbetzin* Judy, is what she wanted to say. In Minneapolis she'd had Friday night sing-a-longs with girls not much younger than the ones in front of her. She'd taught them harmonies and snappy, Israeli melodies. She'd been especially popular with the twelfth-graders.

Lauren introduced her study partner, Dina, an olive-skinned plumpish girl, with lovely dark eyes almost obscured in wire glasses, who conveyed a look of being both scholarly and naive. She wore her hair in a thick dark braid draped over one shoulder like a badger's tail. A macramé vest with soft autumn colors was joined in a fat gold button over her heart. Judy wondered if she'd made the vest herself. "Why don't you read," Dina prompted her.

Judy positioned herself in her chair and read in Hebrew, " 'It is not good for Adam to be alone. I will make him a helpmeet opposite him.' " She couldn't help shaking her head and chuckling.

"What's so funny?" they both demanded.

"I'm a matchmaker," Judy explained. "I couldn't have found a more appropriate verse for my calling."

Their eyes widened. Dina fingered a small hole in her vest. She seemed a little frightened.

"Wow," said Lauren. "You're the first matchmaker I've ever met."

"Not me. I've met maybe ten." Dina added, "I've been on more blind dates than I can count."

Judy took a closer look at her, the half-circles carved around her mouth and the beginning of slackness around the neck area. Here was no college girl, but a woman in her early thirties.

Lauren smoothed down a page that kept flipping over, finally resting the edge of her spiral notebook on it. "So what are the problems with this verse? What hits you?"

Their eyes narrowed on the text. "Well," Dina offered, "the creation of woman sounds like: Man's lonely. God throws in a woman to keep him company, make life better for him."

Judy stared at her. "And what's so terrible about that?"

"It suggests her existence doesn't have intrinsic worth, independent of man." Dina groped in a knapsack. "Wait a second. I'm getting a refill."

Judy's eyes followed her to the hot water urn where other students grouped, exchanging packets of Quaker Instant Oatmeal probably sent in care packages from America, laughing about something she couldn't hear. She peered at the words again. She'd never quite thought of the verse that way. "No one has independent existence," she pronounced when Dina returned. "We're all interconnected."

"Spoken like a true matchmaker. But you have to admit," Lauren pointed a pencil at her, "Eve does come across like an afterthought."

"Hm. I suppose so." A frightening thought occurred to her: Was *she* an afterthought? Dovid didn't see her that way, God forbid. But what about other people? She recalled when her husband had been a rabbi, how the congregants would lean toward him to catch every word, even his offhand remarks. Mostly she'd felt proud, but sometimes she'd had an urge to pinch herself to make sure she wasn't invisible.

"Any other questions?" The clip in Lauren's hair unloosened and Judy watched her tweak and adjust it. Looking at her Judy couldn't help thinking she was too beautiful to truly immerse herself in Torah study.

"I don't know," Dina was muttering to herself. "To tell the truth, this verse makes me angry. How am I supposed to feel? If women were created for the sake of men, or say you understand it mutually, that men, too, were created for the sake of women, then where does that leave me? What place do I and all the other singles have in this world? I'm irrelevant." Her eyes blazed, and for a second Judy thought she might burst into tears. Instead she took a cautious sip of Red Zinger tea.

"You're right, Dina." Judy moved her chair a drop closer. "It really is a kind of Jewish taboo to be single, which is very painful and not very fair. But taboos are useful, you know. They help move people on to the next stage in their life. It's taboo for a four-year-old to wear diapers, so even though he doesn't want to stop wearing diapers, he gets his act together and adjusts to putting on underwear."

"But I *want* to be married," Dina almost wailed. "I don't need a communal push."

"Not you," Judy stage-whispered. "The men. Without the taboo, they'd never get it together. That's why men are commanded to get married, but not the women."

"Back on the ranch." Lauren cleared her throat and tapped the table. "This isn't an actual question," she said, "but I'm just struck by the words, 'Not good.' Till now we've just heard again and again, 'God created light and saw that it was good,' 'God created trees, animals, birds, and saw that it was good.' 'Good.' 'Good.' 'Good.' It keeps repeating throughout the first chapter. And then suddenly, 'It's not good for Adam to be alone.' The words kind of hit your heart with a thud, don't they?"

Judy nodded. "Not Good. It's almost like a slap. All that approval, all that Divine affirmation, and we suddenly bump into Divine displeasure. 'This aloneness is not the way things should be.' "

"Tell me about it." Dina mournfully stroked the tip of her braid.

Judy reached over and patted her arm. "Relax, your besherte's probably reading a book or eating a falafel right now."

"Any other questions?" Lauren asked. Both of them turned their heads toward Judy, who was caught slightly off guard. She gazed at the text, willing herself to come up with something fresh, never been asked before, just like Lauren and Dina had done. But she hadn't been trained to think that way. She almost felt angry at the women for expecting this of her. She was nice-looking, a good mother, a good wife, clever enough, kind, competent. Wasn't that enough to be satisfied in the world? Did she also have to be original? "Well, there's the phrase, 'a helpmeet opposite him.' It sounds contradictory. A helper that opposes you." This was the standard question every commentary remarked on, every rabbi posed when giving a sermon. Hardly original, but Lauren and Dina nodded. "Good. So now let's see what answers we can come up with."

Judy's hand trembled slightly as it gripped her Styrofoam cup. "Excuse me, but isn't this going overboard? I mean, the answers are right here in the commentary. Why bother trying to guess what they said when we could just read them?"

Lauren said, "Did you learn that way in high school?"

Judy nodded. No one expected them to offer their own interpretations. If they understood and could convey what the commentaries said, the teachers were more than satisfied.

"Yes, me too," said Dina. "It wasn't very rewarding. Just try it this way. The text kind of opens to you. Believe me, it'll only enhance your understanding of the commentaries."

Judy shrugged elaborately. Well, she'd do it their way, but she found the idea faintly upsetting. Even sacrilegious. As if she had something to say that hadn't already occurred to the Sages.

Lauren gave a sudden exclamation. "You know, we've been translating this verse wrong! We've been reading it, 'It's not good for Adam to be alone.' It should really read, 'It's not good, this state of Adam

being alone.' " She pointed out the extra word, 'heyot,'—existence—
that had led her in that direction.

"So what's the difference?" Judy asked.

Lauren slumped in her chair. "I don't know. Dina, got any ideas?"

Dina removed her glasses and pressed her hand against her eyes
and forehead. She was silent for a minute and Judy marveled at her
complete concentration. Then Dina smiled and stared out, her face
looking brand-new and vulnerable, like a freshly peeled hard-boiled
egg. " 'Not good for Adam implies woman was created solely with
man in mind, for his benefit. But this translation implies—this state of
man being alone is not beneficial for the universe. It's a cosmological
statement. This aloneness is not good for the world. Woman wasn't
created to complement man but to complete the world."

Lauren was nodding, "I like it, I like it."

"My goodness," said Judy. "That sounds like a huge leap based on
just one word—heyot."

"Maybe it is. Let's see what Rashi has to say now." Three heads
pored over the tiny commentary script. Something was starting to
emerge from the fog. Lauren was murmuring to herself, "an imbalance
in creation, two domains, two authorities" as her finger followed the
small print. She was the first to raise her head, her brows raised in
delight. "She's right, don't you see? Rashi suggests the very same idea!
Until woman was created there was a terrible imbalance in the universe." She half stood in her chair. "Don't you see it now?"

Dina was nodding and grinning. Lauren high-fived her. "You got
it, babe!"

Judy stared at the print. Yes, they were right. Buried in the Rashi
commentary was the very idea that Dina had stated. But she never
would've seen it if they hadn't struggled on their own first. Rashi's
subtle point would've eluded her. A different idea occurred to her
then. "Maybe," she said quietly, thinking out loud, "it's not the creation of the woman that completes the world, but," she hesitated a

moment, "but when a man and woman become reconciled to one another, can live together in a warm connection, *that's* what completes and forms the basis of the entire creation. 'Not good' refers to an absence of connection. God wants here—not a cold peace, but a true reconciliation." As she spoke, her own words resonated deeply inside her. Because her job as a matchmaker was not just to put odd socks together and match them up, but to reconcile man to woman and woman to man.

"You're on a roll, Judy." Lauren was grinning at her. "That kind of answers your question, 'a helpmeet opposite.' It's that reconciliation—as you call it—between opposites, between Man and Woman, that brings us to our deepest good."

Judy smiled, pleased with the way she had taken their idea and run with it, and how Lauren was shaping her idea in turn. Their minds had become intimate. Maybe there was something to this different method of learning, and maybe she did have something new to offer. She would certainly come back.

The young woman with the swishy skirt and Birkenstocks called out, "Phone call for Lauren Nevetsky from New York."

Lauren rose as if pulled by invisible strings, her face alight with anticipation. As she fairly spun out of the room, Dina said in a low voice, "It's her boyfriend. They're practically engaged."

Judy felt her high spirits dip a notch or two as she watched her go. Not enough that Lauren was beautiful and smart. And a boyfriend to boot. Lauren had more Torah knowledge than she, and she was how old? She really did have it all.

※　※　※

Tsippi passed Rochel Leah's Polish roommate, who lay in bed with her earphones on; images of a show called "Dynasty" flitted silently across the screen. Before she entered Rochel Leah's section, she shuddered, as if warding off a sensation of death. She thought of a Talmudic saying—Three kinds of people were considered as dead: a poor person, a blind person, and a childless person. And here, Rochel Leah was practically all three.

"Nu, so what did he say?" was the first thing Rochel Leah asked as Tsippi entered. Color bloomed in the old woman's cheeks. Her boxy hat sat sprightly on her head.

Tsippi fidgeted with her apartment keys. Rochel Leah's eagerness depressed her, because her love was doomed. She might choose to love a corpse, but a corpse could not love back, and that's what she had seen the other day, a virtual corpse with black prayer boxes on his head. She had a soft spot for unrequited love, she always had. She loved a difficult match, especially one that required expert handling, like the Beth-Akiva shidduch which was now underway, may God place His blessing on them, she inwardly intoned. But there would be no joining of two people here. This was a situation of impossible—no, preposterous—love. She regarded the old woman soberly. "He said nothing. He just lay there."

Rochel Leah's eyes blinked a few times, and then she stuck a finger behind her cat's glasses and wiped. "So he didn't read my note," she stated. She did not appear terribly surprised, merely sad.

Tsippi shook her head. "He was covered with notes, though I can't say why, and I don't think he read any of them." She added, "I just don't think he could." Again, Rochel Leah simply sat and blinked. Tsippi went on. "He's no longer in that room, by the way. He was moved to Room 708."

Rochel Leah lifted her two hands and stared at them. Then a cry broke forth from her lips, and she muttered to herself, "No, not there, not *that* floor. He couldn't be worse than before—" Then she said harshly to herself, "Quiet Rochel Leah!" The old woman sat in her bed, a pad of yellow lined paper on her lap, writing, her lips twitching, then falling slack, then twitching some more. In a moment, she thrust out her pointed chin toward the book in Tsippi's arms, and Tsippi opened it to the page with the Israel Museum bookmark.

" 'I will return to you this time next year, said one of the men, and your wife Sarah will have a son.'

" 'Sarah was listening behind the entrance of the tent. Abraham and Sarah were already old, well on in years, and Sarah no longer had female periods. She laughed to herself, saying, Now that I am worn out, shall I have my heart's desire? My husband is old!' "

Tsippi startled. And what of her own desire? she thought. There were many things worth praying for, and she did, turning to God at odd hours of the day, but what could she say was her true heart's desire, anyway? At least Sarah knew what she wanted. Tsippi's mother had always told her, "If you don't know what you want, you get what you don't want." She wanted things for other people—to get married, to have children, to enjoy a life of Torah—but she didn't know what she wanted for herself. She yawned, and suddenly she saw her husband bent over a pile of books. Shlomo was old, but he hadn't always been. During their courtship she had thought it impossible that he would ever age. He had a fire in him in those days—fahbrent. During the war, he had joined the partisans, he had fought, killed Germans and Ukrainian peasants with his two hands. He'd had the body of a bear. And he had had the power to make people laugh. That's how he got the Polish partisans to accept him into their small band, a Jew who could only bring danger to their group. But did she, his own wife, ever hear a joke come from his mouth? Never.

Rochel Leah was banging a spoon on the bed's wood frame. "Don't stop at the good part," she cackled.

Tsippi stifled another yawn. What on earth was she doing here? She lifted the Bible and held it three inches from her face. She read aloud: " 'And God said to Abraham, Why did Sarah laugh and say, "Can I really have a child when I am so old?" Is anything too difficult for God?' " She had a sudden thought—Did God like Rochel Leah? But that question was none of her business.

"He lied, He lied!" Rochel Leah crowed. Tsippi looked at her with alarm and pity.

"No," Tsippi softly corrected her, "not God. It was Sarah who lied. Listen to the following verses: 'Sarah was afraid and she denied it. I did not laugh, she said. Abraham said, You did.' " She looked up at Rochel Leah.

Rochel Leah pointed her spoon. "Foolish girl. Listen, listen to the words. Sarah said her husband was old, but when God spoke to Abraham, He changed it around, saying she called *herself* old. Now why," her neck, which had fused into her chin, stretched taut, "why did He lie?"

"I don't know," Tsippi said in a defeated voice. She felt too scolded and tired to participate in Rochel Leah's little games. "Maybe God is a romantic at heart," she said with a flip of her shoulder, not caring what Rochel Leah thought. "He didn't want Abraham to know Sarah thought he was old, so He worded it differently. He did lie, but for a good reason, to keep them happy with each other."

Rochel Leah said, "Eh . . . not bad, Tsippi-Pippi," unknowingly using the nickname of her youth.

Go to sleep, Tsippi thought, but for a moment she felt good, pleased with the woman's grudging tribute. Yes, she did believe God was a romantic—anyone who read the Bible could see that. But apparently not all were destined for romantic married lives.

Just then Rochel Leah tore off a sheet from the yellow pad that had been resting on her knees, and folded the piece of paper four or five times to a square wedge. She held out a scrawny branch of an arm to Tsippi. "Please, give this to Reb Isaac," she asked, with more humility than Tsippi had ever seen in her face. "Try again," she said. "This time, tell him it's for love. Tell him it's from Rochel Leah."

Tsippi swallowed and, avoiding her companion's eyes, slipped the note into her pocket. She would help if she could, even if it was unseemly. But as she headed toward room 708 her feet lagged. How could she possibly convince a comatose rabbinic gentleman of anything? And even if he weren't insensible, would he *want* a partly bedridden and blind old lady in her mannish hat and foolish glasses? The gentleman appeared to be at least ten years younger than Rochel Leah. But the impossibility—one could say the nobility—of this love made her chest contract for the woman.

With a deep sense of futility, Tsippi knocked on the door, waited, knocked again and entered, and there he lay spread out, stiff. Nothing had changed since she had last seen him except that the notes on the floor had been swept away. She crept closer to the bed. She said quietly in her most heartfelt voice, "This is for you, for love."

A neck muscle jerked. The man blinked, once, twice, and then his eyes slid to the corner and he stared, and in that stare Tsippi saw a question. She added, "From Rochel Leah." At those words the balls of his eyes lost their focus and fell back inside him to some lost place. She put the note in the space between his finger and thumb, but it dropped to the floor. She left, her heart grieving for Rochel Leah.

In the hallway she bumped into a nurse with blue-rimmed eyes.

"What's wrong with that man," Tsippi pointed, "the one in that room?"

The nurse wagged her head from side to side, clucking her tongue. "Oh, so sad, five months ago, a strong healthy man. Then his wife died, and he has not left the bed since. And for a whole week now," her eyes opened wide, "he refuses to talk, refuses to eat!" She wagged her head again, unable to resist the lure of telling over a misfortune.

Tsippi's eyes narrowed. Suddenly Rochel Leah seemed a scheming woman, insensitive, capitalizing on a widower's pain. "Who is he?" she asked. "Everyone seems to know him."

"It's Rabbi Isaac Mordechai," the nurse told her, and seeing

Tsippi's blank look, added, "the kabbalist." She kissed her pursed fingers and touched them to her eyes and, in a fit of modesty, did up the neck button on her uniform. "You never heard of him?" A look part surprise, part sneer crossed her face, a look that said, "What kind of religious person could you possibly be?"

Tsippi shrugged. She had never heard of him. But so great was her amazement that she could barely acknowledge the nurse's disdain. Rochel Leah was sending love notes to a kabbalist widower. Was there no end to this woman's nerve or self-delusion? She was a fool for helping her out, a dupe—that's what she was, making matches among the corpses, groping for life among the almost dead.

Chapter Five

D R. CARMI, BETH'S BOSS, CAME UP TO HER AS SHE WAS REFILLING her mug with hot water, trying to eke out another cup from a bag of chamomile. He was in his early sixties, still handsome, with a head full of dark gray hair which fell to one side, and an upright bearing.

"My wife gave you a compliment the other day," he said.

"Oh?" said Beth, wary. He had a way of throwing her off balance, sneaking up on her in odd ways. She got along well enough with the other co-workers, both secular and religious. Only he irked her. He liked to stand close, a hairsbreadth away, and when she'd give him a look, or remind him that she was a religious woman, he'd step back with exaggerated zeal, his hands raised in the air, and say, "Oh yes, one of the pious untouchables." He liked to read out loud in her presence the racier portions of the Bible. Once she found a photocopy of his hands on her chair.

And now he had a smirk on his face. "My wife said if polygamy ever came back in style, she wouldn't mind having you be the second wife." Beth gave him a puzzled stare. "She said you'd be like a sister to her, someone to do the chores with. There wouldn't have to be any competition."

Beth edged her spoon against the mug and removed the bag of chamomile. "So, you're trying to say I'm the kind of woman who inspires sisterly feelings but not jealousy? Is that what you're suggesting?"

"Actually Beth, I didn't think of that, but—you're right." He let out a guffaw.

Beth smiled grimly and returned to her desk. She hated herself. Did she have to be so helpful? Did she have to even feed him his lines? As she drank her cup of tea, she remembered her date with Akiva, and the thought comforted her.

It was Friday, so work let out early. At two o'clock she washed out her tea mug, bade Dr. Carmi a "Shabbat Shalom," and headed out the door. Two beggars, a man and a woman, sat on the stoop outside the building. The woman had a long face and pointy teeth and was draped in loose layers of clothing. The man beggar was an Arab, broad-shouldered and clean-shaven, with a black yarmulka sitting solidly on his bald head. Except for calling out, "Tzedakkah!" he never said a word, his face impassive, even when the woman grew peeved at his silence and threatened to tell the passersby from the Meah Sh'orrim district that he was an impostor. Today Beth threw in an extra half-shekel, and the long-faced woman sang out, "Shabbat Shalom!" From the bald man she got a flicker of a smile.

She had a thing with beggars. She could never say no. It had something to do with her upbringing. Every Friday night her father would pick out the sickest, most rundown person in the synagogue, and bring home some beggar or schnorrer for a meal and a place to sleep. He'd been doing this from the time she was eight or nine. Sometimes when she'd complain about the old men, their perpetual plegmy throats and loud barking sneezes that their yellowed handkerchiefs never could properly contain, the humps and warts and the general air of misery that they evoked, her father would just say, "Charity saves from death." She remembered exactly how he said it, raising his eyebrows Groucho Marx–style, deadpan, a pretend cigar between his forefinger and thumb. Then there was that terrible week, the week her mother got seriously ill and had to spend Shabbat in the hospital, and she and her father were numb with worry. And still her father brought home a schnorrer to share the Shabbat meal. Later that evening, she found her father sitting on the bed, holding some old socks of her mother's in his hands, and she suddenly said, "Daddy, you don't have to worry! Ma's going to be okay." He said, "What do you mean?" And she said, as if it was obvious, "Charity saves from death!" Her father put down the socks and held her head between his hands. "Don't you know," he said, "charity doesn't save people from dying. It saves God from dying." She looked up at him, frightened. Then he said that God could die inside you but the good things you did kept God alive. That's what he said. Beth used to go back to those words, especially later on when it became her job to make the house ready for Shabbat.

Years later, when her father had died, and it was just her and the beggars, she knew she couldn't do it alone. That's when she decided to move to Jerusalem. Jerusalem became like a parent, gathering Beth into her small suburbs, always watching over her, especially on dates, the trees nodding her on, encouraging her, a mountain peak extending its long hazy arm in the horizon, inviting her to begin again, with yet another. These muted expressions of concern filled tiny little holes inside her. It was as much love as she could bear. Even though it was harder to make a living in Israel, she never regretted her decision to come.

Beth passed another beggar, a lanky American Hassid who looked wolf-like with his scruffy beard and wild peyos dangling past his shoulders. He sang—to the tune of "Found A Peanut"—"Help the schnorrer, help the schnorrer, help the schnorrer—please pay well; help the schnorrer, help the schnorrer, and you won't end up in the other place." He stuck out a bony hand, and she gave him a little extra, for at least he was attempting a sales pitch. "Oy," she heard him say, as she went toward the bus. "Meah Schnorrim."

Later, after she'd lit two Shabbat candles in her apartment, she met with Dina, a single American woman who lived in a neighborhood close by, and they made their way up Levites Street to the Nadvorna Hassidic shul. They had both been invited for a Shabbat meal at a home next to the synagogue. The streets were quiet, the stores were closed, no cars or buses passing, no one waiting at the stops, even no children playing outside. Weekday life had stopped. Only people milling to synagogue, singly, in two's or three's, or entire families, and surrounding them, the Jerusalem hills, hazy, raw and oddly soft in the fading winter light.

Beth had put on a flowery embroidered jalabeeya from the Arab shuk and a gold pendant necklace from her mother. The exotic dress and its long, flowing length aroused a new sense of allure in her, even with the bulky wool sweater and jacket she wore over it to keep warm. She sniffed the air. No baking bread smell from Yussel's Bakery, but the air was thick with Shabbat fare: gefilte fish, cholent or chamin, jachnun and koobana bread, zchug hot sauce, Yerushalmi kugel. She found it difficult to concentrate on her friend, who was lamenting the latest shidduch of the week. Dina had nice big eyes, a good head of soft dark hair and smooth olive cheeks, but her mouth, set primly in her face, made her look pinched and disheartened.

"And you know why he didn't want to go out with me in the end?" Her wire glasses glinted in the fading sun. "He told the lady who introduced us that I don't have enough Yetzer Hara, not enough devil in me." She gave Beth a puzzled stare. "Now what could he mean by that?"

Beth stopped for a moment. "Fire," she said, nodding her head. "I think he meant provocative."

Dina covered her mouth in dismay. "Don't I have any fire?" she asked in a stricken voice.

Beth gave her friend a deep look of apology. "Of course you do," she reassured her. They were silent as they walked up the hill. Beth was wondering about her own capacities for Evil Impulses. She doubted them. Her friends couldn't believe she'd never kissed a man. The ba'al teshuva girlfriends were in awe of her ("You're a saint, Beth!"). The frum from birth friends thought she was crazy ("I never could've lasted that long single" or "But you seem so normal"). I am normal, she'd retort. But was she? She'd once read about an experiment with monkeys who went a long time without being touched and never quite developed normally after that. Had she done damage to herself? She yearned to be married and yet there was no one person in all her years who she had longed to be with. Sometimes she thought a person would have to light a fire underneath her to get her moving in the direction of marriage. But she was looking forward to her meeting with Akiva. No—more than that. Her heart was on tiptoe.

They were passing an industrial area: here a scrap metal yard, there an iron foundry. As they went up an incline they turned into a weedy, rundown section. A robustly handsome, white-bearded man grinned at them from his tiny vine-covered porch. He slouched in a big, wooden chair, a backgammon board resting on a small table. "Ah, here come the righteous women!" he said.

"How do you know we're really righteous?" Beth threw back.

He peered at them from under a cocked white brow. "I can see the Shabbat on your faces," he said.

They both laughed delightedly and walked on, but Beth knew it wasn't only Shabbat that lit up her features.

At two o'clock the next day, there was a knock at Beth's door. She opened it.

There Akiva stood, one arm against the doorpost and the other hand holding a folded jacket. He was wearing a white shirt with a V-neck blue sweater, the sleeves rolled up, and she saw his arms, much whiter and pudgier than she had expected them to be, covered with downy blond hair that made him look feminine. His face was craggier than her last recollection, a little parched. He even had creases between his ears and his temples. As she looked at him, she felt her excitement turn into something dull and sluggish. This couldn't be the man who had inspired all the tangled, wondrous emotions she had experienced a few nights ago. It didn't seem her fate was to change after all.

Akiva straightened. "Hello," he said a bit flatly. "Shabbat Shalom."

"Shabbat Shalom." She climbed down the stairs, holding clumsily on to the rail.

Halfway down, a spasm of twitches and hiccups overcame him. "Excuse me." He wiped his mouth.

"Please, you don't have to excuse yourself," she said quietly.

They walked outside into bright sun and people. It was warm, in the sixties, not unheard-of in Jerusalem in late December. Husbands and wives pushed double strollers down the sidewalk, the women bobbing like proud little hens in their Shabbat wigs. Children dodged in and out of the street, their parents watching indulgently, not worried about cars or buses. Young girls in Empire-waisted flowered dresses walked in tight groups, talking to each other behind cupped hands. The world was out taking an afternoon walk.

Akiva began talking about a Rabbi Yellin, an interesting rabbi he had grown attached to. Beth listened with an abstracted air, barely taking in his words. What if he had an attack before the entire community? He might erupt at any moment. Their last date had taken place in the misty air of Yemin Moshe, with practically no one around to see if he twitched or did somersaults or yelled obscenities at the pigeons. But now they had two blocks to walk till they reached the seclusion of the Jerusalem Forest, their destination. The laughter and talk in the street whirred in her ears. She took fragile steps, blinking at the colored clothing parading in different directions.

"Could we walk faster?" she said.

"Sure." He gave her a faint, quizzical look.

They turned down a steep gravelly path that led into the Jerusalem Forest, and in a matter of minutes they had left all the people behind. On the right, the forest was darkly dense. Then the path split and gave way to a road with weeds and long grass sprouting on either side. Beth began to breathe more slowly. She pressed her hand to her stomach; it was beginning to calm down. She flattened her feet against the earth and delicately stretched her neck.

Akiva bent a knee to the ground. "Tell me what this smells like." He showed her a thin, delicate reed, with tiny yellow buds.

She bent her head to the plant and sniffed. "Licorice! What's it called?"

"Fennel. And this here," pointing to a wild, scruffy-looking plant, "if you pull out the shards, there's a round stalk in the middle. It looks and tastes like celery, but it's much sweeter."

He looked much sweeter himself, she decided, surrounded by all the green, green getting into his beard, between his fingers and legs. He looked good, period. So why couldn't she stop herself from looking so critically at his ears or the crags in his face? She watched him extricate himself from the plants, careful not to uproot or pluck anything that would disturb the peace of Shabbat. She wondered if it was simply easier for her to make him appear unattractive to her than to admit she couldn't handle his twitch.

"Do you see that gray building over there?" She pointed in the distance. "That's a psychiatric institution where I volunteer sometimes."

He nodded. "Good," he said. "If we get thirsty, we can probably go there to get a drink." He brushed down his pants.

A blue car whizzed by. Akiva's head jerked sharply to the right in rapid successions. An arm flopped backward. Two children peered at him through the back window of the car, their little hands pressed to the glass.

Suddenly drained, Beth let out the quietest sigh. "Akiva, could we stop for a while?" she said hesitantly. "I'm feeling a little tired. I think the cholent I ate may be disagreeing with me." After shul she'd gone to the Bartosky's for lunch, where she'd consumed a huge, oily portion of cholent bean stew.

He nodded sympathetically.

They made themselves comfortable under a leafy carob tree. She brought her fingertips to her nose and smelled the scent of licorice on them. She felt his hazel eyes grazing her face.

"Cholent," she said, with mock gravity. "That's one thing I'll never cook."

Akiva started expounding on the holiness of cholent, the holiness of heartburn. "Maybe that's why Shabbat is so special," he said. "It's the only day that can elevate such a greasy mess of food."

She laughed, delighted, clapping her hands.

He leaned on one elbow, stretching out his legs. "What were you like as a little girl? You have a very childlike quality."

"Child*ish* or child*like*?" said Beth.

He snorted. "Childish, we can all do without. That's not what I meant."

"Actually," Beth angled her arms over her head, "I was a strange child." She told him how she used to stand in front of the mirror when she was eight, parting her hair to the left, then the right, finally down the middle, and say solemnly into the mirror, "Beth, the whole world thinks you're ugly, but only you know you're beautiful." Then as soon as the words came out she'd be horrified and try to banish the thought from her head, because she imagined she'd lose whatever prettiness she did have as soon as she expressed her awareness of it.

She looked intently at Akiva. "Does this sound horribly narcissistic?"

He shrugged. "I don't think in those terms. I just liked listening to you."

"What about your childhood?" she asked.

"Well." He sat up straight. "In fourth grade the principal came into class one day and asked us what we wanted to be. After all the firemen and nurses had their say I got up—remember this was in Vancouver—and I said, 'I want to eat the ten commandments.' "

Beth chuckled. "That really is strange. Why did you say that?"

"I don't know." He smiled self-indulgently. "Maybe even then I knew I wanted to integrate the Torah inside me."

"Oh!" She moaned and clutched her stomach. "Please, that's too much. I feel ill." They both fell on the soft grass, laughing. Her black flats had slipped off. Akiva reached over and took one of them into his hands. He held it for a few seconds. Then his fingers slowly went along the sides, stroking the heel, curving around the toe, then the softer insides of the shoe. He turned it over in his knotty hands. Delicately, he placed it back with the other.

"Nice shoe," he said quietly. He closed his eyes.

The nape of her neck felt damp. She breathed in through her nostrils. She felt aware of her lips, their shape and outline, the tips of her fingers. She stared at her arm, at the little hairs raised by a passing breeze, her arm newly alive and dangerous, as if it might reach out and hit him in the gut, or lurch forward and give his beard a hard yank, so hard it would make him jump and twitch like a Mexican bean. What was going on? What had gotten into her? She wrapped her arms around herself and rocked a little. The truth is, her own desire nauseated her. Too real, too gritty, sweaty.

"You seem wistful." His voice was close to her.

She looked up. He had not moved. "No, I'm just . . ." She shook her head. "I'm actually thirsty. Are you?"

"Yes, kind of. Okay, it's to the asylum," he spread an invisible cape with his arm, "where water fountains abound."

"Yes, Sir Galahad, to the asylum." On impulse she asked, "Did you ever act?"

"No. I used to be a clown, though. I'd put on clown shows at children's birthday parties to pick up some spare money." He shucked his beard with his knuckles. "I was pretty good, I think. As you can tell, I'm a ham. It was around that time that my spasms started up. Sometimes in the middle of performing, suddenly I'd start to twitch just like that—out of the blue."

While he spoke she pictured him standing in someone's living room in a polka-dotted costume, his face painted, staring out in bewilderment, not understanding what was happening, the six-year-olds confused, not knowing if the spasms were part of the performance. It was too excruciating to imagine. She wanted to lean over and touch the wrinkly part of his ear.

"By the way, that's my dream house over there. One day when I have my own contracting business, I'd like to fix up that place." He pointed to a lone wooden cottage on the side of a hill.

She turned her gaze from the clothesline. "You come here often?" she asked. "To the Jerusalem Forest?"

"Yeah. Late at night it's really something. A lot of Breslov Hassids come out here for hisbodedus and meditating. Once I overheard someone wailing, 'Help me remember there's another world.' "

A chill went up her spine at these words. He probably meditated, too, she thought, but wasn't so spiritually gauche as to actually announce, Yes, I meditate. She said now to Akiva, "I come here, too, sometimes."

They looked at each other and in the same instant their eyes dropped. He briskly stood to his feet. "Let's go." He shook his right leg, then the left. She slipped her feet into her shoes. They walked quietly toward the large building in the distance set between two small hills, surrounded by eucalyptus and pine trees. At its entrance, a huge sign—Healer of the Broken Souls Institute—hung in granite Hebrew letters followed by gold English ones.

When Akiva and Beth got inside, the main floor was in full gear. Men and women milled around the recreation area and a few patients sat at the small square tables scattered through the room, drinking tea, staring glumly at checker boards or talking to each other. The faded yellow walls were covered with nature posters—the Kinneret Sea, Ein Gedi foliage, the Banyas waterfalls. Akiva and Beth drank water from a gray fountain next to the kitchen. She usually felt relaxed at the institute, mostly because the categories changed, became far simpler. Not immigrant versus sabra, religious versus secular, single versus married, but sane versus insane.

Orna, a Moroccan psychiatric social worker, came forward, slim and alluring in black pants and a rust-colored danskin top, her arms outstretched. "How nice! You came to visit Zahava on Shabbat! She'll be very happy."

"Actually, we came to get something to drink, but—" Beth glanced briefly at Akiva.

"We can stick around a bit," he said. He folded his arms and looked about with mild interest.

"Oh good." The social worker brightened. "Now where is that Zahava?" She tucked an errant bra strap under her shirt and walked quickly down the hall, opening and shutting doors.

Akiva turned to Beth. "Mingle?" he asked, gesturing his jaw toward the tables.

"Mingle," she assented. She knew the patients from her weekly visits and a few lifted their head and stared. She approached a middle-aged Russian man who spoke no Hebrew and little English, and began a dispirited game of checkers with him. Every now and then he reached across and jumped his own men with her pieces. After five minutes she glanced over at Akiva. Old and young women surrounded him, cooing at him, bringing him tea, petit beurre biscuits, peeling him clementines. He stood in the center, his arms folded, turning his head from one to another as they pushed against each other to speak with him. His Hebrew wasn't particularly advanced but he seemed to have no trouble keeping the conversation going. She noticed Zahava among the women, staring at Akiva, fluffing her frizzed black hair. For the first time that day, Beth felt calm.

In the kitchen, a plate or a pot crashed to the floor. Akiva's arm shot out and flung a tea glass to the ground. His head spasmodically moved back and forth. She watched like a mother who had grown accustomed to her young son's wild public antics. Of course, it wasn't wonderful when he twitched. But was it really such a big deal?

"Oy vah voy!" said an old-faced woman with young brunette wig-like hair. "Let me clean this."

Zahava slapped her white thighs and called out, "It's magic! He's like a water sprinkler, like a firecracker, like a dreidel, like an alarm clock, like a—"

"Shut your mouth," said the woman, kicking at the glass with her foot. The younger woman hunched her shoulders.

Beth was about to walk over and console Zahava when Akiva caught her eye. The winter sun had reddened his cheeks slightly, making his eyes look more green than brown. He looked gently at her, and then his lips from the thicket of his beard gave her the smallest smile.

When it was time to leave, the social worker walked them to the door. "They loved you," she exclaimed. "You were a hit!" Akiva smiled and said nothing. "So Beth tells me you do painting work. Any chance of volunteering some time here?" she burbled on. Akiva turned his head and looked at Beth with a measured, slow gaze that predicted all kinds of circumstances that included the two of them. "Yes, there's a good chance of that," he said.

By the time they reached Kinnor Road, the street was quiet and empty. She turned up the hill on Levites Street, passing Judy Bartosky's building on the left, and saw children playing ball in the back lot, near the playground. They turned into Harp Court, walking through the narrow, lump-filled street, and there was Estrella Abutbul sitting on the steps outside her cottage, talking to a neighbor. Estrella's daughter, Miri, sat in a huddle with another girl, shooting dried apricot pits—ajooim, they called them—like marbles.

"Who's that man?" Estrella's son Yisrael called out, staring at Beth and Akiva. He wasn't used to seeing her with a man. He trotted over, holding his ball.

"This is my friend," Beth told Yisrael. Akiva tapped the ball lightly with his forefinger.

Estrella's eyes opened wide. She lowered hers, then looked again. The neighbor also watched.

"Shabbat Shalom, Bet." Estrella slowly stood to her feet. "Shabbat Shalom to you and to—"

Beth turned to face him. "This is Akiva," she said, feeling a new shyness come over her. She gestured to him. "Akiva, this is Estrella Abutbul, my next-door-neighbor."

He took his hands out of his pockets and smiled. "I'm happy to meet—" He stopped. The cords of his neck tensed the way they had the first time he had twitched in Yemin Moshe. He gritted his teeth, straining. A film of sweat dampened his eyebrows.

Estrella stared quizzically. The neighbor squinted and bit into an apple. Beth leaned forward. Just do it, she thought, get it over with. No, don't let others see it, save it for me, no—

He spun into the most violent of spasms she had yet seen, his body flinging in every direction, a sudden pretzel of floppy arms and legs. Hiccups bled from his throat, wild eruptions.

She screamed inside. She turned away. Akiva! Akiva! I can't, Akiva.

"Hashem Yishmor!" yelled the neighbor.

"What—what happened?" Estrella touched her throat, her eyes

round. She held Yisrael close. Yisrael stared, the ball at his feet. "Did a bee sting him?" he asked his mother.

Akiva leaned heavily against the wall, breathing rapidly. Then he pressed hard on his temples and straightened his collar. "No, it's just this muscle I have that jumps now and then," he said, with effort. He wiped the corners of his mouth. "Don't worry, I'm used to it."

"All right," said Estrella, raising her hands appeasingly. "All right. I'm sure you know best." She and the neighbor gave Beth a wondering stare.

Shame swirled around her, running down her back and up and around her throat. Her saliva felt hot in her mouth. She looked down at the steps. She couldn't bear to look up, to see the faces.

"We have to go now," Beth said in a low voice. "Shabbat Shalom."

There was a dead ache in her heart. She knew what she had to say. She didn't know how she could possibly say it.

Akiva and she silently crossed the courtyard to her apartment building. They climbed the two flights of stairs to her apartment.

They stood outside her door. She stared at the porcelain hand-painted Shalom sign hanging on it.

Akiva put his hand on the rail. He cleared his throat. "Sometimes you get very distant," he said, "and sometimes you're right there next to me." He tilted his head expectantly.

"You know," she turned swiftly from the Shalom sign, "I don't think it's going to work."

"What?" he said, stung. "What?" he repeated. His hands dropped to his sides.

Beth faltered, struck by the heat and urgency in his voice. She covered her face with both hands. "I don't really understand it myself," she said from between her hands. "I-I could see being married to you for a few years, but I couldn't see us being married for longer than that."

It was quiet.

His head cocked to the side, staring at her as if she was a painful new thing in his life. "We just met," he said. "Why are you predicting how our marriage would fail?"

She spread out her arms, broken, bent. "It's not you," she said. "It's me. It's my fault." She stared down at her black shoes. Mud was encrusted along the sides. A single grass blade lay stuck to the heel. She couldn't look at him.

A baby's gurgle floated up from one of the apartments.

"You're probably right," Akiva said finally. "It would never work."

The "never" terrified her. She couldn't bear to hear it. She lifted her head to say something, but Akiva was already halfway down the stairs. A moment later, she heard the entrance door slam shut.

PART II

Chapter Six

TSIPPI CROUCHED OVER THE CRATES AT THE STORE'S ENTRANCE-way, unloading the vegetables. A Sephardic man and woman entered the store, and she scuttled behind the counter. The man, who wore his checkered shirt unbuttoned to his chest even with a bitter rain outside, pointed to the bottles behind the counter. "Give me three Araqs, a case of Goldstar beer, and some of that cognac."

Tsippi stood on a little step stool and handed the customer his bottles, one by one. "A bris?" she asked conversationally, as her fingers moved quickly over the register keys. She averted her eyes to avoid looking at the triangle of coarse black-and-white hair coiling outward from his open shirt. She turned to the Sephardic woman, a braid, still black, wound around her mostly gray head, thinking for a moment that the man and woman were a couple, but then deciding no.

"Just a party," the man said. He took three bottles in each hand, holding them by their necks like some unruly chickens, and placed them in his blue shopping basket.

After he paid and left, the bottles clanking against each other, the

Sephardic woman heaved her own items on top of the counter. She pressed her palms against her cheeks and her tongue clucked. "May the Almighty protect us from such parties," she groaned. "You know what goes on at these parties? I'll tell you: Everyone dancing with vases on top of the head." She thumped the counter for emphasis. "Everyone dressed in big fancy kaftans, hoping to hide their fat. Everyone pushing and dancing in circles," the woman swayed her rounded hips, "the husbands forget their wives, the wives forget the husbands, and both are forgetting the children!" Her deep brown eyes blazed. "That's what kind of party!"

Tsippi had plucked a washed kumquat from a bowl on the counter and was about to make the blessing, then stopped, her hand mid-air. Of course, it was none of her business what people did with the food they bought. But it disturbed her that the drinks from her store were being used for lewd gatherings. She threw a worried glance toward the back of the Makolet. Should she mention it to Shlomo later that evening? She considered this: He would get caught up, he would delve into his books, the little time he set aside for her in the evening would be lost in study. Ach, what was the point? She quickly uttered a blessing and bit deeply into the fruit. "Are you sure about this?"

"Yes, I am," the woman said importantly. "I'm making the food for the party. I'm making the egg with malawach, and the chicken with couscous, and the candy cigars." As she mentioned each item, she pointed to the corresponding food on the counter. "Believe me, you Ashkenazim never tasted such delicious food! You see these green and red peppers? And the lemons? Maybe you wonder why so many? This roasted salad takes hours to make and it comes out to so little, but it's worth it, just ask anyone. And no one makes it better than me."

Tsippi eyed her, her head tilted back. Was she joking? How could she sound so appalled at their behavior if she herself was an eager participant? It made no sense at all. Then Tsippi thought: The woman probably wanted credit—for being pious *and* for being a good cook.

Beth walked in, collapsing her orange umbrella shut, and Tsippi's attention diverted. She absently rang up the Sephardic women's things and helped her stuff them into a bag, all the while glancing at Beth. Beth had waved hello to her and was now wandering down the aisle, squeezing an avocado here, prodding a bag of rice there. She looked withered, about ten years older, her skin sad, punished.

As Beth roamed around the room, Tsippi went back to stacking the produce. Now this was a situation that demanded her skill as a matchmaker. Setting up was the easy part. But here was the test—getting each party past their foolish obstacles. Like any shadchan, she had her bag of tricks: homilies, stories and parables crafted to inspire and make them rethink. She could bully, she could flatter, she could hold on until they each agreed to give it another chance. She could understand them so well, they'd have no choice but to listen. "Why did you say no?" she said simply. "What is wrong with you, Bet?" She playfully shook a tomato at her.

"Akiva, you mean?"

Tsippi shrugged and threw her eyes upward. She began arranging the tomatoes, putting the green, hard ones on the bottom and the softer red ones on top.

Beth turned to her with sudden intensity. "I guess it's not possible he just wasn't for me. There has to be something wrong with me, right?"

Tsippi faced her, a tomato in each hand. "What is this?" she said gently.

Beth was silent, sulking, holding her crocheted bag.

"Let me tell you a story," Tsippi said. "This really happened." It was a story she'd heard from a descendant of the Sanz Hassidic dynasty. She'd heard it from other people, too—every group liked to claim it as their own—but she was convinced the true source lay with the holy Sanzers. She rubbed some lotion on her aching fingers. "Once, many years ago, in the times when a bride and groom met for the first time on the day of their wedding, there was a family with a daughter, a beautiful girl, wise and good, and another family with a son, a wise, holy man, saintly, people said. The two were supposed to marry, but on the wedding day the bride saw her groom had a huge, ugly hump on his back. She went into a room and refused to come out, refused to marry him. Finally the groom said to the bride's father, 'Let me have just two minutes alone with her. Then if she says no, I promise to leave and never trouble you again.' "

Beth sighed. She shifted her weight from foot to foot. "Yes?" she said.

"So the groom went into the room. He said to her, 'Before you were born, do you know it was decided in heaven that my soul mate would be humpbacked and very ugly? I saw an image of you, my bride, how sad you were to be ugly and humpbacked, and I prayed to God to make me the humpbacked one instead.' When the bride heard this, she agreed to marry him. That night, with great joy, the wedding took place." Tsippi folded her arms and smiled.

Beth stood still. She was looking away at all the neatly lined cartons of fruits and vegetables. Tsippi saw her throat move up and down, but when she turned to face Tsippi, her eyes were flat. "Well, that's Jewish guilt for you," she said. "If I'm willing to sacrifice for you, the least you can do is marry me. Very clever." She put a bill down on the counter.

"Oh, Bet, Bet." Tsippi rang up the purchases.

"Look, it was a decent try, but it's not a match between Akiva and me. We come from very different backgrounds."

How ridiculous, Tsippi thought. Different backgrounds! How weak. Goodness, some women will find any pretext to get rid of a man. "Maybe," Tsippi ventured, "you should speak to a rabbi about this. Such decisions shouldn't be made without thinking them through carefully. I know someone very nice, Rabbi Yellin, and I think you'd find him helpful."

Beth eyed her. "You're telling me this rabbi specializes in dating troubles?"

"All kinds of problems, religious, emotional, practical. It can't hurt to talk."

Beth shook her head. "He sounds like some kind of guru."

"Goo roo?" Tsippi said blankly.

"Some charismatic figure who's going to solve my problems. Or at least claim to." Beth swept up her groceries in her arms. "Not for me. Thanks for mentioning it, though."

Tsippi watched her go and rubbed more lotion on her hands, pressing between the knuckles. She heated up some water for tea. Her nerves were on edge. The story had stirred her soul, even if it hadn't much affected Beth's. To be spoken to like that, as the humpbacked groom had spoken to his bride. She closed her eyes a moment, imagining Shlomo speaking such words to her. Then she shook her head. Foolishness.

※　※　※

Beth walked up the stairs of her building. She shook out her umbrella, leaving it open in the hallway. It was cold and drafty in the apartment, worse than outside. She could take a shower, but she'd have to wait at least two hours till the water heated up. She muttered to herself. She hardly was aware of what she was saying. She had picked up on Tsippi's scorn—distant signals, but palpable, because she could feel her own shame seeping into her heart. She had become diminished in the matchmaker's eyes. Suggesting a rabbi-therapist—Tsippi must really consider her a sorry case.

She ate her yogurt and read the *Jerusalem Post,* catching up on the country's tensions, and after a while national anxieties edged out her private ones.

The *Jerusalem Post* advertised a concert playing off of King George Street. On impulse she called Estrella, who sounded intrigued.

The band consisted of five women who played religious music only for other women, in keeping with the precept that a man was forbidden to hear and look at a woman while she sang. Beth had heard of this group—they had once been featured on a television program, performing with their faces blocked out. The program was called, "Women Who Want To Be Heard But Not Seen." After she hooked Estrella into coming, Judy Bartosky happened to phone, and Beth convinced her to join them.

On the bus ride over, Estrella was full of questions. "A woman's band? Very strange. Do they practice in the nighttime? And when do they feed their children?"

"I don't know," Beth said. "Maybe their husbands baby-sit. Or maybe they're single."

"Oh." Estrella sat back, her face relaxing. "They're single."

"By the way." Judy was seated opposite her on the bus, and she touched her wrist. "You have regards from Naomi Safran."

"Oh really?" Her heart skipped a moment, recalling her deep respect for her former teacher, but seeing Judy gazing intently at her, she made her face only mildly pleased. "Send my regards back."

"Why don't you study there? At Beit Shifra? They were so impressed with you."

"It doesn't fit into my schedule anymore," she said with a shrug.

"I've been learning there, you know."

Beth was surprised. She hadn't pictured Judy the learning type. Not that she wasn't bright. But she was the kind of woman who needed to be seen as accomplished, in control. And to learn and possibly reveal one's ignorance was something she hadn't thought Judy capable of. Judy went on, "It would be great if you'd join me. I'd love to have a chevrutah who's also a friend."

Beth shook her head. "It's not my focus right now." How could she explain her religious dilemmas? At her age? High school and college was the time for thrashing out issues—belief in God, the veracity of the Torah, suffering in the world—and not now when she was supposed to be beyond that, settled and respectable. She turned her eyes toward the window.

A red sign plastered to a high school building announced: "RACHEL'S SECRETS—EIGHT SHEKELS—FOR WOMEN ONLY." A lean woman in a red beret stood near the ticket collector's table, making sure no man entered. She explained to Estrella, Judy and Beth that last year three teenage boys had managed to sneak past the sign, crouch behind a wall divider and peek at the performers. Halfway into the concert they were caught and thrown out, followed by cries of outraged women in the audience.

Estrella's brow furrowed. "These performers—are they American?"

The woman shrugged and tugged her beret to cover an ear. "All kinds."

An excited energy rested on the throng. Women from every sector of religious life seemed to be in the auditorium—the bewigged, the bereted, the scarved, a few straw-hatted, the bareheaded like herself; all of them in their dresses and skirts covering their knees in keeping with the laws of modesty, some lengths reaching the calf, some swirling down to the ankle, depending on taste. Women, women, a whole colony of them. Beth hunched her shoulders and tried to make her way through the thicket of women. She felt herself contracting, getting smaller and smaller, until she was no more than a dot, an atom bouncing randomly through a swirling cosmos, where each planet and star knew its place. While the married women might like her, be friendly, ask her advice on certain topics and invite her over for Shabbat, still they pitied her. She knew this. She tried pitying them back. Their hands were raw and claw-like from washing mountains of dishes. Some of them hadn't slept six straight hours in years. Some of them surely had miserable marriages and were appalling parents. But here at the gathering no one need know. Here, they got to strut about, confident and sure of their identity, their importance and their place in the world, just because they wore something on their heads. But her shame was public, exposed for anyone to come up and say, "Still nothing doing? Too bad. Maybe I know somebody."

She recognized a friend in the far corner of the auditorium, someone who had been part of her circle years ago, Daniella Stein, and ducked her head to avoid her. They had been friendly for a time, and then Daniella went ahead and got engaged to one of Beth's rejects, a redhead, Yaron, who she had met while volunteering on a kibbutz settlement up north. Beth recalled their first meeting vividly—summertime, kneeling in the moist dirt, rows and rows of carrots between them, his rolled-up shirt sleeves, the knitted yarmulka sloping to one side, his scruffy beard—all the trademarks of a Rav Kooknik, the ultra-Zionist yeshiva that he was attending at the time. He'd quoted her the Talmud and Rashi's commentary that the Messiah would come when the Land yielded produce "b'ayin yaffa," in large, generous amounts, like never before seen in its history. He unearthed a bunch of carrots and dangled them before her. "See? What could be a greater sign of the coming redemption than this?" But Beth had rabbinic quotes of her own, and after work and lunch and showers, the two battled it out in the Beit Medrash study, looking up the sources, arguing out their separate interpretations. She had enjoyed the give and take, felt herself drawn to his fervor, his ardent belief, and maybe he had been drawn to the ardor of her counter-arguments. They had dated. In the end, much as she found aspects of it and him attractive, she couldn't give herself over to his ideology. A one-note band. A music that would ultimately oppress her soul. Also, she had to admit, his nose hair, bristly and wolf-like and far too noticeable, had had a distancing effect. Then Daniella had married him, Daniella the Oxford intellectual, and now here she was with a Rav Kook–style kafiyah covering her hair, and a handsome, alert baby in a sling on her hip.

On stage a woman in a curly brown wig sat stolidly behind a set of drums and cymbals. Next to her stood a lithe woman in a black-and-silver dress, her arms resting on a bass. The clarinetist and guitarist also wore black-and-silver dresses.

"Look Bet!" Estrella pointed to the drummer. "She's married, that woman is wearing a wig!" She put a hand over her mouth.

Judy exchanged a look with Beth.

Finally a tall woman in a long silver dress swept up to the center of the stage. She moved with professional ease, adjusted the mike and turned to give last-minute instructions to the band members.

"My name is Irit," she said in a low, accented voice. Swiss? She tapped the mike lightly and the audience settled into their seats. Irit drew forth three gauzy scarves from her pocket: lime green, yellow and tangerine. She swirled them into the air and they gracefully wafted down, the colors intermingling, misty and harem-like, while she juggled them slow-motion style, keeping them airborne with the swift and clever movements of her hands. Beth softened.

"Jugglers," said Irit into the mike, "that's what we all are, that's what we do every day, our lives are a balancing act of needs, goals and responsibilities as we cross the narrow bridge." She continued to throw and catch the scarves while she spoke, her hands darting in and out like a sorceress. "I welcome you tonight, ladies and"—she paused—"ladies. I welcome all of you able jugglers to 'Rachel's Secrets,' where for the next hour you can let down your hair, you can stop juggling."

She caught the last scarf with a deft swipe at the air and then let all three fall to the floor like petals. "We called our band 'Rachel's Secrets' after the story in the Bible. We all know what Laban wanted to do. After Jacob worked seven years for Laban in order to marry Rachel, his love, Laban wanted to trick him into marrying Leah instead, by switching his daughters underneath the wedding canopy. With the bride covered with a veil, Jacob wouldn't be able to tell the difference until the marriage vows were already pronounced and it was too late.

"The Sages explain that Jacob and Rachel knew of the trick Laban had planned. The couple made secret signs, passwords between them, so that even with the bride covered with the veil, Jacob would be able to distinguish which sister was which. Then just before the wedding, Rachel had a change of heart. She thought: Why should my sister Leah be ashamed before the crowd when Jacob discovers her instead of me? Why should she be exposed to that shame? It isn't her fault.' So Rachel revealed the secret signs to Leah before the wedding, and thus Leah became married to Jacob, and was spared being publicly humiliated. Not only that, but Rachel hid underneath the bridal bed, and in the dark, with every caress of Jacob, Rachel called out and made sounds in place of Leah."

At the mention of beds and caresses, Beth slouched low in her seat. She swallowed and an image flitted through her mind—Akiva's hand moving gently on her shoe, his fingers following its subtle dents and curves. Her body became warm with the memory of that day in the forest and she shook her head, banishing the memory. She saw a few Hassidic women also moving uneasily in their seats, dismayed at Irit's sexual reference. But then they shrugged in resigned acceptance, as if to say: If the holy sages in the Talmud offered this interpretation, how could we object? The Torah wasn't intended for the prudish.

"In every generation," Irit continued, "we women pass secrets to each other, wisdom the men don't know, the hidden Torah, the secrets that create a living tradition, that bind us together." She paused, glancing briefly at the band. "In this spirit, we bring our music to you."

Cymbals crashed. Rock guitar and clarinet filled the room; the bass added a rich undertone. Irit put a hand on her hip and brought the microphone just under her chin. "Her lips utter wisdom, her tongue speaks the Torah of love," she sang, belting out the verse from Proverbs. The room shook as the brown-wigged percussionist expertly slashed at the cymbals and drums with her sticks.

Some of the women simply watched or pointed in astonishment at the musicians. But many clapped their hands and tapped their feet. A group of girls ran to the front of the room and exuberantly danced the hora, their long braids jouncing whip-like in the air.

Estrella stood up, her eyes shiny and reckless, and tugged Beth's hand. "Come, Bet!" she urged.

Judy held out an arm. "Let's dance."

Beth let herself be dragged into a circle of women. The drum pounded. The circle moved faster and faster. Sweat formed on foreheads and necks as scarves and wigs were skewing to the side. Beth whirled, swept up by the beat. One blond-wigged Hassidic woman broke free from the circle, ran to the center, and danced alone, raising her skirt to knee level as she performed what looked like an Irish jig. Beth stared in amazement. She wanted to throw her arms around the woman. Her own feet felt happy and full of jump; she held her head high, and energy flowed through her arms and shoulders. These women and girls around her were her sisters, weren't they? She was not a lone atom bouncing along randomly. At the very least, she was linked to the Jewish women in history. She was part of something.

The band eased into a slower-paced song and the women returned to their places. The tune had a lilting curve that stung at Beth, played in her ears, a kind of tune that made her want to sing and cry at the same time. Irit pursed her lips together, looked down for a second and then sharply drew her head up, at eye level with the audience. She sang:

> "Leah, I am under the bed, under the wood and
>   feathers and wool.
> I am the voice of the wood that has waited, ticking
>   off these seven years in stitches even as fingers.
> I am the feather that knew where it was called, and
>   landed elsewhere.

I am the wool that cries at being sheared from its
　　sister.
I am the voice under the bed, the secrets Jacob
　　arranged with me.
I will clothe you with secrets:

Tell him the Shabbat candle rests only when it is
　　burning.
Repeat that bread rises only to disappear.
Answer that a woman rises from bed to engrave her
　　*form there."**

The music ended and Irit bowed her head. No one clapped. A quiet feeling settled on the crowd, dark and light eyes turned inscrutably inward.

Beth sat in her seat, struck. A thought was growing in her. That wasn't Rachel under the bed. Something else was hidden there. She tried to search it out, looking with her mind's eye. Some dark fluff of dust lay balled in the corner. She saw herself stretching out her arm, trying to touch it, but each time it skittered away, behind the leg of the bed, into another corner, out of reach. She saw now that the dust was desire, dark and covered over, and it was hers. She couldn't touch it but she could see how neglected it was, brushed under a bed, forgotten, stomped on unthinkingly a hundred times a day as she went about doing her other things, thinking she could take out her desire like a piece of jewelry and wear it when the right occasion presented itself. But it lay huddled and hurt, maybe even furious. She felt a shiver take hold of her shoulders. She glanced at a woman in a scarf sitting next to her, and the woman was smiling. This is what a woman looked like who had been touched, loved. How had she, Beth, gone

*by Sherri Mandell

110

unheld all these years? How had she? She was a freak, a trick against nature. She had been offered a ride out of that place, many times, but she'd always said no, it was too crowded, too cold, too warm, too dirty, too dark. The next train, the next, but the trains came less and less often, and before long she'd felt like a fool for waiting. She pressed her fingers into her eyes. When she removed her hands, her fingers were wet. She rubbed them together, feeling the wetness, discovering tears.

※　※　※

Akiva walked along Bar-Nachmani Street, struck, despite his depression, by the beauty of its trees. On his own block, at Shofar Street, the trees were sparse, and the few that could be found stood stiff like soldiers. But in Rechavia and Shaarei Hessed, trees leapt up everywhere, huge overhanging trees that rustled, that moved, that had a little generosity.

He stepped into Teva Natural Foods, setting off a tinkling of wind chimes, badly in need of a carrot, celery and beet juice pick-me-up. Sami, the trim Yemenite assistant manager, gave him a brief smile and scowled back into the phone he was holding. "I asked for six bags of rice," he said. He held up a hand and thumb to an invisible audience. "You gave me five, and one of them crawling with jukim." The assistant listened, sighed, rolled his dark cherry eyes upward and then bleated out a string of guttural sounds.

Akiva waited for Sami to finish his call and start up the juicer. He and Sami had become friendly over the years. He saw a sign hanging on the wall: Melancholy Brew. Herbs to provide equanimity and uplift. It listed melissa, peppermint, licorice root and blessed thistle. Akiva couldn't imagine how anything with a thistle in it could be a balm for depression, but maybe it couldn't hurt to stir up a pot of that brew for himself. Beth's odd rejecting words kept returning during the day to sting him—"I could see being married to you for a couple of years but not longer than that." What did that even mean? Flattering and deeply insulting at the same time. As if he were hers for the taking. Whatever she had been getting at, it still hurt.

Other women he had dated flitted through his mind. There had always been women willing to go out with him, but somehow never willing to bring him back to their friends and families: flawed merchandise. That was all right with him. To his thinking, they were the flawed merchandise and he was grateful to his spasms for having revealed that. He had thought Beth was different. Apparently she wasn't. He remembered his mother pointing a finger at him. "Make a lot of money. Then they won't care so much. You'll see." But he never did see things his parents' way. He remembered their bleakness, their squabbles about the air conditioner, the car, the toaster oven, their complaints about their shoulders, back, legs, their muttered behind-the-door discussions about his 'condition': nothing seemed to work right. He had studied architecture at the community college in Vancouver, hoping for a better life—a bigger life—than his father's tailor salary could afford the family, but one day, while watching a documentary about cows on television—eating grass, sleeping, having sex, getting milked, getting more grass—he'd said to himself, "I'm not a cow, I'm more than a cow." And he'd set off to find that 'more' part, which he no longer believed resided with getting a degree in architecture.

An old woman near the tahini containers was staring at him. She held a tiny book of psalms in the crook of her arm. He stared back, smiling vaguely.

"I know you," she suddenly declared. She spoke to him in Israeli-inflected English.

"You do?"

"You were on that terrible bus . . . the driver threw you off. He said bad things about you, foolish things," she said.

"Ah yes." Akiva nodded philosophically. Kojak. He hadn't come across him in a while. Maybe someone had complained about his behavior and shifted his route. "Don't worry about it," he told her. "These things happen."

She was staring at him with shining eyes. "I almost followed you off the bus. I haven't stopped thinking about you." Her shoulders and head bowed shyly toward him. "I honor you," she said. She spoke in a refined, lilting accent. "You are holy: a tzaddik."

Akiva coughed, his cheeks, neck and chest flushing. Why did she think such a ridiculous thing? Perhaps because she had witnessed his humiliation? He—a tzaddik! A fantastic idea, an absurd one. But was it possible that he was such a holy man that his very humility precluded his own knowledge of it? He had to smile. He doubted that true saints made these calculations, even inwardly.

"I'm no tzaddik," he told the woman. "But thanks for the thought."

"Yes, yes." Her thin, arthritic fingers waved away his words. "Who ever admits to such things?" She lifted her wizened face skyward. "Bless me."

Akiva's head tilted to the side. "Bless you? Excuse me, you've got the wrong man. I'm just a ba'al teshuva, I'm still getting used to all this myself." His arm made a sweeping arc, taking in the Shaarei Hessed neighborhood, the religious bookstores, a Hassid across the street, a poster on a storefront exhorting the passersby: Dress modestly! Give charity! Do not gossip!

The woman gazed back at him steadfastly, and for a moment he became unsure. He put one of his boots up on a stool and bent to tighten the laces. "I'm a house painter." He yanked the strings taut. "My big dream is to be a contractor and have my own business. I play soccer and go to movies now and then. I try not to look at women but most of the time I don't succeed. Maybe I learn a few hours of Torah each day, but that's it."

The woman's jaw set while her eyes stubbornly held his.

"Look." His back straightened. "I can't bless you. But there're other places you can go: to the Altschuler Rebbe, the Shpinker Rebbe, to Rabbi Yellin. I also know some great Rebbetzins." He held a flat hand up to his hairline. "Very high women, besides being easy to talk to. Many of them are just around the corner."

"I'm not leaving this spot till you bless me," she said.

His hand roamed his beard. The more he protested, the more she would attribute it to humility on his part, magnifying him further in her mind. Yet to bless her as if he were a tzaddik would be a lie. Could he say a truthful blessing, in line with the person he was? He stuck a hand inside his knapsack and emerged with a sturdy carrot.

Loudly he intoned, "Blessed are thou, Lord, Master of the Universe, who creates the fruit of the ground." He bit into the carrot, swallowed, removed a fleck that had wedged between his teeth and looked at her. "All right?"

The woman stood motionless, her eyes closed. Then her eyes sprang open and she rubbed her temples. "Now that's a blessing," she said, clapping her hands with a childlike glee. "Fruit of the ground. Isn't that what we all are, fruit of the ground, beginning with Adam and Eve? But this is the first time I have heard this blessing applied to a person." She nodded and bowed her head low. "Now I have something. Now I can leave you." Her lips pulled back into a smile that revealed pinkish gray gums, and though he could not find a single feature of hers that spoke of beauty, he enjoyed looking at her, a woman made attractive—no, handsome—by piety.

She must have seen him from the streets and followed him into the store because she left without buying anything. He watched her cross Bar-Nachmani Street with a surge of well-being in his heart. He'd probably never bump into her again. But he had seen the woman in a way perhaps that others didn't see.

Juice in hand, knapsack across his back, no longer in need of blessed thistle or any herb to lift his spirits, he went outside. He stopped at the traffic intersection and waited for the little man in the traffic light to turn green and signal for him to cross. A cluster of young schoolchildren waited with him. They chirped among themselves, talking self-importantly, with gestures and exclamations, about the unfairness of their teachers, about their lunches, and then inevitably about "HaMatzav"—The Situation—which he had finally decoded after living in Israel for a few years to mean the political predicament of the moment. He kept up with the killings and stabbings (how could he help it?) but he was always mixing up the different political parties and the names of the Arab leaders. Recently, he'd stopped trying to make sense of it all. Not that he didn't care about the fate of his people. He did, terribly. But with so many factions clamoring for their own point of view, for what did they need his puny opinion? Besides, another matter gripped him: transcendence. This was his hunger, his all-consuming need. Once a person tasted it, knew its enchantment, other pleasures paled. Certain things helped: living and eating simply, becoming religious, living in Israel, in Jerusalem no less, the greatest city in the world, as far as he was concerned, for full-time transcendence-seekers.

His spasms helped, too, he couldn't deny it. After one of his convulsions, people couldn't help treating him differently, and this was when he got to see the stock of a person. When he twitched, masks and veils fell away, people unraveled before his eyes: a sometimes vicious side became revealed, or a streak of tenderness emerged from hiding; fear of contagion made the sensible and the kindly recoil. There was no telling the things he might see, often the parts that were a surprise to themselves, to everyone but God. But he, Akiva, got to see. He was like the ancient high priest, the only person permitted entry into the Holy of Holies section of the Temple on Yom Kippur. Yet he, Akiva, the ba'al teshuva, a mere new-comer, got to enter the inner sanctum, the holy of holies of another human being, every day.

The little traffic man blinked green and waved everyone across the street.

Chapter Seven

LATE SHABBAT AFTERNOON, BINYAMIN SAT AT A LONG, NARROW table in a high-ceilinged room, ostensibly waiting for a Rabbi Yellin to appear. Really, he had come to find Rita, the woman in black moire. These past few weeks, he kept hoping he'd bump into her, and then when a dating dry spell hit—unusual for him, but he imagined such spells hit even the most eligible—he decided to be more aggressive about tracking down the elegant beauty from the King Solomon Hotel. A little Divine Providence had led him to the Yellins who in turn had led him to Rita, and now here he was at Rabbi and Rebbetzin Yellins' home for the Shalosh Seudos third meal. He felt like a fool. He had been expecting an intimate meal, the two of them, he and Rita, with the rabbi's family. But there were twenty other people here, a whole mélange. And no Rita. A small-boned, kerchiefed woman placed a platter of browned noodle kugel in the middle of the table, and next to it, slices of pickle spread out like a fan. She looked at Binyamin and smiled, her left eye fluttering slightly. This had to be the rebbetzin, he realized.

Still more people kept straggling in, and with each new one who joined the table, Binyamin's chest lifted then dipped. No Rita. He gazed at a Sephardic man with a doughy belly, then at a woman with her hair pulled back tightly in barrettes, giving her a look of frozen alarm, and next to her a blond man who had just come in and taken a seat, handsome, yes, but his neck didn't seem to fit into his shoulders in a seamless way. So these were the characters the rabbi attracted. He wondered what that said about Rita. What kind of woman was she, anyway? And what did it say about him? What was he doing there? An old Beatles song came back to him: "All the ba'alei teshuva, where do they all come from? All the ba'alei teshuva, where do they all belong?"

At last a little man with a beard that was yellowing at the edges shuffled into the room, slipping into a seat at the head of the table as unobtrusively as a cat. He looked around the table with mild brown eyes, raised two loaves of challah level with his temples, and pronounced the blessing over bread in a high-pitched, resonant voice.

This was Rabbi Yellin. He seemed to blend perfectly with the ragtag crew assembled here. He cut the braided bread into neat parallel slices and, then, with surprising dexterity, carved the loaf lengthwise, from head to toe, the slices falling like dominoes onto a plate. Binyamin watched the rabbi chew his own piece of bread, chew and swallow, until the entire piece was consumed. Then he turned to the person seated to his right, said "Good Shabbes," held out a piece of challah, and nodded his head. The rabbi turned toward the next person, a woman with close-set eyes: "Peaceful Shabbes," he said, and gave another tiny nod and a bread slice. He fixed his gaze on the man sitting next to her: "Sweet Shabbes," and on and on it went, "shining Shabbes, precious Shabbes, holy Shabbes, beloved Shabbes," each person around the table getting their own Shabbat greeting in the rabbi's European-accented English, and a nod and a piece of challah. Binyamin's greeting was "noble Shabbes," and he was pleased with it until he heard the final greeting, which seemed to contain all the others: "Shabbes Shabbes." The Sephardic man with the sagging belly got that one.

The rabbi took a wedge of gefilte fish. He tasted it, chewing slowly, then put down his fork. He peeped at his wife and she peeped back at him. Binyamin wondered what that look meant. Maybe he was like many husbands who needed their wives' go-ahead before venturing the mildest of opinions. The rabbi wiped his mouth with a napkin. "Sometimes, when a person prepares fish for Shabbes," he said, "they're hoping it came out better than their neighbor's, the best fish on the block." He smiled, revealing a flash of small, pretty teeth. The smile was so bashful and winning that Binyamin leaned toward him to catch it before it vanished. "But my wife's fish—I only taste the prayers that went into it, how she hopes it will be delicious to honor the Shabbes."

Binyamin looked down at the gray slab of fish on his own plate. Was Rabbi Yellin speaking metaphorically, or was it really possible to taste the worry or rivalry or good wishes that had gone into the making of food? He chewed deliberately, like the rabbi had done. It was calming to chew slowly, he realized, to relish each crunch, without rushing to swallow. It made him feel settled inside.

Rabbi Yellin began to hum a niggun, a mournful yet plucky "Ai-di-dee-die" that quickly caught one person, tagged another, until everyone was hooked up, suffused with the melody. Binyamin hummed along self-consciously, not sure if he wanted to abandon himself to the mood, but the tune sucked him in, and before long ai-di-dee-dies were coming out of him as easy as air, and then the niggun melted away, leaving a sweet uplift that hung in the room.

Rabbi Yellin turned to a slight, wispy-bearded man sitting next to Binyamin. "Tell me, Yankel, what's higher: a niggun or a spoken word?"

Binyamin carefully regarded the rabbi. What an oddly pleasing question. Not exactly the kind of question the rabbis in the Talmud

119

debated. Too poetic, he thought. Lately, studying the Talmud felt like butting his head against a concrete wall. Those ant-like columns were killing his eyes. And the Aramaic! No one had spoken the language in over five hundred years, and yet he, a newcomer, was expected to master it, and Hebrew of course, and Yiddish phrases like 'nisht kerferlich' and 'geshmack' and 'klohr.' For crying out loud, give a ba'al teshuva a break! But what could he do? Talmud was the bread and butter of Judaism—everything else was whipped cream, or so he'd been taught. He'd be considered a flake if he ignored the Talmud, like the people in this room. Then he turned his head toward Yankel, the slight man at his side, to hear how he would answer the rabbi's question.

Yankel was rocking in his seat, his hands brushing up and down his sides, like a missile about to take off. With his eyes closed, he said, "A niggun, a tune is higher. Speech begins with a thought and comes down to the reality of words, lips, teeth, so it's always a descent into the physical world. But a niggun"—he paused while his fingers played with the air, tracing patterns visible only to him—"it begins in the physical world, but always reaches upward, toward an abstraction, a longing."

Rabbi Yellin nodded. "Yes, a longing." He nodded again, glanced at his wife, and with a little hand movement, signaled for her to pass him a salt shaker. Binyamin watched the rebbetzin hand him a glass salt shaker, her knuckly fingers trembling as they touched his. Was he imagining that the rabbi's fingers arched and fluttered back?

Binyamin sat up in his chair, incredulous. Why, they were flirting! Flirting and no one even knew it. But look at them. They'd been married for years, and they weren't young anymore. Not that romance belonged only to the beautiful. But still, it was strange to see. They reminded him of an episode of *The Newlywed Game* he had watched years ago. There sat this immense Frigidaire of a woman and her pickle-sized husband, clearly having a great time, unable to keep their hands off each other, and next to them a sleek and stunning couple with nothing to say to each other, sullen, blank, not once meeting the other's eye. Nature was full of these tricks. The fat and ugly had their day, too. But it was only an aberration, he decided. Beautiful people really did have more pleasure, as crude as that sounded. No one liked to admit this. Of course the excitement between him and women he'd been involved with had never lasted long, never more than a few months, no matter how stunning the woman, and every time he mourned the dying of those sparks. But Rita promised more than beauty, a certain je ne sais quoi. The front door to the apartment opened and Binyamin looked up.

More chairs were pulled to the table. The four newcomers looked presentable, which pleased Binyamin. He liked Rabbi Yellin and he wanted his devotees to have an air of normality. Then a fifth chair was dragged to the table. He thought his chest was going to burst. Rita! She was as stunning as he had remembered. Her black hair dipped over one brow. She stood still and then with a faint movement of her shoulder her coat slid off in one swoop, and she caught it elegantly with her other hand and draped it over a chair. She wore black again, some glossy material that was a little much for Jerusalem, certainly for this crowd, but they clearly all forgave her, *he* certainly did. How could he not when every gesture, every detail of her proclaimed: Knockout! He tried to get her attention with his eyes. He cast her a look of yearning, "It's me! I'm the one you're supposed to meet!" but she looked blandly out at the crowd, at the embroidered pictures on the wall, at no one, no hint of seeking in her expression. Then it struck him. Maybe she hadn't been told they were to meet! Maybe she knew nothing of his interest or intentions or even his name. He had assumed this was a set-up, the rabbi's wife had said, "Come, she'll be at our table at the third meal, you'll talk and get to know each other," but now he saw he had misunderstood. Well, what did it matter? He could introduce himself to her, offer to walk her home tonight. It was a golden opportunity to make a move.

Someone spoke just then, a blond-bearded man, the handsome one with the stiff neck who had come late. "Rabbi Yellin, you said last week 'It is forbidden to be depressed, but it is necessary to be brokenhearted.' "

Rabbi Yellin, with a duck of his head, motioned, "Go on."

"But I'm confused." The man's head tilted in a likable way. "How can I tell the difference? What if I'm only fooling myself that I'm brokenhearted, when really I'm just depressed?"

Yes! Binyamin thought. He wanted to know the answer. He saw other people around the table nodding. The blond man's question had become everyone's question. Rita was nodding, too, though he wasn't sure she'd really heard the question. She was half-turned in her seat, reaching into the pocket of her coat.

Rabbi Yellin gave a shrug that started with his hands and traveled to his shoulders. "The depressed person sees only his own sorrow. The brokenhearted one sees everyone's sorrow and shares their broken heart."

Something snapped in the air. Binyamin startled. It was Rita, chewing gum—he could actually see it, pink when she opened her mouth between chews. Binyamin stared at her. Then he thought: So she chews gum, so what? A natural woman. Anyway, he could hardly register this. He was still mulling the rabbi's words. "The brokenhearted one sees everyone's sorrow." He couldn't remember the last time he had cried over another person's sorrow. A sigh broke loose from his throat. Suddenly, he wanted a broken heart, too. He heard another person exhale heavily at the end of the table. It was the blond-bearded man who had asked the question. There was something engaging about him. Binyamin regarded him. Then he saw the man's neck jerk, once, twice, three times, in rapid succession.

Binyamin sat still as a rock. What was this, a hallucination, a trick of the eyes? No one else was reacting, though. Except for a wince from the Sephardic man, it was ignored. Poor fellow, he thought. He probably had Tourette's.

Another spasm overtook the blond man. His arm shot out, his entire body jiggled uncontrollably. After a few seconds, the spasm passed and his arms and legs relaxed, floppy-like. Binyamin glanced over at Rita. She had put a fist into her mouth, but her eyes were wide and bright, her nose flared, her face was red with the effort of suppressing something. Then it erupted: Her laughter sprayed the table, bounced off the chairs, filled the room. She squeezed her eyes shut and placed her head on the table, her shoulders shaking. The woman with the barrettes patted her back and murmured, "Brokenhearted, she's brokenhearted."

Rita lifted her head a moment, then gazed foggily around. They had mistaken her laughter for tears. Her head flopped back onto the table, and she began to snort. This was nothing like the modulated laughter from the hotel, but some coarse, phlegmy gurgling. Binyamin averted his eyes and put his hands on his ears. No. No. This couldn't be Rita. It just couldn't be. Would the rabbi invite such an insensitive airhead to his home? Well, the rabbi might. From what he could surmise the place was a spiritual free-for-all. Still, maybe Binyamin had caught her at an off moment. He hoped that was the case.

Later, after everyone sang the Grace After Meal, and people began dispersing or breaking into groups of two, Binyamin found himself standing next to the blond man with the twitch. "I really like this rabbi," he confided. "Does he give any classes during the week?"

The blond man shook his head regretfully. "He doesn't teach. Anyway, he's a straight Gemara man. If he gave a class, it would be nothing like what you heard today."

"Too bad. I wish they taught this way in my yeshiva." He liked the after-feeling here. He could sense the static inside him giving way to an inner alignment, a humility that didn't sting, a kind of yearning that created its own fullness. He took out a navy blue book and flipped through it.

"I know." They both stood awkwardly, looking at the departing guests, and after a moment or two they introduced themselves and told each other where they studied. The blond man snapped his fingers. "Actually, there's a place up in Safed that learns like, well, like women do—Bible, Medrash, philosophy, and once you've gotten your feet wet, some Hassidus and mysticism. I hear they have an eclectic staff."

"Really?" Binyamin slid the book back into the wall unit. He looked at the blond man. "What's this yeshiva called?"

"I used to know it." The man, Akiva, squeezed his eyes shut. "No, wait, it's coming to me—" He held his palm up, as if halting traffic. "The Holy Beggars Institute."

"The Holy Beggars Institute," Binyamin repeated in a dubious voice. "No Talmud there, I suppose?"

"Very little."

"No Talmud," he muttered. It sounded like a blessing—to be spared Aramaic! To learn the parts of the Torah that really spoke to his soul!—and yet a curse. He might as well declare himself illiterate. Self-respecting Jewish males knew how to figure out a page of Gemara. There was no getting around that. If he learned at that institute, the rabbis might look down on him. The women surely would. His stock was sure to plummet. "I'll file that name away for the future," he told Akiva. He looked around the room, catching snippets of conversation ("His talk is like Jell-o. You just can't hold on to it.") wondering how he might approach Rita to make sure he hadn't gotten the wrong impression. She was standing at the entrance to the apartment, staring rather dreamily at a picture on the wall. He maneuvered nimbly between the chairs and people, his steps quick. "Excuse me," he said, and then he stopped and stared at her. She was planted in front of a mirror—not a picture. The dreamy, faintly arch expression was reserved for her own reflection, not for some enigmatic scene. Her self-absorption both sickened and compelled him. (After all, women he'd dated had accused him of the same trait. One ex had called him a legend in his own mind. Bitter woman.) Rita raised her eyes a moment and looked at him. He'd never seen her so close, full-face. Her eyes were dull pennies. There was no light in them. He felt a sudden cramp in his stomach. The dead eyes made the rest of her features look as if they had no connection to each other, as if no animating force held all the parts together. Pretty, yes; lovely, no. To look at her was to be disappointed. How had he missed this? He felt his cramp radiating outward, and he pressed a hand into his stomach as he went to get his coat.

Rita turned slightly toward him. "You say something?"

He shook his head, aggrieved. Never had a fantasy woman evaporated so quickly, so thoroughly, before his very eyes. "Sorry," he mumbled. "I thought you were someone else."

※　※　※

Judy heaved her Midrash Rabbah and Sefer Mechilta onto the shelf with her cookbooks. She had just returned from a late Friday afternoon learning session with her chevrutah partner, Lauren, a meeting that made no sense at all given that she had a cholent stew yet to prepare, a salad to make, and a kugel that was only halfway assembled for baking. These college girls were oblivious to the demands of reality. At least she'd had the white beans in water for a few hours and wouldn't have to resort to a quick soak. She peeled onions and threw them into a pot with oil, along with some spottily peeled potatoes and sweet potatoes (skins were good for you anyway), then a turkey neck or two and some barley and beans and water and, there, the cholent was basically set. She'd spice it just before she put it on the metal blech where it would stay heating all of Shabbat. She began dicing cucumbers, tomatoes, onions and pickles. Her hands moved in jerky stops and starts.

Dovid entered and washed his hands carefully under the faucet. He dried them with a white-and-blue-striped dish towel (gone were the days of going through two Bounty rolls a week). He began opening a Pyrex casserole dish here, a Crock-Pot there, sampling an eggplant dip, annoying Judy with his wanderings in their tiny kitchen.

"Dovid, help me out here," she said, handing him the knife, more to get him standing in one place than because she wanted his help.

"Where are the kids?"

She pointed a thumb backward over her shoulder. "At the neighbors," she said, and smiled. For a change, a nice, sane pre-Shabbat moment just for the two of them.

"How's school?" he said.

"Oh, pretty good." Judy stood at his side, picking out the larger chunks from the salad bowl, making criss-cross lines in the cucumber, dicing them further. "But I'll tell you, these girls at Beit Shifra, they're a different breed. They're so"—she groped for the right word—"so fierce when they study, so determined to understand. How come I never see anyone smiling?"

"Do I smile when I'm learning in yeshiva?" Dovid asked. He tried out a small smile, mentally weighed it, and tried on a broader one. "No, I don't smile when I'm learning." He shrugged. "That doesn't mean I'm not enjoying myself."

"And you should see the way some of these girls dress!" Judy went on. "A banana fell on a girl's skirt, making a stain. The next day she was still wearing the skirt with the same stain."

"Think of them as running a marathon," Dovid offered. "They don't have time for trivialities."

"Looking good is never a triviality. Especially when you're in the marriage market. But who has time to date? They're so busy learning Torah," she said. "Who has time to think about clothes, food and other necessities like bathing?"

Dovid put down his knife and turned his head sideways. "Judy, are you enjoying yourself at this place? No one's forcing you, you know."

She wiped her hands on a batik apron hanging on a hook with the word "Rebbetzin" etched into the material. "I do want to be there," she told Dovid as she slipped the apron over her neck. "The classes, I like. Really like. The other Torah classes they offer in the community, I'm just a passive listener. I get more information, more ideas, more knowledge, but who needs me? At Beit Shifra, it's as if I'd been going to basketball games for years, watching from the sides, and one day someone invites me on the court to actually play."

Dovid nodded emphatically. He was a sports fan.

"But it's the girls that get to me." She sat down rather forlornly at the table and spread out a white plastic bag from SuperSol. She began gathering scraps of discarded vegetables and putting them into the bag. "They all have these plans for themselves," she said at last. "Some of them are just these take-charge, be-the-best-at-everything types, so as long as they're here they'll excel in their studies. But the others, and there's a bunch of them—Lauren and Arielle and Dina—they know what they want. Lauren wants to do research on medrash, translate old books that no one's looked at in years. Arielle wants to write textbooks that promote ethical growth using Biblical passages." She ticked off their plans on her fingers. "Dina intends to sit and study for the next few years and see where it takes her." She turned wonderingly to Dovid. "How come I never had any plans like that?"

Dovid let out a careful, controlled sigh. "In your day—" he began.

"Ages and ages ago—" she said mockingly.

"Well, seventeen years ago, to be exact, most women didn't take having a career so seriously."

"Oh, Dovid," she smacked his wrist lightly, "it's not just a career I'm talking about. A lawyer, a doctor, a computer programmer, occupational therapist. Everybody does that. But these women are on some kind of life mission. Each one is an innovator in her own way. They're blazing a new path. Nobody's mother or grandmother learned Torah like this before. Not just to know what to do in terms of Torah practice, but for the pure love of learning. They're on a path of scholarship which makes no sense monetarily or even socially. No one's going to consider them more desirable marriage-wise as a result. Yet they do it. Why? They love it. Torah does something for them."

"And you?"

She was holding her red spiral notebook, flipping absently through the pages. She liked the effect it had on her. She felt more collected as a person, sturdier, steadier, and at the same time fresh and alive. She could practically feel the neural pathways in her brain buzzing when she studied. Torah thoughts followed her through the day, in the middle of sorting socks, or while she was waiting in line at the post office. But when friends asked what she was doing, she always minimized the time she spent at Beit Shifra, fearing to openly declare her passion. Many women took Torah classes here and there, but to devote five hours a day was unusual, and she couldn't quite separate herself from what the neighbors would think. "Yes," she said finally. "I love Torah study. I just don't think . . . well, I don't know if I have anything new to contribute. Maybe I know how to take someone else's idea and dress it up, but I don't know how to create something fresh, something of my own." And here was the real source of her insecurity. To put forth an idea or theory of her own seemed beyond her.

Dovid bit into a chunk of cucumber. "I always thought you had a good, sharp mind." He nudged her with his elbow. "You think I would've married a dull woman?" he said out of the side of his mouth. "The truth is, anyone who could make matches like you has to be original. First there's nothing, and then there's a couple. It's the highest form of creation—something from nothing."

"Very funny," she murmured, and began wiping down the counter with a rag. Dovid held out his palms, his fingers cupped as if weighing grapefruits. "Just study Torah! Stop thinking about if you have what it takes to succeed. *Hafoch bah, hafoch bah, dekula bah*—turn it, turn it," he translated from the Aramaic, "because everything is contained inside it."

Judy squeezed out the rag and draped it over the faucet. The other day in the Beit Medrash, she had been rereading the Adam and Eve account in the Garden of Eden. If Chavah had sinned by eating from the tree, why was her husband's reaction to her so positive after God cursed them? Mother of all Life, he'd called her. A germ of an idea was tickling inside her brain. Maybe she'd take a deeper look, check out some sources. She didn't know what might come up. But that was half the fun of it, she thought, or at least Lauren would say so.

✳ ✳ ✳

Rochel Leah asked her to put wool socks on her feet, and after that, a pair of cotton ones—for the circulation, she insisted. Then she held out her plate of sunflower hulls for Tsippi to empty.

"Well, what did Rabbi Isaac say when you gave him my note?" she asked.

Tsippi remembered his response precisely. She couldn't help it: those eyes, the way they stared, then disappeared on her. She reported back to the old woman exactly what had happened, not mincing words, including her observation that the sound of Rochel Leah's name had meant little to him. Rochel Leah sat still, except for her fingers, which twitched in her lap.

"Come here," she said to Tsippi. "Closer, closer," she motioned with her hand. She patted her bed and Tsippi stepped up. Rochel Leah peered intently with her good eye into Tsippi's face, then reached up with her hand and began sliding her fingers over Tsippi's skin, deftly touching her eyes, her cheek, her jaw and neck and chin, then squeezed her arm and hip. Tsippi blushed and twisted away. "Why—!" she stammered.

"You're good-looking!" Rochel Leah announced. "Not too fat or thin either."

Absurd gratification swept over Tsippi. She *was* good-looking. But no one had told her that in years. Certainly not Shlomo. Then she said with some asperity, "Does that surprise you?"

"A little," Rochel Leah said. "From the sound of your voice, I thought you'd be squat and plain. But it seems you look well."

Tsippi began to smile, then stopped, unsure if she'd been flung an insult or a compliment.

"Here is what I need from you," Rochel Leah said. "I can sense that Reb Isaac likes you. Talk to him, not like a Hassid follower who wants crumbs of holiness from a Rebbe, but like a woman who finds him handsome."

Tsippi's head felt woozy. "But—but this is the one *you* want. Isn't it?" She stared at Rochel Leah. "What about those notes? What place do I have in your—ah, courtship?" she ended delicately.

Rochel Leah shook her head and chuckled sadly. "No, this is not for my sake. I do this for the sake of the world, for the sake of his Torah study, which has been interrupted these last months." She twined her fingers together, the two forefingers, propping her little chin. "You see, Reb Isaac is a kabbalist. But he has lost his way because of sad circumstances, and no one can rouse him out of it. And now I hear he's taken a turn for the worse." Her silver brows rose, then fell with sudden ferocity. "They all take the wrong way with him! They bring him their problems, their notes, their petitions to God, even the silly nurses. He needs a woman's desire for him, that's what he needs."

Stunned, Tsippi backed away from Rochel Leah's bed. She fell into a chair, her eyes darting about the room, at the sturdy walker poised next to the night table, at a huge silver-plated book of Psalms studded with aqua-colored stones, at the television set in the corner, unused except as a shelf which held a vase of pussy willows. The television of Rochel Leah's roommate blared for a few seconds (some program she was always watching called *Boat of Love*) and became mute. It wasn't true, then. Rochel Leah wasn't making a doomed play for a man. She felt almost disappointed. "But he's a kabbalist, you say. A saintly human being. What does he care about a woman's . . ." she flushed, "desire?"

"He's also a man."

"But—but why me?" Tsippi asked. She felt a damp sweat break out behind her ears. "Why not you?"

"Ach, all I know how to do is dote on him. I have no effect on him at all. But I think . . ." She paused. "I think he likes you, Tsippi. He looked at you—remember that. You roused him out of his stupor."

A giggle exploded from Tsippi's throat, and she gritted her teeth, clamping down on any other eruptions. "I can't see why you'd think he'd like me. I didn't get a real response, anyway. But it doesn't matter: I can't do what you want. I'm a married woman."

"Still married, eh?" Rochel Leah absently picked something off her tooth. "I forgot about that. So go tell your husband. He wouldn't mind if he knew it was for the great kabbalist Reb Isaac. It's an honor, I tell you. I would do it myself, for the sake of the Torah he has yet to share with the world."

The woman was serious. Tsippi lifted the collar of her dress away from her neck. Her entire body needed air. "No, you'll have to ask someone else. Get one of the pretty nurses."

"They won't do, I tell you." Her fist tightened. "They are too coarse. Everyone else considers herself too holy. You are exactly the right person—it all just came to me today. I beg you, Tsippi-Pippi, I beg you, please, take care of this. You wouldn't have to do anything forbidden. It's like talking to a stove or a radiator. He just lies there. Try to make an old man feel good. Go to him. It's a mitzvah, a good deed that will never be forgotten."

A good deed, Tsippi thought. Her being rose in horror at offering herself—like Ruth before Boaz!—before a man not her husband. The whole thing was nonsense—she had never even thought of another man besides her husband. Yet some distant part of her was moved by the idea. To save a kabbalist from despair! She, her very self! Any Torah wisdom he brought to the world would be credited to her (and also to Rochel Leah, she had to acknowledge). She would rouse him from his abyss. But the whole scheme was absurd.

"I'll think it over," she said. Just to be kind.

Later that evening Tsippi set a cup of tea and a plate of petit beurre biscuits in front of her husband. "Shlomo! I wish to ask you something," she said.

He lifted his head, then nodded.

"Rochel Leah, the woman in the nursing home," she began, "well, she—" Tsippi stopped, watching him wedge a slice of napkin into his Talmud before he shut it. She said, "No, what I wanted to ask is—If I was in danger, let's say drowning, or maybe in a leper's colony, yes, held hostage in a leper's colony. Would you risk becoming a leper yourself to save me?" She peeked at him, lowered her eyes and peeked again. It was the closest she'd come to asking, "Do you love me, do you really?"

He looked at her and pulled on his lower lip, bunching it as he thought. "You ask an interesting question," he said. "There's a similar case, the famous case in the Talmud with the two men and the one flask of water. 'Whose blood is redder, yours or mine?' Yes, but where did I read it?" Muttering to himself, he got to his feet and his eyes scanned the bookshelf.

Tsippi watched how he scratched his stout hip absently, how his finger ran along the spines of the many Talmuds ("looking with my hands" he called it). Her eyes gazed at his white beard, searching for the few strands of red left, but they seemed to have disappeared. Minutes passed. Tsippi waited. And she waited again, looking for some emotion to pass his face. She ached.

He pulled mildly on his ear and shook his head. "I wish I knew where it was. It's somewhat well-known."

"Never mind," she told him. "I'm sure it's somewhere." She tucked her chin under and took out chicken from the freezer. Then she soaked some beans for the Shabbat cholent she would prepare tomorrow. A cholent, and yet another cholent. All the cholents that she would make and eat together with Shlomo stretched out before her, an unbearably long row of pots.

When she returned the next day, Rochel Leah was daintily cleaning out her ears with a swab of cotton.

"Well, and what did you decide?" Rochel Leah asked, businesslike.

Tsippi sat in her chair as she took off her jacket and folded it over her knees. "I've thought it over. I can't do this. It's a kind of adultery, what you're asking me to do, an adultery of the heart."

"Did you know," Rochel Leah said, reaching for the sunflower seeds on the night table, "that the saintly man, Rabbi Aryeh HaCohen, he used to pay a visit to the widows of Jerusalem every Friday night before going home to make the Kiddush? He knew that's when they'd be missing their husbands the most, so he went out of his way every Friday night to flirt with them, to make them happy. Did you know that?"

"Well good for him!" Tsippi burst out. "Maybe his marriage was better than mine!"

Rochel Leah chewed on the seeds. "And what's so wrong with your marriage?" she asked.

"Nothing, nothing at all," Tsippi muttered, astonished at the words that had risen from her mouth. There was nothing wrong with her marriage. "We're a good couple, but we're the practical sort," she said, looking down at her knees. "Passion, passion is for . . . others." She closed her eyes for a moment, scared she might burst into tears, but the moment passed. She didn't know why it was so hard for her to say this.

Rochel Leah wiped her fingers with a moistened paper towel. "Youth brings out passion in people. Married life," her hand opened and shut, "married life does not. So," she said, "will you go to Reb Isaac?"

Tsippi blurted, "No! Send someone else." She seized the Book of Genesis and a bookmark fell out. She flicked through the pages and read out loud, "The men turned from where they were and headed toward Sodom. Abraham was still standing before God. He came forward and said, 'Will you actually wipe out the innocent together with the guilty? Suppose there are fifty innocent people in the city, would you still destroy it? Shall the whole world's Judge not act justly?'

" 'God said,—' "

"Stop!" Rochel Leah made a lurching motion from the bed. Sunflower seeds sprayed the sheets. "Stop, here is the answer. Listen to Abraham. Listen how he spoke to God. Can you believe his nerve—accusing God of being unjust? It wasn't like you or me talking. He had a special connection with God, he had nearness, closeness, he was the holiest man on earth, and still he was willing to risk his relationship to God, all the closeness and holiness he had achieved—which wasn't easy, mind you—and he did it because he loved people more. It was an act of holy chutzpah."

The slyness of the old woman's argument astonished Tsippi. Comparing her dilemma to Abraham's! She sat clenching and unclenching the hem of her dress. "Why are you doing this?" she demanded. "Why do you love him so much? Who is this man to you?"

Rochel Leah lay crumpled in bed like a collapsed parachute. She said, "He's my little brother, Itzik Muttel."

Tsippi felt her breath go out of her in a whoosh. "Your brother?"

The old woman nodded. She removed her glasses and wiped her eye with the back of her wrist. "My mother always asked me to take care of him. I looked after him when hoodlums would try to beat him up, I looked after him in the first war, as a young girl, when the family got separated, and then in the second war, too, when the Nazis ripped his beard from his face, I was the one who tended to him. Then he married and he didn't need me so much but I still kept my eye on him from afar, but now he needs me, that's why I'm here, to love and take care of him, but I didn't figure out exactly what kind of love he needed or how to do it until you came."

Tsippi's eyes moved over Rochel Leah's face. The old woman's chin was trembling, her eyes liquidy behind the cat glasses, her cheeks hanging in loose flaps. Rochel Leah! She wanted to throttle her for all her winding deception, for her ridiculous devotion. She wanted to cry. Rochel Leah and her little brother, the kabbalist. "I'll do it," she said slowly, and before her eyes she saw Rochel Leah revive.

Tsippi washed her face in the sink and rearranged the scarf on her head, tying it to one side, making it look as if a lavender flower had sprung over her right ear—the one coquettish ploy she would allow herself.

As she climbed down the stairs, she felt ridiculous. What was she doing? She remembered a match she had arranged between the elderly professor who owned the rabbits and a certain young and beautiful Yemenite waitress. Oddly, they had liked each other. Who could tell in these matters? But this! This was more ludicrous than anybody could ever imagine.

She continued to mutter to herself as she walked, glad that no one could see or hear her in the stairwell. "Let some good come from this and not just my own humiliation." She squeezed her eyes shut. What would Shlomo say if she were to tell him? Maybe he would find a Talmudic source that compared her function to that of a nurse, administering to a sick person's needs. "It is permitted!" he would announce. She thought of Abraham serving food to the three strangers. They were angels, and he didn't know it. Was Rochel Leah some kind of devil unbeknownst to her? Nothing made sense, not Rochel Leah, not herself, nor the absurd path she had taken. But she would do this deed and hope it was good.

Tsippi stood outside Rabbi Isaac's door and leaned her head against the wall. Then she opened the door to room 708. The shades were drawn, the room almost dark. She stood before the kabbalist's bed. The black tefillin boxes had been removed from his head and she saw the red indentations on his forehead. She coughed and just then his eyes fluttered. The lids continued to hover between open and closed; then the sides of his forehead squeezed together and his pale brown eyes remained open, turned in the direction of Tsippi.

He seemed to wake up. He seemed to notice her. He seemed to be looking her over. Maybe she did have a special effect on him. Like Rochel Leah told her, "a man is a man," kabbalist or not, and she a woman. Something was going on.

But he was a man of God! The secrets of the universe he knew, but what of the secrets of desire? Then she thought: What were the secrets of desire if not the very secrets of the universe?

She stared at the skin on his lower face where his beard would have been if it had not been ripped out during the war. The skin was scarred and jagged. She felt a shiver pass between her shoulders. She was in the presence of a holy man. He moved his head. Could he be beckoning her to come forward? She felt something stirring inside her.

Then she saw a movement under the bed covers. Tsippi froze. The kabbalist was leaning on one side, his neck raised, a grimace on his face. He said: "Go home." She blinked, twice. His face turned red and rageful. He pointed a finger. "Go home!"

Tsippi gasped and rushed from the room, her hands plucking at her heart, picking up her poor legs as if chased by a devil.

It was chilly outside, the air unusually still. She tried to put on her jacket but her arm and the sleeve kept missing each other. She tried to walk fast, faster, to put distance between the two of them, but her legs weren't working right and she kept stumbling. Her inner organs were in upheaval. Her neck was damp. It hurt to breathe. The air had become thick with her secrets. She bumped into a tree and touched its bark with wonder. There were heavy clouds, bunched together. There was a pulsing all around her. The tree branches stretched out their arms, the leaves whispered, "Come here, Tsippi." She yearned. But for what, for whom? She hurried past the trees, her fingers trembling, her knees aching, scared and alone.

Chapter Eight

BINYAMIN SPRAWLED ON HIS BED, FACEDOWN, AND LISTENED TO his phone messages for the second time. Two Shabbat invitations, an artist who wanted to collaborate on a show in the Old City, a rabbi from his yeshiva who wanted to discuss his Talmudic progress (or lack thereof, he thought, wincing), a call from his bank. That was it. No call back from Etti, the matchmaker he had phoned the other day. For the life of him, he couldn't understand this dry spell. Not a single date—or even a phone call—in over three weeks. Well, what other matchmakers could he call?

He began to dial Mrs. Bartosky but stopped after the fourth number. She'd seemed slightly miffed at him, he recalled. About Talya the nurse. The spunky, witty, pretty one. No, Talya couldn't be called outright pretty. Nice looking, cute, was more like it. She did have something to her in the looks department, just not enough to inspire him toward marriage. In his olden, pre-religious days, she would've made perfect filler till someone more compelling turned up.

He flipped through the little black book he kept on his night table under the answering machine.

"Mrs. Vunder? It's me, Binyamin."

"Hello, Binyamin."

He stared at his painting of the Ten Commandments while he waited for her to say something more.

"How are you feeling?" Binyamin asked, awkwardly. He had never had to ask before.

"Fine, thank God. I'm a little tired, but it will pass."

Binyamin yawned into his hand. Why didn't she begin with the names already? He didn't want to be doing this, making these calls in the first place. And now she was going to force him to ask: Do you have anyone for me? Well, he wouldn't. It was too much like being a beggar. "Well, I hope you get some rest," he said finally. "I'll be in touch later."

"Fine. Good-bye, then."

He grimaced at himself in the mirror. That was an odd call. But Mrs. Vunder, she had her odd habits and moments. He'd been a guest at her house a few times and had observed her—small things like blinking frequently, scratching at her knee. Once he caught her pulling out an eyelash. Little things that would've driven him crazy had he been forced to be in permanent close contact.

He began to dial Shani Applebaum's number. Shani was young, blond, petite and energetic, and she usually bombarded him with so many names he couldn't help feeling flattered. Sometimes she'd joke and say, "Binyamin, your problem is, you need someone like me." He'd call Shani. She'd make him feel good. She'd have someone on her fingertips. Other matchmakers sometimes lagged between the idea and the execution, but not her.

"Shani? It's me, Binyamin."

"Binyamin! Hi!" He held the receiver an inch or two from his ear. Her pert blond energy crackled through the phone. "Got a million things going on right now! Just made two successful shidduchs in the past week, can you believe it? I'm busy with the engagement party and the parents and you wouldn't believe." She burbled on and on. Her voice got fainter as she spoke, as if she was being sucked up into some vast tunnel.

He broke in. "Have anyone in mind for me?" His cheeks burned above his beard.

All Shani said was, "I'm swamped! Later! Later!"

"Okay! Okay!" he said, matching her tone. He called two more women. One said, with annoyance, "I told you, I don't have anybody right now," though he hadn't remembered speaking to her in the longest time, and the other conveyed through her child that she was taking a break from making shidduchs and at the moment was grouting her bathtub. With each call, Binyamin drooped lower and lower. He never should've followed Tuvia's advice. Putting himself out there was too raw, too humiliating. But what choice did he have? His fate and future happiness rested in the hands of these women. Enough with the ladies. He didn't think he could take any more just now. He dialed Pedro the Shadchan. Pedro was affable, low energy, not the most organized matchmaker, but pretty decent, with a decent pool of women.

"Hallo?" said a little girl.

"Can you get me your father?"

"No spik Anglit." The little girl giggled.

Damned Hebrew. Damned females. "Daa-dee," he enunciated. "Ab-ba, Tah-tee. Get him."

There was a scuffling noise and a cry. A boy's voice seized control. "What you wanting?"

"A woman!" he almost screamed. "A wife!" Instead, he said slowly, his voice on edge, "Your father."

"Abba!" hollered the boy.

Moments later, Pedro said breezily, "Who is speaking?"

"It's me. Binyamin Harris." He closed his eyes.

"Ah, yes, Binyamin." He paused. "What can I be doing for you?"

Binyamin pinched his chin, hard. "Isn't it obvious? Why do you think I'm calling?"

Pedro sighed, twice. "You are calling for a shidduch, then," he said gently.

"Of course. Is this new or something?"

"No. But you leave me then with sad news for you. Sad news."

His mother, his father, his sister—someone had died. But that was crazy. Pedro had nothing to do with that. He spoke into his pillow. "What is it?" he asked, his voice muffled.

"No more shidduchs for you. That is what I must tell you."

Bullets of fear shot into the lower region of his stomach. "What? What are you saying?"

"The matchmakers, they got together and decided—no one will set you up anymore. That is it. Fineeto."

"Wait—" he tried to speak, but his throat was clogged with cement. "Why?" He sat up in bed, his bare feet on the tile floor. "What's going on?"

"All right, I tell you. But don't get angry with me. Every month, all the matchmakers get together. We see how we're doing and we give each other names and we discuss cases. You know how it is among professionals. Everyone talks and talks. And your name came up. It was decided then. That you are not responsible, not ready for this step maybe, I don't remember exactly."

Binyamin stood groggily to his feet. "A bunch of yentas got together and decided I'm not ready to get married? How dare they? Who do they think they are?" He raised a fist and stared at it, more in puzzlement than in rage. "Are they therapists, people with degrees? And I thought they were my friends," he said with bitterness. He couldn't fathom it. "Do they all feel this way? They all blacklisted me?"

"All."

"You, too?"

"Yes, me, too, Binyamin."

A whip of hatred unfurled inside him. "If you think you can stop me from dating, you can tell those sharks they're out of their minds. No one can stop me. I'm too eligible. I've got friends, acquaintances. They can't control all of Jerusalem, as much as they'd like to. Go tell them that. Barracudas. All of them!"

"Please," Pedro said wearily. "It is not necessary to speak that way. I regret that it must be this way. Good luck to you, my friend."

Binyamin's knees foundered and he collapsed into bed. He lay there frozen, too struck to even replace the receiver. He had been blacklisted. They had discussed him, analyzed him and found him wanting, unworthy of the Jerusalem women. He rammed the phone into his pillow, again and again. Damn them, damn them all. "I'll eat pig," he shouted at the walls. "I'll break Shabbat, all thirty-nine violations! Then you'll be sorry!"

※   ※   ※

The bus moved in fits and starts through Kings of Israel Street. Beth hung on to a bar for support, and with her other hand she removed a slip of paper with an address: Rabbi Yellin, 45/2 Hosea Street. Just yesterday she had bumped into a teacher from the Beit Shifra Yeshiva. "When are you coming back?" the teacher had asked her. "Naomi Safran keeps asking about you." The anxiety that shot through her intestines was so excruciating that she decided then and there—what did she need to carry around her religious questions and doubts for? If you had a headache, you took a pill, if you had crooked teeth you got braces, if you had trouble believing in the Torah, you spoke to someone. Since this rabbi, according to Tsippi, handled all kinds of troubles, he probably wouldn't be too startled by hers. But she definitely would not discuss her social life with a perfect stranger. God and Torah, yes; love—no.

"Hosea Street!" bellowed the bus driver. "Who wanted Hosea Street?"

"Me, me!" Beth called out, and quickly scrambled off the bus. It was dark outside and the advertisements placed inside the bus shelters let off a neon ethereal glow. During lunch hour that day, she'd seen a few trucks bearing Tel-Aviv license plates go up and down the streets, unfurling posters, unscrewing the glass panes off the shelters, and affixing huge colorful ads. Now, as she walked down an incline to get to Hosea Street, she stopped to get a closer look. At the bus shelter in front of the Religious Books and Articles store was a poster of a thickly muscled man eating a candy bar and whirling a basketball on the tip of his finger. Opposite Schwartz's Hat Shop, Beth spotted a poster of Miss Ramat Gan, looking smug in a Subaru, and further along an ad for Bank Mizrachi. Near Shalom's Glatt Kosher Butcher store, a woman with bursting breasts, wearing tight shorts, was advertising a watch.

The Hareidim and Hassids in their dark suits or kaftans averted their eyes whenever they passed a shelter, some clutching their black hats or fur-brimmed shtreimels. A few Hassidic boys huddled in front of the basketball ad, a younger boy pointing in amazement at the finger spinning the ball. She saw an old, mottled-complexioned woman, as old as the Western Wall, look at a poster—the one with the woman's bursting breasts. The old woman stared fiercely, like a hawk, craggy hands on hips, then wiped the corners of her eyes and said, "Oy Jerusalem."

Beth became swept up in the neighborhood's agitation. Her eyes went from shelter to shelter, scanning for even more scandalous posters. She felt sorry for the Geula and Meah Sh'orrim residents. It wasn't right for a Tel-Aviv ad agency to come in, with no respect for the mores of this community, and bring their crassness. If she had known that the new plastic shelters were paving the way for the posters, she would have preferred that the old, corroded shelters would have stayed. And yet some part of her was greatly aroused by the scene. It was a historic moment. The Meah Sh'orrim residents were brushing up against the world of television, and women in bikinis. What would they do now? She wondered what Akiva would have made of this scene.

She turned into Hosea Street, where a dusty row of bread-colored stone buildings were made less shabby by the ivy and bougainvillea clinging to the walls. Through a window Beth saw a young kerchiefed woman holding up a lettuce leaf to a kitchen light, probing the veiny folds for tiny insects. Beth found the rabbi's building and went up to the second floor.

Two Hassids, one with long scraggly peyos, the other one's shorter and neatly curled, stuck their heads out from behind a scratched wooden door.

"So, what's your problem?" the neatly-curled Hassid asked.

Beth flushed. "Look, it's personal. Do I have to tell you?"

Curly shrugged. "No. But there's a line of people waiting to get in. Maybe your question can be handled better by someone else." They looked at her, beefy arms folded over their stomachs.

She stared back. Hassidic bouncers, that's what they were. She'd have to give them something. "I was asked to be a teacher of young women, to teach Torah, but I'm having trouble believing in it myself, and I'm scared of the damage I might cause." She stopped and let out her breath. She had exaggerated a little to dramatize her case. She was here purely for herself: She couldn't stand living in internal spiritual limbo. The Hassids consulted each other with their eyes, nodded briefly, then opened the door to let her in. They showed her to a room with chairs, a faded couch, a huge crammed bookcase, and a table that seemed to go on forever. "But you'll have to wait here. The men are waiting in the other room."

So she was the only woman. She sat demurely at the table, hands in her lap, conscious of her femaleness, even if there were no men to see her. It was a plain-looking room, straight hard lines, no fabrics or bric-a-brac to distract the eye, no big easy chair to hide in. Bare walls, except for a black-and-white etching of the famed Chofetz Chaim rabbi, and there next to a ledge that held a silver candelabra—an intricately embroidered picture of Rachel the Matriarch's grave. It was eight-fifteen. She heard a door open and voices in the hallway, a faucet turning on and off. She didn't have a book, not even a piece of paper to write on. Now it was eight-thirty; now eight forty-five. As she sat and waited, it occurred to her that she didn't really mind sitting there doing nothing. It felt pleasant, expectant. Maybe, she thought, this was what it was like to wait, while you were pregnant. You might sit there doing nothing, hands in lap, but no matter how still you were there was a churning inside, a ripening, something was getting created. She yawned hard and looked at her watch: nine-thirty. She tried to compose her thoughts and frame the questions she would ask the rabbi. It occurred to her that her problems in belief had started when she'd been asked to be a teacher. Something about the idea of going public had frightened her and stirred her doubts. She probably wouldn't be in this room if Naomi Safran hadn't approached her that day in the Beit Medrash. She yawned again and took herself to the couch, which was surprisingly comfortable, and before she knew it, she'd fallen asleep.

At ten-fifteen the Hassidic bouncers called out, "You can go in now!" and she jumped awake and removed a quilt that someone—the rebbetzin probably—had put on her while she'd slept. Her head fogged for a moment. "Do you want to go later?" Curly asked.

"No, no. I'll be ready in a second." She went to a sink and washed her hands and splashed water on her face. She returned to the room, stood next to the table, sat down, then stood again uncertainly.

The rabbi came walking in, his body half-turned toward the doorway, making a "Relax, relax!" hand motion to someone in the hallway she couldn't see. He had the requisite long white beard that these rabbis in Jerusalem tended to sport, but it had a luster to it, as if he brushed it a hundred strokes every night. Did men shampoo their

144

beards? she wondered, then shook her head. He was smiling at her right now with a sweet gravity, his cheeks above his beard bunching into two walnuts. So small and cute and approachable, she thought, with his tiny elf-like build and crinkling walnut cheeks. She wanted to reach over and pinch one of them. She shook her head again. This was a rav. He deserved the greatest respect.

He sat catty-corner to her seat at the table. "So you teach Torah?" he said in regular English. It wasn't an American voice or an Israeli voice or an accent from any one country that she could recall. It was a Jewish voice, inflected with years of Talmudic study, mournful, cheerful, pragmatic and slightly nasal.

"Not yet," she said. "I was supposed to but these religious issues—they got in the way."

"So tell me." He motioned with his shoulder.

Tell me. He made it sound simple and cozy. Well, she'd try one or two out on him. "I'm having difficulty with some of the rabbinic commentaries. Take the verse, 'an eye for an eye, a tooth for a tooth.' A frightening verse. Think of how it's been misused throughout the centuries."

"Well, as you know, we have the Mishna and Talmud that explains: an eye in exchange for—monetary compensation. If you knock out someone's eye, you have to compensate them financially."

"So why didn't the verse say so? Nothing in the text suggests an eye in exchange for money. What's the textual basis for that?"

Rabbi Yellin bunched his fist into his beard, his eyes shut. He said, "Have you heard the Vilna Gaon's interpretation that 'eye' actually hints toward money if you switch—"

"I'm sorry," Beth said, "I've heard that idea, and it's clever, but doesn't really satisfy me."

The rabbi nodded and pulled out a book. "You realize that the Torah never intended for you to knock out someone's tooth or eye in revenge. Ever. And I can prove it to you." He began turning pages.

145

"Let me show you in Leviticus, Chapter Twenty, verse twenty-three."
As he spoke, he began to pull out Ksav veHakaballah, Moreh
Nevuchim, the Maharitz Chjas, the Rashash and Maharam Shif, books
and tiny commentaries lurking in the back of the Talmud, sages she'd
heard of but never actually read. "Come, let's look."

They sat and studied.

Curly peered into the room. He looked at Rabbi Yellin and Beth.
His face said, "What, you're still with her?"

Rabbi Yellin nodded at the Hassid and held up his hand suggesting an indeterminate amount of time. The Hassid left the room.

Other questions came up, Reuven sleeping with Bilhah, King
Solomon and his many wives, the role of Aaron the priest in making
the Golden Calf, Canaanite slaves. It would've been the best forty
minutes of learning she'd ever had if not for the bouncers who kept
sticking in their heads and saying, "Nu?"; pointing to their watches
and stretching out invisible lines in the air of all the people waiting to
see him. Even though Rabbi Yellin kept making his "relax, relax,"
hand motion, Beth knew her good luck couldn't last.

She braced herself. "Rabbi Yellin, please give me a blessing I
should succeed in finding my husband, my besherte." Saying those
words out loud, she almost burst into tears.

Just then, the bouncers, Curly and Scraggly, entered the room and
began walking, grim-faced, toward Rabbi Yellin. The rabbi gave them
a half-alarmed look, then turned to Beth. "Maybe you already met
him," he said in a low voice. "Maybe you said no."

Her neck stiffened. She felt her body go red. "Wait, what do you
mean?" But now the Hassidic bouncers were on either side of him,
urging the rabbi away to the next room, the next meeting, next, next,
next. "Don't worry," he called over his shoulder. "Everything's going
to be good." His eyes peered at her like little Hanukkah candles. Then
he was gone.

She folded up the quilt and returned it to the rebbetzin, thanking her, and with a nod to Curly and Scraggly who'd resumed their spots at the door, she left the apartment. Outside, the moon shone with a cool brilliance on the Jerusalem stone apartments. She was shivering, and starving, too, she realized. Her needs seemed to pierce her, pure in their intensity, and she walked vigorously, shaking off the chill, until she found a kiosk open, where she bought a bag of french fries. She was still mulling the rabbi's words when the bus came. Of course, he could've meant anybody, Beth realized as she settled herself into a seat by the window. Akiva wasn't the first man she had rejected. Through the years, she'd had some almost-proposals which she'd cut short when she'd seen where things were heading. It didn't have to mean Akiva.

The bald driver everyone called Kojak smiled at her in the mirror. The bus was practically empty. He gestured with his shoulder. "So pretty, no?"

Beth followed the line of his shoulder. He meant the bus shelter outside, the one with a thin woman in a bathing suit drinking a can of Tropeet guava juice, while bobbing on the Dead Sea. "Nice," she said indifferently. She dipped her hand into a bag in her purse and took out a fat french fry. She munched on it and let out a sigh that seemed to take out a few chunks from her soul. The story of the humpbacked man—the story Tsippi had told her—floated through her mind. She saw the groom approaching the bride. She saw him looking at her, telling her that he had prayed long ago for him to have the hump instead of her, and the slow transformation on the bride's face as he uttered his words. What was the groom really doing? For a moment he had offered her a different set of eyes: noble eyes, Jerusalem eyes, and once she had a glimpse through them she never wanted to return again to the old way of seeing things. Yes, it was clear—that was why the humpbacked groom had aroused the love and desire of his bride. She thought of Akiva. He also had offered her a different set of eyes, rare, prince-like and truthful ones, but she had not shown herself capable of looking through them. He had tried to arouse the latent nobility inside her, and she had turned away.

"Why so sad?" the driver said.

She barely lifted a shoulder, not even bothering to rearrange her expression into something more amiable.

"How's your love life?" he asked suddenly.

Beth made a *comme ci, comme ça* with her wrist. "Close your eyes. What do you see?"

"Nothing. Hah! Now I understand." The bus swerved past the Merkaz Hotel and a lone Arab laborer got on with a paint-encrusted pail. Kojak's eyes followed him to his seat. "Well, why can't you find anybody? What's taking you so long?" he said with a shade of irritation, as if her single status was an insult to him. "You're smart, you're nice-looking, you're nice. Why aren't you married by now?"

"Because I'm an idiot, I can't find someone to love," she burst out, then groaned, cursing her slip of the tongue. She knew how to finesse that question in ten different ways. What did she have to be honest with Kojak for? But now the driver was kneading his jaw, his eyes narrowed with calculation.

"I know somebody," he announced. "Don't say no," he shook a finger at Beth when he saw the look on her face. "Do you know I made a shidduch between a yeshiva student and the daughter of the Chief Rabbi of Belgium?" He nodded importantly. "So don't laugh. This man I'm thinking of—he paints pictures, some kind of artist—his name's Binyamin. An American. I just spoke with him the other day."

She'd heard of him. How many American artists in Jerusalem went by that name? Judy had once mentioned the artist in passing but had never suggested a date. It probably wasn't worth it. Well, what could it hurt, she thought. Plenty. These days, who needed a fresh disturbance? But the fact that the suggestion came from Kojak gave the shidduch a larkish feel. Really, Beth, she scolded herself. What was the big deal? On the heels of the rabbi's good wishes to her, it seemed criminal not to seize the moment.

Three stops later, the Arab painter got off. Kojak stopped the bus, staggered to the back, and kneeling heavily, thrust his head underneath the painter's seat, poking around. No bombs; nothing but pink bus slips. Beth scribbled on her bag of chips and tore off a corner. "Give him my number," she said as he sheepishly walked past, and handed him the scrap of paper.

※　※　※

Akiva was running late. He entered the stone, shack-like structure just in time for the Yishtabach prayers. He fastened his tefillin in place, draped his tallis over his head, and hurried through the morning blessings, the sacrifices and the psalms, catching up just as the worshipers called out: "Hear O Israel." The chazzan called out, "Redeemer of Israel!"—the signal that they were about to begin the Silent Devotion. Akiva took three steps backward, three steps forward, his feet coming together like an angel's, for this was the Silent Devotion, the culmination of the entire morning's prayers. He held himself throughout the eighteen benedictions, keeping his thoughts on the words, using all his strength to focus, to climb the mountain of prayer. One slip and he'd fall. But if he held on, curled his tongue around the words till they rang strong and sweet inside him, he just might get to the top. It had never happened, but he had come close a few times. A purple light had exploded in the back of his head and he'd had the sensation of overhearing God's thoughts about the people in his world. Unfortunately, he couldn't remember what they were.

In front of him someone moaned, a large man with delicate hands. This man always let out a whimper somewhere near the end of the Silent Devotion. He was beset with financial problems, Akiva knew. Next to him someone rocked and swayed and flailed their arms, like a man who'd fallen into a hole in the ice and was desperately trying to extricate himself. Behind him someone hummed the benedictions, making rhythmic, clickety noises with his tongue, like a train. Everyone had their own style of prayer. As for himself, he liked to stand still and silent like a candle. Sometimes though, he couldn't help but twitch through the sheer effort of trying to remain spiritually attuned.

One paragraph from the end, as he said the Guard My Tongue From Evil meditation, his eyes fell on a man standing two feet away from him, wearing a black yarmulka that didn't quite cover a huge crater-like bald spot. He looks like Dr. Sorscher, Akiva thought, but it couldn't be; Dr. Sorscher wasn't religious. Well, maybe someone in his family had died and the doctor had come to recite Kaddish. While he craned his neck and tried to see more, his thoughts jumped back to a time five years ago. A medical specialist, Dr. Sorscher had given him the pamphaldamine drug which he had reluctantly tried. It brought on a sweating light-headedness, a nausea in the pit of his stomach. It also turned his eyes yellow.

"I can adjust this—easily," the doctor had told him. "By the third time, you won't feel anything; your reaction has been excellent." But then the doctor revealed that extended use of the drug caused impotence in twenty percent of the men who used it.

Akiva's mouth went dry. "What's extended use?" he asked.

"Five years, but the condition is reversible," the doctor quickly added. "When they stop taking the drug, the impotence disappears."

Akiva turned away, sickened to his depths. He never tried the drug again. How ironic that the bus driver, Kojak, the one who had thrown him off the bus, had branded him a drug user, of all things.

As he unwound his tefillin straps from his arm, he casually took a few steps to the Bimah, then walked back, looking in the bald man's direction. No, not Dr. Sorscher, not even a look-alike. He recalled what he had told Beth about his experience with pamphaldamine. He had felt free to share these details with her on their first date. Of course, he hadn't reported the doctor's recommendation—*that* he had omitted, along with the other complication the drug would cause. What was the point, at the start of a relationship? The drug with its looming cloud of impotence revolted him. He had never brought it up with anyone, ever.

He felt a spasm coming, about thirty seconds away, but he clenched his jaw and breathed evenly, expelling air from between his teeth. The spasm passed. Akiva tucked the black leather boxes and straps into a cloth pouch, folded his prayer shawl and returned it to the wooden shelf set aside for these articles.

Chapter Nine

J UDY LEANED OVER TO FASTEN A CHINESE STRING BARRETTE IN
Beth's hair. She had forty-five minutes to get her ready for the
date. "And as long as we were talking about Beit Shifra, I have a
question to ask you—about belief." She stopped. "Beth, are you listening?"

"Uh huh." Beth turned her head to glimpse her profile in the mirror. Catching Judy's frown, she gave her a chastened smile and sat up
with exaggerated erectness.

"Okay. So, here's what I'm trying to say. I learn Torah, I work
hard at understanding what's written, with the assumption that there
are layers of meaning buried in the text. The depth, the wisdom, that's
the payoff, right?" Her eyes closed in thought. "But what if—I don't
mean to be sacrilegious—what if I assumed meaning in a cake recipe.
Would the meaning get revealed there, too?"

"Hah. That's a good one." Beth swiveled around in her chair.
"What you're asking is, does meaning exist objectively, waiting to
be unearthed, or is it simply a projection of—your own desire for
meaning?"

"Exactly." Judy felt relieved to be understood. "It's possible that the attention and devotion—the belief that I bring to the table, maybe that's what creates the meaning."

Beth was staring at her.

Judy flushed. Then she said, "Not that I really think that. I'm just playing with the possibility." She looked down, gazing critically at her fingers. There she went again, retreating from an idea she'd expressed. She noticed in class how tentative she was when she ventured a concept. As if she was only allowed certainty in the area of relationships. She unfastened the barrette, brushed out Beth's hair, and began to arrange it again.

"That's a good one," Beth repeated, her eyes thoughtful. Her hand shot up. "Ouch! That hurts! Give it up, Judy. My hair's too fine to do the things you want it to." She pulled off the barrette and shook out her hair. The brown strands crackled and snapped.

Judy cast her eyes upward, but decided it wasn't worth the fight. She had more important battles right now. For instance, Beth's velveteen burgundy dress. Appealing, yes, for 1966. Her musings would have to wait.

"This is pretty," she said, fingering a sleeve, "but not for tonight. Look, you tell me this guy's intense and spiritual? Wear something sexy."

"But it's my favorite!" Beth's shoulders hunched up defensively.

Judy faced her grimly, hands on hips. "You're not going out in that dress," she told her.

She looked stricken.

"Beth, listen to me. Men need a certain amount of . . . you know. And looks go a long way." Beth's eyes glazed over. Judy went on, "Didn't God package apples and oranges in bright beautiful colors just to entice the appetite?"

Beth had a disgusted look on her face. "The whole world acts like—If you're good-*looking,* therefore you're *good.* I reject that."

"You're right. Looks are over-valued. But you can't ignore reality." A new thought struck her. "I know you." Judy pointed the brush at her. "You're still thinking about that guy, Akiva. You turned him down, right? It's over, remember?"

"Over," Beth repeated. She sighed and began brushing her own hair.

"Open your eyes. Time to move on. There's a world of people out there for you to meet. It could happen in a flash. One minute you're walking down the street, and then—By the way, do you remember the bomb that went off on the number twelve bus? Going to Bayit Vegan?"

"Sure." She stopped brushing. "That was over two months ago."

"But you didn't hear the story, did you?" Judy's eyes gleamed. "So after the explosion all the injured people were taken to the hospital, and two of them—a man and woman in their twenties—got acquainted while recovering at Shaarei Tzedek. Well," she paused, "they just got engaged. Think of that next time you're on a bus."

"Mazal tov for them." Beth set the brush down on the table. "All right, all right. Let's see what you have."

Judy looked through her closet. She had maybe a minute before her window of opportunity shut. There! Her turquoise dress—her most slinky and unRebbetzinlike—was perfect. She held it out, her hand on the neck of the hanger.

"Oh Judy." Beth swatted it away. "I'm not glamorous like you."

"Then this." Judy showed her a flowing olive-tan dress—part classic, part earthy Bohemian—that she had bought from a J. Jill catalogue back in the States before making Aliyah. Beth agreed to try it on. Judy began to work on her face, and Beth stiffly held up her head, eyes squeezed shut, as if submitting to something painful.

"Great bones!" Judy said. She smoothed on moisturizer and patted on foundation, then blush, eye shadow—"No blue," Beth called out—then eye pencil, lip pencil, lipstick, the works. The foundation at the jawline needed to be better blended. She fixed it with a damp sponge and stepped back to examine her work. Beth's face had gone from flat to three-dimensional, from somewhat attractive to truly lovely. Judy bit her lower lip and ducked her head so Beth wouldn't see the tears forming in her eyes. Her beauty had been silenced years ago. How little it took to bring out the softer lights of her face, the allure in her eyes, the sensuality of her lips, but no one had taken the time or interest: not Beth, not her friends; certainly not her mother, that much was clear. Then she remembered: Beth's mother had died when she was twelve or thirteen, but had the woman left no legacy of femininity to her daughter? There wasn't any reason Beth couldn't have been a beauty. She must've gotten by on her good features and no effort, but now she had reached the age where effort was crucial. As the French say: There are no ugly women, just lazy ones.

She watched Beth as she looked at herself in the mirror from various angles. To Judy her face seemed almost inwardly lit. "That's not me," Beth said finally. "I look like a Sicilian bride." She began to wipe away the lipstick with the back of her wrist.

Judy lifted her arms toward the ceiling. *"Hab rachmones! Hab rachmones!"* she beseeched in a ringing voice that surprised even herself. Compassion, just a bit of compassion.

And Beth, taking the compassion to be for Judy's sake, not her own, said, "Okay, I'll keep the rest, but the lipstick has to go."

"Okay." As Beth went into the bathroom to try on the coffee-colored dress, Judy's thoughts drifted back to her earlier musings. Did belief serve as a tool to reveal meaning, or did it actually create it? And what did the word *belief* even mean? She'd heard her learning partner, Lauren, talk about a willingness to humble oneself before a sacred text, to put parentheses around one's doubts, to hold them in abeyance even if only momentarily, in order to understand the words in front of you. This made her think of a medrashic saying about water. The greatest amount of water collected in the deepest hole; wisdom gathered in the most humble person. The deeper the hole, the more water it could contain. People who made no room inside themselves would never hold much beyond their own preconceived ideas. Belief didn't create meaning, she concluded, it just made room for it.

She heard Beth wrestling in the bathroom with the dress. It was a complicated outfit to put on, she remembered. Maybe the French were wrong, and not every woman could be made beautiful through sheer effort and will. She had seen attractive become pretty, and pretty become beautiful, certainly ugly become adequate, through the applied effort of makeup, but rare was the woman who skipped a step and went from ugly to truly pretty through her cosmetic exertions. The groundwork had to be there. Beauty, like meaning, couldn't be a complete figment of the imagination, not entirely an invention.

Now Beth, she thought, had all the groundwork, but not enough will. If it had been herself in her situation, she would've fought with every means available to track down her besherte: looked her best at all times, gone to an image consultant, found the best therapist money could buy, asked the help and advice of every matchmaker in the book, flown to America, Belgium, England for fresh prospects—whatever it took. For all Beth's fine qualities—her decency and fair-mindedness, a sharpness and curiosity and a sweetness, too—what came to mind when she saw her was an image of a drifting log in the ocean, taken by this stream or that, bumping along with no purpose. She was willing to get herself wet, but not really immerse herself— choose a man, a dynamic career, or immerse herself in Torah study, or even a specific religious path. Beth herself thought the fact of her very impartiality and her lack of clear definition made her accessible and open. True, she was welcome at any home and could fit in everywhere. But essentially she belonged nowhere. She just refused to commit herself.

Beth appeared in the doorway in the J. Jill catalogue dress. It wasn't quite right, Judy saw. Something in the hip area didn't drape

the way she would've liked. The burgundy dress, for all its quaint out-
datedness, had suited her better. But Beth was clearly elated with the
dress, much as she tried to downplay her delight. She posed in a mock
Betty Crocker preen, hands on hips. "Vell? Vat do you tink?"

Judy surveyed her. "Beautiful," she said finally. "Just beautiful. By
the way, who's the guy?"

Beth shrugged. "Nobody you'd know."

※ ※ ※

Beth waited a little anxiously at the bus shelter, Judy's bus story still
vivid in her mind. Only Judy could come up with a bomb explosion
story with an upbeat shidduch message, though she hoped it wouldn't
be necessary for people to die or lose a limb in order for her to get
married. She felt a little guilty not letting Judy know who her date was.
Since Judy knew both of them and had never set them up, she probably didn't think it was such a good idea to begin with. But Judy didn't
know her as well as she thought she did, and Beth didn't want the date
nixed before they'd even met. Suddenly she noticed a poster on the
shelter, a picture of a long-necked ballerina posed with her arms in an
arc over her head. So the Tel-Aviv ad agency had finally made it to
Levites Street. She put her head up close and read: "You're a woman
of the times. You deserve freedom, comfort, ease. Buy Nashit—fra-
grant and discreet." Beth looked uneasily at the picture. The ballerina's leg was perched precariously on a sanitary napkin. And at the
bottom, in italics, she read: *"Cotton was for Grandma's times!"* Beth
looked up and saw the other bus-goers standing at least ten feet away,
shunning the shelter, and she skittered away to where they stood.

She met Binyamin in the lobby of the Jerusalem Plaza Hotel, but
since they were both starving they decided to go to the Shalom Ori-
enta restaurant down the block. A Vietnamese waiter told them the
house specials in a lilting Hebrew, and they both listened, charmed. In
the center of the table flowered a red Chinese fan with a picture of the

Western Wall and a Torah scroll etched in gold. The black-slippered steps of the waiters, the smell of ginger in the air, the olive-shaded mural of fragile trees and kimono-clad women gazing at vases, all filled Beth with a soft benevolence toward Binyamin. He was dark-bearded with silver-threaded hair and thin lips, thin wrists, and thin eyebrows, an ascetically handsome man. Score one for Kojak, she thought. He did look younger than forty-two, though. Something in his expression that she couldn't pinpoint, an unanchored quality.

For the first twenty minutes, they discussed the Sephardic enclave where Beth lived. Though Binyamin lived across the street in the Beit Morris complex (he joked, "to think I left New Jersey and came to Israel only to live in an apartment building called 'House of Morris' "), he'd had some contact with the Sephardic people who lived on Beth's side. A few times he'd prayed in their little hut of a synagogue. His impressions were amusing.

"I like them," he declared. "There's an honesty they have. When a Sephardi sins, he admits it. He sinned, his desires got in the way. When an Ashkenazi sins, he claims there's no God."

Beth laughed appreciatively. He had caught the difference between the two in a sentence. "Well put!"

"Actually, my rabbi told me that line," Binyamin acceded.

Beth smiled at him. "See, you're honest, too." She glimpsed herself in a wall mirror and was struck by how relaxed and pretty she looked.

As the waiter padded away with their orders, Binyamin leaned toward her. "Beth, tell me something you like about yourself that's invisible." He settled back into his wicker seat and smiled.

She froze, feeling the pressure to conjure up something witty and truthful. Suddenly she couldn't think of anything invisible in the entire world, except her soul, which was too obvious.

"Oh," she said, pulling a wrapper off a pair of chopsticks, "my appetite."

He looked startled. Then he closed his eyes, breathed in and exhaled. "That's profound."

"Are you joking, maybe?" She tapped the tip of a chopstick against her lip.

"No, Beth."

She looked at him sideways. What was all the Beth-this, and Beth-that talk? Her father once told her it was an old salesman's trick to use someone's name at the earliest opportunity to gain the person's trust. Akiva—he never flung her name around. The few times he actually called her by name felt like a rare offering. But Binyamin was a nice guy, quite decent and nice-looking, she had to admit. She smiled engagingly at him.

"Would you mind drawing me a tree?" he said.

"What?"

"It's a game," he told her, and unfolded a sheet of paper flat on the table. "Just draw any tree that comes to your mind."

She shrugged. "Fine, but I'm no artist."

"Beth, it doesn't matter whether it looks good or not."

He sat quietly, his lips pursed, while she sketched a thick-trunked tree. She drew with a child's absorption, making large cauliflower-like heads sprout from the branches, a few blades of grass near the tree's gnarly roots, a jagged hole in the middle of the trunk.

"Okay, that's enough," he called, his hand on the sheet, but she managed to add a nest in a tree branch before he took the paper into his long pink fingers.

He bent over it, murmuring and shaking his head. His cheek muscles knotted and unknotted.

She took another glance at the tree. What was the big deal? It seemed harmless enough, not a great drawing, but certainly not terrible.

"You yearn for the infinite," he said finally, "but you're on the lazy side."

"No, I'm not."

"Okay," he amended. "These lines over here," he pointed to the fine lines she had drawn along the trunk, "they do show energy, but it's a selective kind."

She placed her hands flat on the table. "So—you analyze trees? I don't understand. Is there a basis for that?"

"A tree is like a person," Binyamin began to explain, his chest expanding with his delivery. The waiter suddenly appeared at their side with two porcelain bowls of wonton soup cradled in his arms. He hovered over the table until they had sampled the broth.

"Very good," she said, and Binyamin nodded his agreement.

He shot his soup with soy sauce and continued, "The trunk is the heart, the leaves are the head, and the roots are—ah, the lower region, the libido of the person. Actually, you can tell a lot from these drawings."

"All right," said Beth, "tell me."

"Well," he peered at the drawing from various angles, and then held it up to the light, "you see yourself as very alone, apart from others. You set yourself above people in sneaky ways. This, along with a critical streak, prevents you from having more joy in your life. Also, there's a basic nurturing you didn't get when you were growing up. Hmm, look at this," he pointed at the tangled roots. "You're deeply insecure about your femininity."

Beth clicked her nails sharply against the table. "That's ridiculous."

He glanced down at the giveaway tree roots and shrugged. With the edge of his spoon he sliced his wonton in two and scooped it into his mouth.

"Did something terribly shocking happen to you when you were eleven or twelve?" he asked, his eyes returning to the drawing. "Did you experience a great loss, someone close to you?"

Her eyes lowered. "Well, yes, my mother died."

"Yes, it's pretty obvious. I can see it here." He pointed at the black hole in the lower center of the tree trunk. "That explains the lack of nurturing and possibly the feminine insecurity," he mused.

She flinched and dropped her head. "Will you stop it?" she choked.

"I'm just trying to get to know you," he said, a little plaintively.

She undid the red cloth napkin shaped into a boat and wiped at her eyes with the tips.

"You just want to disqualify me, is that it?" she said, noting he hadn't said her name from the moment he'd laid eyes on her drawing. "All this"—her hand made circles over the paper—"it's just some screening device. You don't really want to know me, do you?"

He took an empty glass into his hands and said gently, "Come. There's no need to be defensive about your problems. Besides," he persisted, turning the glass to catch the light, "why not use shortcuts if it'll help you know if the person's right for you, the one you should marry? I want to get the show on the road. What's wrong with that?"

It all sounded reasonable and mature, but then she glanced at the unruly tree roots. "Maybe that it's fallible and manipulative?"

He sulked in his chair, loosened his collar and began looking at the other couples in the restaurant.

The waiter arrived, delicately setting down their plates of food, as if he sensed the precarious shifting winds of the shidduch. She ate her sesame chicken with the green and red peppers spread confetti-like over the fowl. Binyamin picked at his plate of moo goo gai pan with his chopsticks, then discarded them and went at it with fork and knife. They ate noisily, rapidly.

Halfway into the meal Beth remembered Binyamin and raised her head to look at him. His cheeks seemed wider, a rosy magnanimous fog expanding his features. She tapped the side of her chin to signal that a Chinese noodle twig had entangled itself in his beard. He sheepishly removed it and they began to talk.

He confided that he possessed a kind of yellow pages of saints, Rebbes and tzaddiks, and had actually visited a few. He shared a few episodes, and as he related some of the Torah discussions he'd had with them, he rose beyond the gimmicky and actually sounded appealing and sincere. She couldn't imagine what he was doing studying at his yeshiva in the Old City. It was far too analytic and Talmud-based for him. She could picture him fitting into two other yeshivas she knew with a more individualistic, possibly mystical bent that would channel his creativity.

Beth considered telling him she also had gone to see a rabbi for enlightenment, though she didn't think Rabbi Yellin qualified as a Rebbe or mystic. Even though she hadn't gotten her questions fully answered—how could she in forty minutes?—she'd felt better knowing he hadn't regarded her questions as particularly new or shocking. Anyway, she wasn't seeking answers, exactly. She was seeking an approach, a direction. How to be both fully intellectual and truly pious. The people who spoke the language of intellectual honesty— where was their passion for mitzvahs? Why did so few of them relish the details? Why did they rush through prayer, as if it were a heavy baggage they couldn't wait to unload? And the people who devoted themselves to every detail of God's Torah, the ones who were capable of crying during prayer—why did they turn numb and rigid at the idea of critical thinking? As if their brains had committed suicide? Could a person be inside and outside at the same time? It would've been nice to discuss these thoughts with her date, but Binyamin struck her as at the very beginning of his religious journey; he probably would only be confused by her spiritual issues. So instead she arched her eyebrows high, encouraging him on with his Rebbe sagas.

By the time they started on the lychee dessert the rhythm of talk had quickened. He was a good shmoozer, and she couldn't help being drawn in. She even began to feel a certain need to rescue him from his present yeshiva and direct him to one better suited to him. But she had played that role of savior in the past and didn't quite feel up to it. He spoke some more while she ate the last bits of lychee on her plate. He gestured with his hand for her to finish his, and she did.

At the end of the evening, he folded her cauliflower tree in two, tipped the waiter who was clearing away the plates and walked her to the bus stop. He apologized for not taking her home—he was sleeping over at a friend's in the Old City, he said.

"The problem is we both have too much in common," he said, as the bus arrived. "We cancel each other out. We're both cynical idealists."

Beth nodded absently and boarded the number fifteen. Let him say what he wanted.

"There wasn't much chemistry either," he added, standing in front of the bus door. It was about to shut. She reached out and plucked the drawing from his hand. "Can't I keep it?" he said as the door closed. "I analyzed it!"

"No," she mouthed through the door. She smiled and shook her head at him as the bus carried her away.

She sat, lulled by her thoughts and the steady embryonic rumble of the bus.

When the bus let her off, she saw the sanitary napkin ad. It had been damaged in her absence. The ballerina's upper arms and thighs had been spray-painted blue. Probably some Hareidi zealot, the ones she was always reading about in the *Jerusalem Post,* had obliterated those parts of the body with paint. The ballerina's limbs had been darkened, but instead of erasing those parts, they had been crudely emphasized, adding a charge of sexuality. And why not the breasts? she thought. She became conscious of her own arms, thighs, breasts, the place of the womb, and lower still. She felt guilty—of what, she didn't know. Of being a woman? Of menstruating? Unfortunately, those years were numbered, with no man in sight. She walked quickly past the shelter.

Back at the apartment she went through her mail. She carefully removed the coffee-colored dress and examined it for stains. None. She headed for the shower, even though she had taken one that morning. Her date with Binyamin—or was it the sanitary napkin ad?—had left her feeling unclean.

Beth reached down and handed her another wet T-shirt which she hung on the clothesline. They were standing on Judy's porch balcony. The sky was a marbled gray, but the forecasters had predicted no rain. "And then he said, 'There wasn't much chemistry, either.' " She turned her palms outward. "So I got on the bus, and that was that."

"So that was that." Judy shook a wrinkled dress, pulling out the twisted sleeves from the body. "Well," she said in a somewhat forbidding voice, "did you flirt with this man at all?"

"Flirt?" Beth had been expecting sympathy. She was rubbing a sore muscle in her shoulder. "I tried to, but he was such a goon."

Judy hung a sheet on the line. "It kills me, you know, seeing you in this situation again and again. I mean, how many times do you have to go through this, year after year, season after season? I would go mad."

Beth turned her back and leaned out the window, staring at all the clothing Judy had hung in the past half hour—six children's worth, not to mention her own clothing and her husband's. At the apartment building across the way other women were clamping similarly vast quantities of laundry on swaying clotheslines. Her own line of laundry was meager. "What can I do?" Beth bit her lip. Married people were always finding something wrong with her, some factor on which they could blame her spinsterhood: her hair was too long, her body was too plump, she didn't floss her teeth often enough, she was too busy or not busy enough, too sharp, too dull, too self-absorbed, too selfless. "I try, I try so hard."

"Yes, I know." Judy looked at her. "But why do you have to have such high standards? We all made our compromises, and whoever says they didn't is just self-deceiving. So why can't you get on with it like everybody else?"

"You think it's arrogance that keeps me single?" Beth's nose scrunched. "Haven't you seen what's out there?" She shook her head at the lunacy of married people.

"Why not join a club with men in it, a book club, a nature walk group? Talk to men. Find out what men like. Flirt. Take a chance. Buy bikini underwear." She gave her a sideways look. "Don't be so defensive."

Beth blew a strand of hair upward. "Now you sound like my date. He called me defensive, too."

"Beth, I say this with all the love in the world." Her fingers pursed, she touched her heart. "If ten people tell you you're drunk, you'd better lie down."

Beth said nothing. Her eyes rested on Judy's clothesline. "Hey." She pointed to some diaphanous peach thing swaying in the wind. "Where'd you get this?"

"Hm." Judy crossed an arm over her stomach, her other fist pressed into her hip. "Victoria's Secret," she said. "But don't worry. I know a good place in Jerusalem to take you."

At the store's entrance, an elderly guard cheerfully asked Beth and Judy to open their bags, which he then squeezed and prodded, poking for bombs and other suspicious lumps. "You can go in," he pronounced. Delilah's Lair was having an end-of-season Purim sale. Under fluorescent lights negligees shimmered. Frothy pale undergarments lay coiled in sunken tables. Mounds of bikini panties towered in a corner. A blond-haired mannequin with outrageous cleavage wore a tiger-striped bra and a matching G-string.

"Remember," Judy said, "it's not a museum. You're here to buy, not just look. Oh!" Her eyes fixed on the discount rack. "I see something I like! Meet you later."

Well, a little privacy wouldn't hurt.

She dipped her hand into a jumble of items she couldn't identify. A red garter belt wrapped itself around her wrist, and she undid it, recoiling slightly. None of the stuff appealed to her, but what did she expect? They were sale items that packs of women had already pawed over. The nicer things were hanging, and some of the really exquisite negligees were behind the counter, zipped up in heavy plastic, not for anyone but the serious customer. She smiled to herself. This reminded her of one of the sayings of the Sages: "A blessed thing is hidden from the eye." Some parts of you were too precious to casually expose to the crowds passing by.

She wandered in and out, fingering the slips, frowning as she eyed the displays. The shop struck her as pathetic and offensive. All that lavish attention devoted to fulfilling men's fantasies. And what about women's fantasies? Where were the shops catering to females' desires?

She spotted Judy with a pile of silky short robes draped over one arm making her way to the dressing room. Beth stopped at a particularly attractive bra and panty set in a perky tangerine. The underwear was high cut, and without even trying it on she knew it would offer a whole new look to her thighs. Did she even have fantasies? She couldn't think of any, not to save her life. A few times she had tried to actually invent a fantasy, having read in a magazine that it was a must for women. But when she tried to carry an image through from beginning to end, say a tall, dark, muscular man carrying her off to some desert island, something was always going wrong: The man suddenly got a nosebleed, with basins of blood everywhere; or an army of pygmies descended to attack them; it could be anything. It hurt her brain to work a fantasy so she stopped trying.

"Nu?"

She glanced up. Two small dour eyes were trained on her. A Hassidic woman in a black dress and thick seamed stockings stood pointing at the tangerine bra and panties. "Do you want it—yes or no?"

Beth stared at her. "Is this your store?" she blurted.

"Oh yes," said the woman. "I have the biggest selection of any store in Jerusalem. Only the best here."

Beth took a step closer. "Do you mind if I ask," she lowered her voice, "do you wear these things yourself?"

The Hassidic woman looked affronted. "But of course. Why shouldn't I?" She lifted the edge of her shapeless black dress and showed the lacy slip she was wearing beneath it. "And you should see what's under the slip!" She adjusted her wig, which had fallen low on her hairline. "It's a mitzvah to dress this way for your husband. It's the first thing I tell my daughters when they get engaged." She reached for a bunch of black satin bras and began affixing them to hangers with little silver pins. "Look around," she said, pins in her mouth, "see what else you like. For brides, I give discounts."

So underneath black, dour Hassidic clothing lurked a pack of slinky sex kittens? Beth could hardly believe it. Well, she'd buy the bikini panties and bra and be done with it. She turned to go to the register and she saw a satiny negligee in hunter green, draping from a hanger by the thinnest spaghetti straps. Suddenly she longed to be inside it. She pawed through the rack till she found one in her size and, blushing, took it into the dressing room. Her shoulders! They were stupendous. Lovely white hills that anyone would want to caress. She did a Yemenite step before the mirror and the negligee glittered on her body like a waterfall. She stretched out an arm, tango style, her neck held high. "Kiss me, you fool," she said to the mirror.

Beth and Judy paid for their purchases, but just before Beth left the store she tucked the bag with hearts on it into a larger bag with the words "Glatt Kosher Meat" in bold letters. Judy laughed.

Later Beth went alone to Steimetsky's Bookstore where she bought herself *The Flirter's Handbook.* She read it straight through in three hours, snorting and guffawing as she tried to imagine herself imitating the sinewy movements of a cat, as one chapter actually sug-

167

gested. It made fun reading. Afterward, she added to her list of Daily Habits: Give a compliment to one man a day.

A few days later, she stood in line at the Post Office to buy stamps. A few yards away an auction was taking place for all abandoned, unclaimed postal items—a twice-yearly event. It was unclear if her particular line was being attended by the clerk, and another customer, paunchy in an Israeli masculine way, kept calling out, "Are you open?" but the clerk didn't even lift his head in acknowledgment. He seemed to be distracted by the auctioneer who was holding up a box and calling out, "Tea towels. Fifty shekels for a set of tea towels."

Finally Beth leaned on the edge of the counter. "Can I buy stamps here?" Her voice was light and sweet.

The clerk lifted his head. "Yes, in just two minutes," he said kindly.

The other customer hitched his pants up by the loops and turned to her. "With a pretty voice like that, no wonder he answered you and not me."

She laughed, delighted. She was wearing her tangerine underwear and felt daring. "Ah, you're just the wrong sex," she pacified him. "If I'd been the clerk," her arm gave a magnanimous sweep, "I definitely would've answered you."

"Would you now?" He looked at her penetratingly.

Her eyes froze. He was flirting with her. In the background she heard the clerk calling out, "Reading glasses, thirty shekels for a box of reading glasses." She tried to think up a witty, deflecting response. But why deflect him? Or why deflect him now? She could always send him on his way in two minutes, instead of stopping it short as she usually did. "Uh huh," she said stupidly, but it seemed to be enough because he was already hiking up his elbow on the counter and smiling down at her. Was this all it took? The clerk was calling out now with extra fervor, "American deodorant and toothpaste! Ninety shekels."

His eyes moved slowly over her, taking in her bulky sweater, long brown skirt, and finally settling for an interminable time on her flat, rain-proof shoe boots. She cringed. She knew she looked dowdy. "Too bad you're religious," he said finally. "Otherwise I'd start up with you in a second."

She blinked, taken aback. Then she slapped her cheek lightly. "How'd you guess my deep dark secret?"

"The shoes. That's what they all wear." And he went off, shaking his head regretfully, muttering, "Too bad, too bad."

Beth watched him leave, her chest buoyant. A little blond boy in a knitted kipa walked by and she could've sworn he winked at her.

Chapter Ten

B INYAMIN, YOU LOOK LIKE DEATH," HIS CHEVRUTAH, TUVIA, TOLD him. Tuvia had just shown him the proofs for his wedding invitation and gotten the blankest of responses. "Worse than death. Purgatory."

Binyamin slouched in his chair, his head sunk into his shoulders, appearing as if he had no neck at all. He was tired. His soul was tired in every way. The thought of cranking out yet another painting with a glaring Jewish symbol on it made him feel cynical to the point of self-disgust. Then lately, he kept dreaming about a yeshiva in Safed, the Holy Beggars Institute, a mystical place he'd heard about, but way too funky for the yeshiva world he inhabited. Many mornings he could barely pull himself out of bed to go to his yeshiva. His learning made him feel like he was drawing water with a sieve. He might get credit for his effort, but how long could he delude himself that he was retaining anything? The rare times he understood the Talmud, he felt lit up, powerful and connected in history. But mostly, when he looked into a page of Talmud he felt autistic, and depressed. He'd never been depressed in his life! And to top it all off his last date had been a bomb. The strange thing was, as much as he hadn't gone for her, she hadn't gone for him. Maybe he was losing his appeal. It had happened to a friend of his in the States, a real stud. One day he looked into the mirror, and whatever it was he'd had—that buzz he gave off that made women want to know him—was gone. "Another one of those dates," he said out loud. "A decent woman, but no spark, really." He lifted his hand, about to say more, but dropped it futilely on the table. "No spark."

Tuvia twiddled a growing earlock. "I fell asleep on my first date with Chani." He laughed. "Talk about no spark! And now I can't wait till the wedding, when I get her alone in the Yichud room. These things need patience sometimes."

Binyamin barely lifted his eyes, too dispirited to disparage Tuvia's dating tips.

"So you had a bad date." Tuvia gathered up his wedding invitation proofs and put them into an envelope. "So what? There's lots of women out there."

"Maybe for others, but not for me." He flicked glumly at some paint on his fingernail.

Tuvia removed his glasses and began to wipe them with the edge of his shirt. "What are you talking about?"

"Well, if you have to know—I've been blacklisted." He explained how the matchmakers had banded together and put a ban on setting him up further.

Tuvia put a hand to his cheek, his mouth open. For once, he didn't have a ready aphorism. "Wow," he said finally. He let out his breath. "I can't believe they did that. That's awesome—I mean, awful," he corrected himself.

Binyamin shot him a murderous look.

"I mean, what power they have. I had no idea! These matchmakers, they could ruin your life." His small, dark eyes darted here and there. "It's frightening." He reached over and held Binyamin by the wrists. "What are you going to do?"

"I'm rather desperate," Binyamin admitted. "I'm thinking of calling Mrs. Bartosky."

"Oh, you mean that matchmaker in your neighborhood?" Tuvia replaced his glasses carefully and blinked a few times. "Why her?"

"My hunch is, she's behind this plot. After all, the last person who set me up was her. I've got to talk to her, reason with her, let her know I'm not the creep she thinks I am." He heaved a sigh and looked out bleakly. "What else is there to do?"

"Call her. Call now. You've got to fight this."

Binyamin nodded.

"Call now. Go." Tuvia made a shoving motion in the air.

Binyamin's head emerged from between his shoulders, cautious and turtle-like. "Now?"

"Yep."

The yeshiva public phone was out of order, so he went outside to the phone booth just under the Jewish Quarter Cafe and fumbled in his pocket for an asimone token.

Someone answered on the first ring. "Hello?" the voice whispered.

"May I speak to Mrs. Bartosky?"

"That's me," she said hoarsely. "Someone's taking a nap. Trying to keep the volume down." She stopped. "Who is this?" Then, awkwardly: "Binyamin Harris?"

"Yes." He paused dramatically. "That Guy." He tried to inject a note of lightness: "So. What's all this talk I hear about refusing to set me up?" He could only hold the tone for a few seconds before sliding into resentment. "What have I done to deserve this treatment? I turned my life around, became religious, to be treated like the worst scum? Is that right?"

She coughed.

"I know this was your idea. What do you have against me?" He tried to calm his erratic breathing.

"Binyamin, I have nothing against—"

"Then set me up! Get rid of this ridiculous ban."

"I can't help you," she said. "I see where you're headed, and I just can't help you."

He stared at a billboard advertisement for Hadar pickles, at the pretty dark-skinned Jewess who smiled broadly over a cucumber field. "Why not? Is it because I want someone beautiful? Should I marry a woman I'm not attracted to, just to be a mensch, to be nice? What would be the point of that?"

"No point," she said gently. "But the more I talk to you, the more I see I can't help you."

"But you can. You could introduce me to a wonderful, beautiful religious woman."

He could hear her fingers clicking against the receiver. "I already have," she said. "I've introduced you to the most gorgeous women in Jerusalem, the most intelligent, the nicest. Somehow you arouse their interest, and then before it's even started, it's over. This one, her wrists were too thick, that one, her eyebrows too close together, another, her voice too emphatic. No one is good enough." She spoke blandly, without accusation, as if relating simple facts.

Binyamin stood rock still. No one is good enough. The phrase kept striking his brain, releasing sparks, images from the past, old girlfriends who hadn't measured up. "Look, you've got me all wrong. I'm not some arrogant jerk who thinks he deserves the best." He leaned into the next sentence: "The truth is—I *need* the best. Call it a sickness, call it what you want. If she's not stunning, I couldn't make her happy." His voice cracked. "That's who I am, the way I'm built, and there's nothing I can do." It was true. In this area of his life, he had no control of himself. He was helpless in the face of his need. Surely she would have compassion. He had been this way from time immemorial, from the womb. It wasn't his fault.

His hand was damp and he wiped it against a pants pocket. Then a memory hit him like a karate chop at the back of his neck. He remembered his parents going out for the evening, and he, a boy of five, watching his mother slowly descend the stairs, her hair in a high bun, thinking her the most exquisite, magical being his eyes could ever imagine. He was absolutely captivated by her beauty. And then a few summers later, he overheard a lifeguard making a crack about her ragged armpits and cellulite thighs as she sprang off the diving board. He didn't even know what cellulite meant, but he had felt a scalding shame that instantly reversed the way he saw his mother forever. She had never been beautiful, he realized, looking at old photos. He had been tricked by love into seeing beauty where none existed. Well, he would never be made a fool of again.

"When I hear men talking that way—"

The matchmaker's words came to him like an echo from the end of a long tunnel. "What way?" he stammered.

"Binyamin." Her voice was bereft of inflection. "You're talking like a man who's planning on being a bachelor for a few more years. You just haven't suffered enough."

He held the receiver against his chest. Suffered! He had no intention of suffering any more than he had, any more than the matchmakers had already made him suffer. But her words sliced into him. "You hate me."

"Ridiculous! Why would I introduce you to the best women I know, some of them friends?" She paused. "Tell me, Binyamin. Has there ever been anyone you really liked, someone you actually knew?"

"Sure there have," he said.

"Tell me."

He considered this. "You're asking about anyone," he said finally, "anyone I've met, not necessarily on a blind date?"

"Yes, anyone."

"Well, if you want to know," he said slowly. He rubbed an eyelid. He thought of their conversations, the Shabbat meals he had eaten at her home, the fluidity and ease with which she moved from one task to the next, setting the table, putting a shoe back on a child's foot, saying "no" to a neighbor who asked her to watch her children but in the pleasantest most good-humored way possible, turning the simplest deeds into acts of poetry. He realized then what it was he was seeking: an air, an attitude that went along with the beauty, the sort of woman who could lift a home into finer atmosphere and render it holy, graceful. *That's what it was.* Beth, Rita, Talya, the others—these women all lacked grace. "If you really want to know, I'd have to say it was you." He felt points of heat along his cheeks and neck. Well, it was true. There was no point in being embarrassed. She was just the woman he was looking for: capable, clever, devout. And absolutely stunning.

He waited, his chin pressed into the receiver. A cold sweat moistened his beard. Then the phone vibrated with laughter—the matchmaker couldn't stop giggling. Every time she seemed to stop, another wave of laughter carried her out to sea. Her hilarity refused to ebb. "Do you have any idea," she said between chuckles, "any idea," she choked, "what the stomach of a woman who's borne six children looks like?" She let out a final laugh that cut into his throat. "I wouldn't last one week in your regime. Now excuse me, I'm very tired. I must go. Good-bye." She hung up.

Binyamin replaced the receiver, so thoroughly abashed that he couldn't help glancing around the different shops in the area to see if anyone had witnessed the effect her laughter and words had had on him. No witness except for the smiling woman in the pickle advertisement. He began walking toward the benches in the Cardo Plaza. After a few steps, he noticed he was walking askew, almost with a limp. He shook his right leg and straightened himself, but still there was a groan in his body. He stopped at a juice stand and bought a strawberry banana smoothie, then walked over to the courtyard with the benches and the squared fountain that never gushed water, no matter what time of year. He sipped the smoothie, and looked at the Roman pillars, the statue halves jutting up from the stone ground. Judy Bartosky had misunderstood him. Of course he hadn't meant to be taken literally. He could never handle a war zone of a stomach, six children and the rest.

He sucked long and hard on the straw and the cup made a hissing, spitting sound. He had reached the bottom. From his bench in the Cardo Plaza he could still see the sweet dark-skinned woman in the pickle advertisement. His eyes strained as he stared at it. Except for the dark skin, the woman looked like Talya, feature for feature. Her broad bland smile burned into him. He shuddered. What was this, the phantom of Talya? Take her away! he ranted silently at the billboard. He didn't want her, well—not enough, that much he knew. Fragments of his conversation with the matchmaker kept rushing through his brain. Binyamin squashed the smoothie cup with the butt of his palm.

His neck bones ached. He wanted to lie down on the bench but it was too public, with all the yeshiva students and maroon-bereted soldiers and mothers passing by importantly with their baby carriages. If only he were alone, he thought. But how could he be more alone than he was now? There was no woman in his life, not even the possibility of a date. The endless stream of women, the consultations with Mrs. Bartosky and other matchmakers, they all had given him the illusion of company, of purpose and friendship, a coterie of women surrounding him with their insights, their feedback, their sympathetic voices, their concern. All that was gone now. And even if he were no longer to be blacklisted, even if he were to meet that perfect knock-out woman, there would come the moment when he would notice the one thing— a too grating laugh, hairy knuckles, runned stockings—and she would shame him, embarrass him, expose him the way every woman had the power to do, as his mother had. He couldn't rid himself of this fear. He'd always had it, and he could easily be in the same position in ten years: no children, no wife, no life.

"God, help me." He felt great pain—the pain of being far from women, of being far from himself, from God, from Torah, his family, his art, with nothing to show for his life. "Help me, God!" Each word sliced into him and all of his skin tingled with a sort of joy.

✺   ✺   ✺

At work, as Beth passed Dr. Carmi's office, she could have sworn she heard him say on the phone, "And that sow of a woman never washes her hair." Her face whitened. What was a sow? A pig? An adult female pig. She thrust her head into the office. Dr. Carmi pressed the phone to his chest and looked at her with bored, heavy-lidded eyes. "No, Beth, Dr. Bar-Chaim and I are not discussing you," he said, and resumed his conversation.

She scowled outside his office. Who cared what that Carmi thought? He was hardly worth the effort. And what did the others think? Did Sareet the typist laugh at her behind her back? And what about Eva the office manager? Did they not confide in her? Didn't they tell her their day to day problems, their dating and marriage woes? Though once when she offered an insight, Eva had said, "And which magazine did you read that in, Beth?" as if her own life could not possibly be the source.

After work she stopped in on Zahava at Broken Souls. Zahava was in the "Normalization Room," frying potatoes; she wore a short pink dress, beige stockings with two-inch-thick runs going up her thighs, and her hair tied back in a sock. A high-functioning patient, she was allowed a few such supervised hours in a small kitchen and living room, away from the other patients. Orna, the psychiatric social worker, hovered close by, her face a network of coy winks and smiles. Beth soon discovered the source of her joy: Akiva had been volunteering a few hours a week to paint the walls and ceiling, she said. The Institute's walls gleamed like they never had before.

"Nu, so when is the chuppah?" Orna gave Beth a sidelong look. "Do you think a man gives five hours a week because he is nice? Feh! Two hours, maybe. Five hours, no."

Beth coughed. "We're not seeing each other."

"Really?" Orna's brows lifted.

Zahava pointed a wooden spatula at her. "I am very angry at you, Bet."

"Why?"

"Because if you don't want the firecracker man, give him to me. Don't worry, I'll find you someone else to marry."

But I don't want anyone else. The words almost leapt from her throat. Then she sensed something. Yes, she had to get to the Makolet. She had to speak with Tsippi. "I have to go," she said. "I'm sorry, but there's something I have to do."

"Such a touchy girl," Orna called after her. Beth sped down the corridor and fifteen minutes later she huffed her way into the grocery store. Behind the counter stood Tsippi's son, Mutti, bent over a maroon volume of the Talmud, which he'd propped up against the cash register.

She approached the counter and he drew his eyes from the book. "Excuse me, do you know when Tsippi, ah, I mean, your mother, do you know when she'll be coming to the Makolet? It's very important that I speak to her."

Mutti fingered a single white thread in his dark beard, and shook his head with regret. "My mother is away—not for one day, not two days," his arm swept the Makolet, "but for the entire week! I am sorry," he said.

"Oh." Her shoulders sank. Tsippi was gone. Beth had come to depend on bumping into her at least three times during the course of the week. She looked around, at a loss, almost asked Mutti for advice, then turned to go.

Her eye caught on a man in the grain aisle. He wore a parka and his head tilted in a familiar way. It was Akiva, holding a bag of split peas. Impossible! A dried paintbrush sticking out of his pocket removed all doubt. Akiva. She moved toward him. "Akiva!"

He raised his head. His neck muscles went taut as if before a spasm, but instead he sneezed into a handkerchief, and then blinked two or three times. "Hello," he said in a pleasant, even voice, and folded the handkerchief into a pocket.

"Hi!" She couldn't stop grinning. "Where have you been these days?"

He tossed the bag of split peas onto a shelf, and it nestled in with the other bags. "Just around."

"I see." She looked at the boxes of Telma Chicken Soup Mix lined neatly in the next aisle. She touched her hair, fluffing it out from behind her ears. Akiva looked different, better than she remembered, in loose American-looking pants. A slice of green sweater was outlined under his thick jacket. It occurred to her that the last time they'd met had been on a Shabbat.

"Orna tells me you've been volunteering quite a few hours at Broken Souls," she said.

"That's right. She knows how to strike a hard bargain, that Orna. But I don't mind the hours. It's kind of fun there."

Beth nodded. They stood there silently.

"Do you know," she took an awkward step closer, "I was wondering if I'd ever see you again, I was really wondering."

He spread out his arms, striking an ironic pose. "Well, here I am." Something in the way he said it made the warmth leak out of her.

"Yes." As an afterthought she said, "And here I am."

"Okay." He absently scratched his beard.

Was he smiling faintly? No, she decided, this was the way his face usually appeared in repose, a look of quiet, open-hearted regard.

"I had a dream about you," she offered, and stopped, mortified at her forwardness.

He merely put a hand into his pocket and looked back at her, his eyes flatter than usual.

"Please, you are making this very difficult for me," she said in a low voice.

Akiva propped his foot on a lower shelf. "Frankly," he said, "I don't know what you're getting at. This is a little too cryptic for me."

She rubbed the space between her brows. "I just was hoping we could get together sometime. Maybe things ended too abruptly between us." She let out her breath and drew her jacket more tightly around her.

He said nothing. His eyes bent inward, as if checking an inner authority, an inner pulse. He was gone to her.

"Get together," he said in a thinking-aloud tone. "I see."

The huge gray metal refrigerator hummed. A little girl stood quizzically in front of a stack of cereal boxes. Behind them, Mutti laughed with a customer.

Akiva brought his hands flat together and rested the butt of his chin on his fingertips. "Actually," he said, after a minute, "I don't think it's such a good idea."

Her mouth dropped. She stared at him. She put her hand flat against the refrigerator, stunned.

"Not a good idea?" she asked.

He lowered his head, blew his nose.

She looked at him. "Why isn't it a good idea?"

He opened his hands.

"Maybe you don't find me—" She broke off. "I'm not attractive enough, is that it?"

He shook his head. "I think you're—" He lifted his shoulder, didn't complete the thought.

"Are you seeing someone else?"

Again, he shook his head.

Now, he turned slightly and his eyes wandered over the assorted grains on the shelf, vague and distant. It dawned on her: Maybe he didn't believe she really wanted him. She had to make it abundantly clear that she did. And why would he believe her? Hadn't she rejected him? She positioned herself in such a way that he would have to look at her. All they needed was one plain, true look to set matters straight. But he kept his gaze on the bags of grain in front of him.

"It doesn't bother me," Beth blurted. "Your twitch, your asperclonus, whatever it is. Look, this hasn't been easy for either of us, but I think we really have to see if it can work. We owe ourselves that much."

His eyes widened. "So you've decided we owe it to ourselves," he said, and she nodded and was about to elaborate, but she saw something in his eyes: Don't grace me with your Lady Bountiful acceptance, my spasms don't concern me as much as they seem to concern you. Her cheeks and forehead stung with embarrassment.

"I'm sorry," Akiva said finally, in a kind voice. "It just isn't right."

He zipped his jacket and lifted a hand in a cautious good-bye. She watched him walk down the aisle, past the frozen foods, past Mutti and the cash register and out the door.

She leaned against the refrigerator and stood there until a woman tapped lightly on the door. Dazed, she stepped to the side and watched the woman open the door and take out three plastic bags of milk. Beth rubbed the edges of her eyes. She started for home. Her back was chilled.

※ ※ ※

Tsippi found out the news while polishing the candlesticks. They were intricately flowered and difficult to clean, 'miracle candlesticks' she called them, because they'd been retrieved after the war, unearthed from the hiding place under the steps of her parents' old house in Lublin. She twisted her mitt up and down the neck of the candlestick, glancing at the smudged newspaper which lay under it. The dining room table was stacked high with Shlomo's books accumulated from the week. He'd yet to clear them off and return them to the shelves so she could set the table for Shabbat. A name from the newspaper jumped out at her, and as she leaned closer to read more, an obituary at the bottom of the page caught her eye, an announcement of Rabbi Isaac Mordechai's death and funeral.

She gasped and muttered, "Blessed is the true Judge," and then she felt something odd under her right rib, as if a bone had dislodged. She turned away, pressing against the spot. He had died. She folded back the newspaper, searching for its date. Yesterday had been his funeral. She eased herself into a chair. The news didn't enter her head properly. Just eight days ago she'd seen him. She closed her eyes, and an image of his red, apoplectic face bobbled before her in her mind. The great kabbalist, Rabbi Isaac Mordechai, gone from the world. She pressed her knuckle into the corner of her eye. She wanted to weep, but she didn't know what to weep for. She had come to rouse him from his coma, but instead—wasn't it the truth?—he had roused her. Since then, she'd been in a state of torment. She kept noticing the men, her own Shlomo, too, and others, she couldn't stop herself: how they jiggled keys in their pockets, or twisted and turned their necks or rubbed their jaws, their hands and arms shot through with veins. When a certain Sephardic customer sneezed, she felt it in her throat. She was undone. She had wanted to curse Rav Isaac, for the troubles he had caused her (consciously or not, she'd never know), but now that he was gone she didn't know what to feel.

The funeral! She slapped her face with the silver mitt. She had missed the funeral! Why was she sitting here wasting time? Rochel Leah was sitting shiva, and she had to pay her respects! She pulled off the gloves. She reached for her purse and for the keys hanging behind the door. Poor Rochel Leah, entirely bereft in the world, and she had missed the funeral!

She walked along Kinnor Road until she reached the long stretch that wended through the Jerusalem Forest. The scent of evergreen and eucalyptus trees invigorated her, and she walked quickly. As she passed the tombstone factory, she recalled Rochel Leah's devotion to her brother. What would the old woman do now that he was gone? She remembered the rabbi's words to her and wondered if she had been the last person he'd spoken to. That thought filled her with such gravity that she suddenly sat down on one of the boulders that lay strewn like severed heads. Was it possible she had set him back in some way? A white cat with a black Hitler-style mustache slithered out between two boulders, and she jumped up, mumbling and talking out loud. Maybe—here, her fingers began to shake—maybe she had hastened him to his own death! She let out a strange noise. She pressed her palm to her heart and hurried on.

When she entered room 909 at the geriatric home, Rochel Leah was sitting up, giving commands to a nurse's aide. The aide was going through the closets, packing clothing and books into a large bag. "Ah, Tsippi," was all Rochel Leah said when she came through the door.

Tsippi put her arms around Rochel Leah and embraced her so hard that the old woman was thrown back against the pillow. Rochel Leah carefully righted herself. "I'm so sorry," Tsippi said, with great feeling, her arms still clasped awkwardly around the old woman's waist.

"Yes, me too." Rochel Leah's hand groped behind her and fingered a long, cream-colored tassel. Tsippi noticed it was attached to an ancient-looking tallis that was folded neatly on her pillow, probably her brother's tallis, she thought. Rochel Leah stroked the tassel, and a muscle above her right cheek twitched. "Well, who's going to argue with That One?" She pointed to the flaking ceiling. She disentangled Tsippi's arms and gently pushed her off. "Did you put the books in the same bag as the boots?" she asked the aide. "I told you not to." She turned her head, staring out from her good eye to have a better view, then gave up. She said, "Let me pack." She slid her two legs to the floor, her nightgown sliding above her knees, and Tsippi couldn't help noticing her legs which were surprisingly well-formed, with none of the blue crater marks of age. Then again, she'd never had children. "Maybe I can do this with no walker," she murmured as her feet groped for slippers. Tsippi watched in amazement as Rochel Leah stood, holding on to the radiator for a moment and then letting go. "You should've seen me at the funeral," she told Tsippi. "I hardly needed a walker at all. You missed a splendid funeral, you should know. The way they spoke about my brother Itzik," both hands pressed against her cheek flaps, "the world will never forget."

At the mention of the kabbalist's name, Tsippi's eyes blurred and her nostrils went moist. "Forgive me," she whispered. "You must forgive me."

"Why? Because you didn't make the funeral? Don't worry so much." Rochel Leah slowly made her way to the chair at the foot of the bed, one hand braced against the bed for support. The aide's arms hovered close by, cradling the air in case she fell.

"No, you don't understand." Tsippi wiped at her eyes with the hanging loops of her head scarf. "Maybe it was me, maybe it was my fault that he died."

The aide, her arms still outstretched, let out a shocked snort.

"You? Tsippi?" Rochel Leah stopped and stared at her through her cat's-eye glasses which were slipping down her nose. "Why would you think that? He was in a coma, he was practically a vegetable, they didn't expect him to revive." She took up her laborious walk, and when she reached the chair, she hunched her shoulders and backed herself into the seat.

"But he did revive. He opened his eyes, he said to me, actually he shouted it, 'Go home!' He said it twice," Tsippi admitted reluctantly, and she looked down at the nubbled bedspread, sensing the aide's eyes on her, wishing Rochel Leah would excuse her from the room.

Instead the old woman shook her head, smiling. "Oh that Itzik Muttel. And did you?"

"Did I what?"

"Did you go home?"

"I don't remember." Tsippi shrugged weakly. "I suppose I did. Where else do I have to go?"

Rochel Leah slapped the air near her face. "You didn't listen! His last words to you, the last words he ever spoke, and you didn't listen!"

"No, no. I think I did go home," she suddenly insisted, alarmed at Rochel Leah's vehemence. She put a finger between her brows. "Yes, I definitely went home."

"Ach! Did you think he was telling you to go home and bake challah? Vey iz mir! 'Eyes they have, but they don't see, ears but they don't hear,' " she quoted from the Psalms. "My brother was telling you to go to your husband."

Tsippi stood, the air punched out of her heart. Go to your husband. Go home. She again felt the pain under her rib. "And do what?" she said hoarsely.

"Do what," she echoed mockingly. "Ach, why did he waste his last words on you, why did he even bother?" she asked, staring disgustedly at her fingernails. Then she pointed to the door. "Go!"

"Still—I—you—" she wanted to ask about her packed bags, was she leaving, was she merely switching rooms?—"tell me," she blurted, "what about our chevrutah, what about learning Torah together?" but Rochel Leah kept her bony finger aimed at the door. So she went.

There was a feeling of urgency in the air, like before a huge rainstorm, negative ions gathering in the atmosphere, but halfway home, when the rain began to fall, it came down so lightly she hardly needed a hood. A row of carob trees stood out starkly, leaves trembling on branches, thousands of shimmering little green fish. She heard the distant crack of a rifle going off. It was the firing range just a kilometer away. The pain under her rib was gone, and the rain was sweet against her face and throat, like mist from a bottle. Go home, go home: the words kept striking her brain, her heart, compelling her faster. But who was there waiting for her at home? Only Shlomo. Just Shlomo. Shlomo. She walked fast, and then slow, dream-like.

When she entered the apartment, the dining room table was clear, all books returned to their shelves. She heard the shower running. She stood listening, and remembered something from thirty-nine years ago. She had been married just a few short weeks, and she was taking a shower. Shlomo had kept trying to peek his head into the stall, and she kept dodging him, ducking behind the curtains, asking him to leave, when suddenly, in a fury, she pulled down the curtains, ripped them from their hooks, and wrapped the material around her body and, in a trembling, indignant voice said, "Now, now will you leave?" He left. As she stood next to the bathroom door, she felt a blush spreading across her face like a rash, a blush from thirty-nine years ago.

She knocked softly on the door. "Shlomo? Shlomo, it's me." There was no answer. She put her hand on the doorknob. "Shlomo, I'm coming in," she called, and she opened the door.

He had placed his dark pants and white shirt neatly over the toilet seat. A shower curtain with a leaf pattern went around the tub. She began to undress rapidly with a swiftness that made her feel young when she heard his voice mutter from the shower, "Tsippi?"—a muffled, querulous sound that almost stopped her in her tracks. But she blocked it out as she undressed. A gust of cool air came into the room from an open window high above the sink. Her skin shivered, then she pushed aside the shower curtains and stepped into the tub. Her husband turned. She saw the loose flesh of his arms and stomach, his massive body gone slack since he no longer worked as a shochet, the body that had once been strong enough to convince the Partisans to let him join and fight. The water hit her face, blurring her eyes so she couldn't see the expression on his face; she only heard him say 'hunh!' as if someone had punched his lower belly. She put an arm around his waist; his hand seized her shoulder. They stood there, the warm water falling on them, their knees bumping against each other.

Chapter Eleven

JUDY SAT ON HER TINY SQUARE OF BALCONY. SHE WAS TRYING OUT a huge wicker rocking chair Dovid had just picked up in the Arab shuk. The glide wasn't smooth—she had to really throw her body into it to make it rock at all—but she liked sitting in it anyway. It was dark outside with a slight wind, and the smell of evergreens blew in from the Jerusalem Forest, making her feel calm and alert. Under the street lights she could make out the white flowers of almond trees which had begun to blossom two weeks ago. A couple stood under one of them. She suddenly wondered if Beth would actually wear the bikini underwear she had bought at the boutique, or if it just was the idea of buying bikini underwear that appealed to her. Beth was one frustrating woman, she thought. She rocked some more and looked out.

The moon looked very simple in the sky, cold and beautiful. The wind played with her scarf, making the tail end loop around her neck. She felt a peculiar distance from herself.

"Judy, why are you sitting up there all alone?"

It was Estrella down below in a housecoat, waving her arms S.O.S.-like, a bag of garbage at her feet.

"Just enjoying the night air," she called down.

"Ah yes, 'The air of Israel makes one wise,' " Estrella quoted from the Talmud, nodding sagely as she tossed her bag of garbage into a huge metal vat shared by the people of Harp Court and Beit Morris.

"Hasn't improved *my* I.Q.," Judy said. She slipped her arms into an L.L.Bean sweater draped around her shoulders.

"What are you saying?" Estrella made a snorting noise. "Beth tells me that every day you are learning Torah at that school." She quoted again, " 'Torah's the best merchandise in the world.' What could be a smarter thing to do? You're not wasting time like us, with cooking, children, the laundry, you are choosing wisely."

Judy peered down at her. Was her neighbor being sarcastic, giving her a subtle reproach for not being more devoted to the home? She didn't think so. But she felt a little anxious that Estrella knew how she was spending her days. Her and who else? Then she pinched herself. Grow up, Judy, she thought. Release yourself from the tyranny of what people think. Take a stand. Be something. "So, why don't you learn Torah, too?" she asked, though she knew Estrella would claim she didn't have the time.

"Me? I go to a class every Tuesday night on the laws of gossip. Since I've learned the laws, I'm much more careful."

Judy stood up, put her hands on the balcony rail and looked down. Bougainvillea plants climbed extravagantly up the four-story apartment building. Not very long ago, a lecture one night of the week had been enough for her, too. When she studied, it was like she was building roads in her brain, and every now and then she was rewarded with a road that reached and wobbled toward God. But roads didn't get built in a single hour out of the week. "Why not more classes?"

Estrella fingered a button on her housecoat. "Maybe people will say I am a show-off," she said lamely. "I was never too good at it in high school." She wiped her hands against her sides. "Well, good night."

From below, Judy heard the door to the building open and shut.

Was that what people secretly thought about her—a show-off? She winced, picturing herself being discussed. After all, who was she to think she could devote herself full-time to Torah study? Was she that talented at it, that passionate? Was she clever like Lauren, reflective and studious like Dina? She still hadn't gotten around to writing that article on Eve, though she'd researched it a bit. She didn't take her ideas seriously like they did. She was still mucking around. She imagined her friends saying, "Oh poor Judy. Her childbearing days are over so she's desperate to fill up time. Matchmaking isn't quite her thing anymore. She doesn't know what to do with herself."

Not far off the mark. She *didn't* know what to do with herself, exactly. . . . She wanted to spend more time on the Eve account, though. She had an idea that seemed radical, even absurd. And yet the more she thrashed it around in her brain, the more it made sense to her. But a theory needed textual support. Judy took out a pen from her apron pocket and a receipt from SuperSol and began to write down some of her thoughts. She felt a small thrill at committing the beginnings of her theory to words. A little space was opening up inside her mind. A sweet wind.

Dovid stuck his head through the door. "Want some Turkish coffee, Judes?"

"I'll take some Wisotsky tea," she said, putting down her pen. As he was leaving, she called out, "Dovid, tell me, what struck you about me when you first met me?" She was looking straight ahead, at the apartment across the parking lot.

"Your smile," Dovid said promptly.

She swatted at the air. "No, not my looks. What impressed you about me?"

Dovid coughed. "Well, let's see. You were very articulate. Mature. I liked that. You had a clarity about you. You had an idea of what you wanted, the kind of life you wanted to lead, where you wanted to live it. It bowled me over."

"Thank you," she said from the rocking chair. "No sugar in my tea this time."

"Is that it?" He peered over the rocking chair, and she tilted her chin up and gazed at him. She nodded. "Okay. Wisotsky with no sugar. I'll be back soon."

She gave an ironic smile. Men were easy to impress. She had known she wanted to live in Israel (her mother's dream, which she'd assimilated into her own) and that certainty had cast all her actions under a spell of clarity. The one thing she could say with certainty now was how little she knew about herself and what most enlivened her. She rocked vigorously. She hadn't had a clue. It wasn't as if she had been miserable; she had just shlepped along, like everyone else, some days more productive, some days less. Why did she feel superior to Beth? Because she had a few kids?

She turned over the receipt from SuperSol. She wrote: "Things I am Passionate About:." "Learning Torah," she wrote. Her hand paused. Then it scrawled, "Setting people up." Yes, here was a good thing, too.

A laughing woman's voice drifted upward. Judy leaned forward in the rocking chair. A man's chuckle soon followed. Everyone was seeking a connection of some kind. She squinted at the sky, and from a certain angle it seemed that impossibly thin gossamer strings were extending from each star down to the city below, crossing and crisscrossing through the dark blue of the night, until the entirety of Jerusalem was covered in a latticework of lines. Shidduchs and more shidduchs. A shidduch to get the right fit between neighbors, to reconcile between friends and parents and children, between husbands and wives, to reconcile one country to another. The whole world was a shidduch. And she was on a shidduch, too, if she dared, with her self.

❊   ❊   ❊

During the day she was fine, but at night she thought her body would split in two. She'd taken to prowling around her apartment just before she went to bed, cleaning, sorting, flipping through old magazines. She didn't know what to do with her hands. She felt a pressure in the air; she wanted to jump out of her bones. What was this?

One night when Beth couldn't bear staying in her apartment a moment longer, she went over to her neighbor's. Estrella answered the door looking spent, her howling nine-month-old held in a football clutch under her arm. Beth offered to hold the child. She clasped her against her shoulder, the baby's cheek next to hers, and began pacing the floor—ten feet forward, about face, ten feet back—chanting rhythmic poetry as she paced. After ten minutes she eased into a waltz and sang a lullaby. She sang and waltzed and after half an hour the baby had drifted into sleep and she had calmed enough to go to sleep herself.

Suddenly, she started baking bread again. One night she found herself flinging open cupboards, taking out the bread baking ingredients and the bowls and cooking supplies. She poured hot water on her wrist to test the temperature for yeast, put a dab of honey into the yeast mixture to help it rise, and soon after her hands and wrists were gritted with dried flour and dough which she punched down and let rise only to punch down again.

She rolled the dough into four long fat fingers, braided them into challah and then coated it with beaten egg and sesame seeds. The challah looked pristine and sensual sitting there on the gray baking sheet. Her hand hovered over the smooth shiny curves, enjoying the challah artistry, and then gave a sudden smash into the center. She hit the dough again and again, her knuckles smacking against the skin. Each sock sent a thrill through her arm. She slapped a doughy cheek. She punched a smooth expanse of belly. She pummeled with two fists, then with a moan heaved the entire mangled mess into the oven, heaved the door shut and waited.

That's what the pressure felt like, a terrible waiting.

Lately, when she went to the forest with her can of mango juice

191

and Egozi candy bar and a determination to connect to God through her prayers, all she had were questions and complaints. She'd followed the Torah laws faithfully. But maybe if she hadn't kept the laws so meticulously, if she had allowed a man to touch her, it would have melted those toughened places inside her and helped her overlook the hard parts in another person. Maybe she'd be less religious but she'd be married. Did God approve of the barren life she was leading? What did He really want?

She went through a list of men and could come up with no one who she would've wanted to touch in the first place. Or else there was no one she didn't *not* want to touch, from a craving to be normal, from a desire to know herself through being with a man, any man, from sheer physical craziness. She lurched between the two extremes, fussiness and desperation, and had settled into an attitude of indifference which was simpler to manage. Maybe that's why she hated dolling up for a date. The act of dressing up was a public declaration: She wanted a man. But why should she expose her need to the world when the chances of getting satisfied were small? To say—I want, I need—was so hard, much harder than being permanently anxious. Oh, she was stubborn, a case. God couldn't be blamed entirely for her situation. She knew this was true. But why wasn't His heart breaking for her, just a little? It was as if He had agreed—'So you want to stay single? So stay.' He had stopped caring about her love life, and so she had stopped caring about the Torah, His creation of love.

Beth decided to take a bus to the Kotel. It had been three weeks since she'd last gone to the Western Wall. Too long.

But when she picked up a rain-battered book of Psalms at the Western Wall, she couldn't pray. She had no words in her heart, and she couldn't bring herself to utter the words in the book. Surrounded by all those stones, she felt like stone herself. A dark-skinned woman in a dress of long flowing material and a vibrantly-colored headdress, one of the recent Ethiopian immigrants, was standing erect before the

192

wall, making fluttering hourglass motions with her hands, now and then touching her fingers to her eyes. Her bearing bespoke great dignity, as if she was approaching the Wall as an equal: "You, Wall, should have been destroyed long ago, yet miraculously you remain standing. I, too, have escaped my destroyers. I, too." The Ethiopian woman's presence touched Beth, but still she had nothing to say to God. How could she need and want so much and still have nothing to say?

She sat on a cement bench off to the side. Old lady beggars prowled around the Kotel, alternately reading from prayer books and eyeing stray worshipers to collect money for orphan brides, for a man who had corns on his feet and couldn't work, a child who required a bone marrow transplant and needed airfare to Boston, Massachusetts—Beth listened to all their pitches. Over in the corner, by the huge tuft of hanging moss, was a woman who she identified as a clerk from the Post Office, and then a bride in an off-the-shoulder ball gown appeared, her hands clasped in a devotional pose as a photographer snapped her picture. A teenage soldier adjusted her beret and peeked through the slats of the plastic wall divider at the other side. Then she tentatively approached the Kotel and touched its nubbly surface as if it was the face of a man she was deciding if she liked. Farther down, an old woman in a sparkly scarf was moving her lips and smiling, the only person smiling at the Kotel, a hand grasping a tuft of grass growing between the huge stones. Beth watched her pray. The woman was fierce in her words as if she were giving God a tough piece of her mind, and then her manner changed and became almost congenial, as if God were a friend sitting across from her kitchen table, a bowl of fruit between them, and then a moment later she turned inward, quiet, covering her face with her gray crackly hands. Beth had never seen anyone pray like that.

With a shock she realized it was Tsippi, the Makolet woman. She had been so transfixed by the sight that she hadn't even recognized her. Tsippi. She felt a sudden upwelling of awe for the old woman, and love, for her and all the women here. She walked up to the Wall, turned her face sideways and put her cheek flat on the warm, craggy stone. She stood like that, taking in the tiny pings of love coming off the Kotel's stones, a hundred massive ancient breasts, wrinkled by the tears, flattened by the cheeks of thousands. She still had nothing to say, but maybe, she thought, God likes the prayers of a stone.

She returned the book of Psalms to a wooden shelf, and found, there among the other psalm books, a faded blue Bible. She picked it up and looked along the spine: the book of Shmos. Exodus, her favorite. She knew many of the verses by heart, and was familiar with a good number of the Rashis, Rambans and Kli Yakars and Sfornos and Ohr HaChaims. Not to mention the commentators on Rashi, the Mizrachi, the mystical Gur Aryeh and so many others. She read a few verses to herself from Chapter Three, the burning bush section, letting the words hit her as if hearing them for the first time, letting a question rise up, then fall as an answer revealed itself, and letting another question come forward in its place. This was a dance she knew well. How long had it been since she'd looked inside? Eleven months, a year, if she didn't include the visit to Rabbi Yellin? It felt inhuman to have been away so long, and suddenly incomprehensible to her, as if she'd decided out of the blue to forego salads, clean socks, singing. To what end? So she still had her Questions, her Torah Issues. Couldn't she have them and still stay connected? Ambivalence never killed anybody. A phrase from the Talmud drifted into her thoughts: "Better you should reject Me, saith the Lord, than ignore My Torah." She felt the beginning of tears. Too long she'd deprived herself. Too long.

She washed her hands at the stone water fountain, and took the bus outside Dung Gate directly to Broken Souls, to Zahava.

In the Normalization Room, Beth and Zahava peeled and cut potatoes for frying. She taught Zahava a word game and they played it while tending to the potatoes, stirring and coddling them along with a wooden spatula. Beth felt a certain affection, even compassion, for the potatoes as she watched them fry. They were so cared for and waited for, these smooth brown potatoes, as were all the vegetables in the shuk. Hadn't the land of Israel lain dormant, desolate, for hundreds of years, waiting to be tilled, waiting to flower and come to life under the right hands? No one had the right touch, maybe because God had cursed the land. And then in this century the settlers had transformed the desert, worked it, loved it, brought the land to life. And here they were, the potatoes. How could she not feel a tenderness for each vegetable that had struggled and finally emerged from the ground, soon to be eaten and forgotten?

She took a slice of fried potato, said, "Blessed is God master of the world who creates the fruit of the ground." She blessed it strong, each word brimming with feeling, so the potato's holy travels would not have been in vain. The potato might be gone, but at least, she consoled herself, her thoughts about the potato would remain.

As she went to the cabinet to get plates, she noticed a prayer book lying on a shelf. She read the inscription inside and saw it belonged to Zahava. The sun was going down, streaking the sky with color, and it was now or never if she wanted to recite the Minchah afternoon prayer. Oh why not, she thought, and began to chant the "Happy are those that dwell" psalm. Zahava sat in a sofa chair and blew smoke rings in her direction as Beth readied herself for the Silent Devotion. She bent her knees and bowed, and from the corner of her eye she saw Zahava still watching her, looking bored, her smoky breath filling the room.

Suddenly Zahava called out from her chair, "Bet, don't cry. Don't cry, Bet."

Beth stopped, startled. Was this woman her prayer cheerleader? She tried to get back on track. ". . . rebuild Jerusalem quickly, in our lifetime, an eternal structure, as You promised . . ." In her mind, she saw the women praying at the Kotel, each uttering the same words said by Jews over two thousand years ago. This parched city of jagged stone. But more than tree, rock and stone. A thorny, Biblical verse, that's what this city was, a verse that cried out, "Explain me!" begging to be interpreted by all who came to her, demanding a personal response. "You may not pass through unchanged." It would not be possible. Beth had seen the women pray at the wall.

The sixteenth prayer read: Blessed is God who listens. It didn't say, "Who answers, who gives you exactly what you ask for." Only that God listened, took note. She believed that. She liked the honesty of it, that it didn't raise false hopes. But she'd had friends who'd insisted on certain things from God, pestered and persisted, and against all expectation, God had delivered, outrageously, with great abundance, practically with signs and wonders. Why couldn't she noodge like them?

"Don't cry. You'll get married, I know you will. You'll be happy."

Beth raised her lids, gave her a stunned look, then lowered her eyes. She picked up speed during the last four benedictions.

She took three steps back and three steps forward. "The Holy One who makes peace on high, make peace upon us below and upon all of Israel." She closed her prayer book and kissed the cover. She peeked at Zahava from behind her prayerbook. She felt connected to her, as if they had prayed as one body.

Zahava held a cigarette loosely between her fingers and crossed her legs. "Do you know when I feel close to God?"

"When?" Beth regarded her.

"When I'm smoking cigarettes. I talk to God when I'm smoking."

Beth rubbed the edge of her prayer book along her jaw. "So what do you say?"

Zahava ground the cigarette into the armchair. "None of your damn business." Then she got up and together they set out plates, napkins and a salt shaker. Beth went to the main kitchen to get the utensils.

A man was kneeling on the floor. It was Akiva, stooped under the kitchen sink, a pail of paint at his side. Her throat turned hot. She wanted to flee. Then she braced herself. She'd done nothing wrong in asking him out. She had nothing to be ashamed of. She took a step toward the utensil drawer.

Just then he raised his paintbrush and glanced at her. He nodded, his eyes far away. Beth nodded back, curtly shutting the utensil drawer. Who needed him? she thought in sudden rage. As she walked from the room, she saw his neck roll and then jerk backward. A tremor passed through her own body. A lone hiccup sounded loudly through the halls.

She walked straight into Orna in the corridor.

"Bet!" The social worker seized her by the shoulders. "You look very funny, very," Orna's fingers fluttered, "shaky. Come into my office. Drink some water. I want to ask you something."

"Yes?" Beth asked, alert.

"We are having a Purim party for the patients. There will be music and dancing, and hamentaschen pastry, also maybe a little bit of wine. Please—invite all your friends. We will make"—Orna snapped her fingers in the air—"*simcha*, lots of celebration! But really, we want to make it a special party for the patients, so be sure to come."

Beth shrugged, relieved. "Certainly. I'll bring whoever I can. It should be nice." She turned to go.

Orna called after her, "And tell everyone they must come in costumes. No costume, no entrance. I'll make a good Spanish dancer, yes?" She posed with a folder over her face, and batted her lids.

"Perfecto!" Beth smiled.

It was dark outside, with a mild breeze blowing as she walked home. In another month or so the winter rains would end. A wind blew gustily on a fig tree, separating the leaves this way and that, making pathways of air, then sweeping up the leaves together in bunches. Beth zipped her jacket. The day had been so mild she had walked outside with the flaps open. She felt the breeze between her fingers and let herself be pushed along by the wind. She thought of a plastic bag she had once seen drifting about in someone's living room, first settling on a sofa, then wrapping itself around a table leg, finally resting square in the middle of the room. Beth had reached to the floor to throw it out, but the lady of the house, a prematurely white-haired sweet-mannered woman, had said, "No, let's just let it stay there, I'd like to see where it will go next." A little pulse of faith warmed Beth just then, the sensation of not knowing what was in store, but letting her feet carry her just the same.

PART III

Chapter Twelve

TSIPPI CIRCLED SHLOMO, STAPLER IN HAND, HER SILKY PURPLE cape undulating around her. She fixed a green doily to the top of her head and affected a coquettish pose. "So how do I look?"

Shlomo was sitting at the dining room table, assembling the Purim shaloch manos food baskets for the next day. Scissors, tape, glue, cardboard paper and tubes of paint lay scattered across the table. She had put him to work and he was painstakingly writing little Purim cards to the neighbors. In the center of the table some poppies and jonquils drooped from an old yahrtzeit glass. It charmed her that Shlomo had picked them himself and not bought them. In the past week or so, he had shifted in tiny, significant ways, and she could only hope his romantic overtures would continue. Go home, Rochel Leah had told her. And she had returned, to her shock and delight, to a husband quite willing to match her new frame of mind. She slanted her doily at a daring angle. "I said, how do I look?"

Shlomo lifted his head. He squinted at her. "You make a beautiful broccoli," he said. "You'll be the prettiest one at the party."

"Broccoli?" She stepped back. "I'm not a broccoli! Can't you see I'm an eggplant?"

"Eggplant, broccoli—" he waved his hand vaguely over the table. "What difference does it make? It's Purim!"

She fixed him with a sharp look. "It makes a difference to me."

He reached over the table and fingered the shiny material of her cape. "Come here." He held out two arms and still sitting, positioned her between his knees. Tsippi stood still, felt his arms around her, and broke away.

He scratched under his brow, his head tilted, puzzled. "Is something the matter, Tsippi?"

She shook her head, surprised at the mood that had come over her. "Nothing, nothing." She held back a great sigh. Romantic or not, he was still . . . thick, impenetrable, she didn't know what exactly, as dense and unknowable as the Talmud he pored over.

He stared at her, his fingers plucking at the tips of his beard. "You've been working yourself to the bone," he said finally. "You need a rest, a vacation. Didn't I tell you you should have a vacation?"

"Ach, it's just a big headache to arrange." Tsippi tore off a piece of scotch tape and attached a Purim card to a basket.

"Is that what you're worried about? I could arrange the whole thing. We could go together."

Tsippi was looking for another basket to tape a card to. She stopped now and looked at Shlomo, rather stunned. "But you never went with me before on a vacation. Would you even know how to make the arrangements?"

"What's to know? I make some phone calls, I get a hotel reservation. We could go to Safed maybe. Or Tiberias. We could go to the spring waters. There's a nice strictly kosher hotel we could stay at. Maimonides' grave is close by. Or if you like," he said in a rush, "maybe to the Banyas, it's very pretty over there."

"Oh really? How would you know?"

He stared at her, bewildered by her tone. "I heard," he said lamely. "Yehudah Kess went with his family last Pesach."

Tsippi set the Scotch tape on the table and it made a sharp smacking sound. She turned her eyes on her husband. "All these years you didn't go with me, and now yes?"

"Why, I just—"

A rage flared inside. "All these years, every vacation you never came with us. The boys and I went on our own trips. And now you offer me half a cup of water and expect me to . . . jump, to be happy?" She had never before spoken to him like this.

He blinked several times and let out an astonished grunt. "I didn't know you wanted me to come on the trips. I thought it made you proud that I spent the time in the Beit Medrash. Your husband wasn't just a simple shochet. Weren't you proud?" he asked, almost pleadingly.

"Yes, but you could've asked me what I wanted," she said in a low voice. She shut her eyes. He had never acted selfishly and yet he had never asked what she wanted. He had kept her far, and she had kept herself far, too. Couples should be together, she thought, at least some of the time. No matter how many pretty words and caresses that he lately had begun pressing on her, she and Shlomo were still separate, living in separate rooms, because their minds were so far, one from the other. He had never included her. And she hadn't known how to ask, how or where to even begin. She muttered, "A man and wife should know how the other one thinks and feels."

"What is it, Tsippi? Tell me, what did you say?" He touched a hollow point between her shoulder bone and neck.

"Oh nothing." What could she say? She felt completely drained. She folded her hands and set them on the table. "I saw Rochel Leah today."

"I hope she's doing well." Shlomo stood and brushed off his pants, letting fly tiny scraps of paper.

"Well enough. She came into a modest amount of money from her brother, and she's not at the geriatric home anymore." She picked at some dried glue on the table. "She's quite busy settling her brother's estate. She doesn't even have time to learn anymore."

Shlomo said, "That's a relief, right? You said you wanted to stop learning with her, but didn't know how."

"Well, I changed my mind," she said curtly. She was surprised at the loss she had felt, worse than when her sons had stopped learning Torah with her. She hadn't enjoyed the foolish missions Rochel Leah had sent her on, but despite the old woman's overbearing manner she'd looked forward to the learning part. "It wasn't the perfect situation, but she was my chevrutah, after all. We learned together. Something is better than nothing." She began gathering all the art supplies into a pile. She wanted to say something else, but stopped a moment, distracted by the sound of the toilet running in the next room.

Shlomo pondered this. "Oh Chevrusah oh meesusah—give me a chevrutah or give me death," he translated from the Aramaic. "Or, actually, did the rabbis mean 'give me friendship or give me death'? I'd have to see the Gemara."

Tsippi suppressed a sigh as he went over to the bookshelves and took out a huge tome. He stood, his large squarish head bent over, his hands flipping through the pages. She gathered more odd scraps from the table and waited. "So did you find it?" she asked. He shook his head, pulling on his lower lip, distracted by something else as he sat down. Presently, she walked over and stood near him. She could hear a faint gurgle in his stomach. The orange juice that he'd taken after the Purim fast must have disagreed with him. Her eyes went down the page, trying to see if she could recognize or understand anything. The Aramaic was beyond her, as usual. "Oh!" She pointed at the middle of the page. "I think I know that word. Be'ah. Egg. Right?"

Shlomo followed her finger. "Yes." He smiled. "Very good."

"And this phrase I also know—Eretz Yisrael." She shrugged. "But that's in Hebrew. And what's this word doing here—a kittel?"

"Oh no." He shook his head. "It means to kill. 'They killed it.' "

Tsippi's brows lifted. "What's going on in that Gemara?"

"It's a somewhat strange Aggadata," Shlomo admitted. He translated, " 'Realize,' said the prophet, 'that if you kill Temptation, illicit desire, the world goes down.' Instead, the Sages imprisoned Temptation for three days, and then they looked in the whole land of Israel for a fresh egg and could not find one. Thereupon the Sages said—"

Tsippi broke in, "But what does temptation have to do with eggs?"

"Temptation is sexual desire. The Talmud is saying, without sexual desire the world would not exist. Even eggs would not get laid." He wiped his forehead with one of the napkins from the Purim basket. "Should I continue?" Tsippi waved him on.

"The Sages said, 'What should we do now—kill Temptation? Then the world goes down. Should we beg for half-mercy? They do not grant "halves" in heaven.' So they put out its eyes—"

She felt a mounting excitement as she tried to comprehend. "For goodness sake, what are they talking about now—halves in heaven, putting out eyes. This hardly sounds legalistic or plausible to me."

"It's not, it's Aggadata. But the halves in heaven—what could that mean?" He put his face to the tiny column of print running toward the middle. "Oh, I see," he said after a minute, and he chuckled. "The Sages asked if sexual desire could remain but only be directed each person to his spouse. But the Heavens said no. To ask the tempter to live but not tempt is a thing Heaven will not grant."

Tsippi looked pensively at the black Aramaic print. "So, the rabbis are saying that sexual desire is at the root of everything, whether I know it or not? The hidden motive behind all our actions?"

"Yes, this is correct."

She nodded to herself. The secret of desire was indeed the secret of the universe. She peeked at Shlomo. He looked commanding and powerful, sitting there with his hands resting solidly on the page. Like a conqueror, she thought. Like the partisan warrior she had married. But now traversing pages, not lands, conquering ideas, not Nazis in a forest. Perhaps not as outwardly dramatic and exciting, but still vital— explicating God's will, the way Jewish men had fought throughout the years of exile. Jewish valor. "Yes, it makes sense," she pronounced. "But what's this odd business about putting out the eyes?"

Shlomo reached over and adjusted the green doily on her head. "Come." He smiled at her. "Let's see what Rashi and Tosafos have to say." She touched her collarbone. You're asking me? she almost exclaimed. And before he might change his mind, she slid down next to him, on the same chair, and they sat learning, and there was room for both.

Later, on the way to the Purim party, gripping Shlomo's arm, Tsippi thought of his chevrutah, Yehudah. No more chevrutahs meeting in the evening, she decided. At night, his mind and bones belonged to her. She would be his night chevrutah. She would make sure. She closed her eyes and in her mind she thought she saw Rochel Leah laughing. Rochel Leah. Look what she had wrought. The woman was an angel, and she, Tsippi, hadn't known.

✳ ✳ ✳

Beth shifted the straps of her get-up. Her head hurt. She had just returned from synagogue where the Book of Esther had been read. Every time the Megillah reader mentioned Haman the villain's name, over two hundred men, women and children shook noisemakers and stomped their feet. As a child she had looked forward to the boisterous holiday. But now she found herself siding with the Megillah reader, who kept trying to glide over each of the fifty-two times Haman's name was mentioned without the children noticing every time. The children always caught him and shook their noisemakers with extra gusto and glee, as if to punish him for even entertaining the idea of skipping Haman's name.

Beth straightened her yellow yarn wig so that a fat braid rested evenly on each of her shoulders. She had painted loud, big freckles across her cheeks, and her lips were a vivid pink pout on her face. On her eyes she'd stuck thick, false eyelashes. In her high spiked heels and bobby socks she looked like a cross between Raggedy Ann and Mae West. She'd hung a huge poster on herself: "Virgin Reject Number 314 from the Court of King Ahashvueres."

Dina covered her mouth and snickered. "That looks pretty bad." She herself was dressed in feathers and a fringed jacket-dress, her dark hair going in a braid down her back, an alluring olive-skinned Pocahontas.

"Thanks." Beth glumly fingered her false eyelashes.

"Well, isn't that the idea? I mean, aren't you supposed to look pathetic and all?"

"It's supposed to be *funny*. The Persian king throws a beauty contest for all the virgins in the province. This one doesn't make it to the finals. I thought you'd laugh, not snicker."

"I'm sorry." Dina lowered her eyes.

Beth put her hands on her hips, trying to strike a pose, achieve an air, but the right attitude eluded her. The idea had seemed clever and outrageous last week, but now she wasn't sure she could carry it off. And how would she be able to dance? She searched through a desk drawer and found a stapler, then stapled the strings of the poster to her shirt and bra straps.

There was a knock at the door. Estrella stood in the hall wearing a scarf and housecoat and a bulbous fake nose and round glasses. Yisrael appeared behind her, dressed as a skeleton. "I'm Haman's skeleton," he said. He screwed up his face. "Arghhhhhh!"

The women drew back, screaming in feigned terror. He laughed and skittered away.

"Those children," said Estrella, sitting down on the stool next to the phone. "I begged Yisrael to come as something nice. Be a Mordechai, even King Ahashvueres, or a cowboy. But he had to come as Haman." She lifted her eyes. "Very nice," she said, looking at Dina's costume. She glanced at Beth and her eyes widened. "Virgin Reject Number—" she read the rest silently and gave Beth an alarmed look.

"Hashem Yishmor!"

"Isn't it funny?" said Beth.

"No, it's not funny at all!" Estrella unwrapped the black glasses from around her ears and flung off her fake nose. She rubbed her eye with her thumb. "It's forbidden to speak evil of oneself, to show yourself in such a way, looking so . . . so foolish."

"I told her the same thing," Dina added.

Estrella rocked her head from side to side. "No, no, I will not let you go out like that. Also, it's not proper to use such immodest words."

Beth slumped against the wall. It was true. She *was* casting herself in a ridiculous, demeaning light. It was too close to her real situation to not appear as a parody of her own life. She looked pathetic to everyone, not outrageous.

"How can I get another costume this late?" she said finally. "The party's in less than an hour."

Minutes later, Estrella returned with some masks, glossy fabric, wands and veils falling from her arms and tossed everything onto the sofa. "Pick something!"

Beth waded through the articles and she lifted a piece of shiny, yellow material. "What's this?"

Estrella smiled. "A hamentaschen—the filling is poppy seeds. I sewed it myself for Miri. The costume would look very fine on you— it's big enough for an adult!"

Beth said, "Uh uh," and continued looking. She picked up a gorilla mask and stared thoughtfully at it. It was a professional-looking mask, with fur and pliable rubber skin, an opening for the mouth, the ears and nose finely detailed. The expression on its face was savage and at the same time bashful. She fingered its dark brown fur.

"I'll take this," she said, "and this." She grabbed an ornate fan and long black gloves that reached up to the elbows.

Estrella spread her hands open. "All right, Bet. You know best." She declined the party invitation, insisting she had to stay at home to make Purim food baskets for the next day.

Forty-five minutes later Dina and Beth were waiting outside for the number twenty-seven to Broken Souls. Beth wore the gorilla mask, its lips now rouged and false eyelashes pasted to its eyes. She'd hung a strand of pearls around her neck. She wore a long, silky turquoise caftan from the Arab shuk and high heels, a thick, white shawl draped over her shoulders. She leaned carefully against the pole of the bus stop. There was no place to sit. All that remained of the bus shelter were four cement poles and a charred seat and wall. A bunch of shelters had been torched a week ago, burnt and razed to the ground. Her feet ached in the high heels.

"Farewell, Tinkerbell," Beth remarked, touching the charred spot where the pretty ballerina had cavorted on the poster.

"Who do you think did it?" Dina asked.

"Burned the shelters?" She kicked at one of the cement poles. "You know." Many rabbis had denounced the bus burners, and while not naming them, people suspected they—the rigorously devout Hareidim—had done it, just as they had spray-painted the ads that featured undressed women. To destroy property was a serious sin, an act of theft, the rabbis had said, denouncing the perpetrators. Truthfully, she hadn't been sorry to see the ballerina and her sanitary napkin go.

"There's rumors that Ayala Rimoni is behind this," Dina told her. Ayala was a Knesset member known for her radical feminism. "More than rumors. The radio said she made a coalition with the Hareidim. They did the spray painting, and she and her pals did the burnings."

"And I heard the President of The Society for the Conservation of Nature was taking responsibility." She shook her head. "What a country. They all want credit for vandalism."

The bus pulled up and the two of them boarded the number twenty-seven. Now Beth removed her slinky glove and withdrew a limp bus card from her purse for the driver to punch.

"Whoo whoo!" The driver whistled at her.

Someone else called out, "Dahleenk, you breaking my heart!"

Beth lifted her head high and coolly took her seat, teetering slightly on her heels. She removed a fan from her beaded purse. "I need some air!" she said to Dina. She crossed her legs and fanned her neck.

※　　※　　※

Binyamin stood in front of the mirror looking at his face. The boys at yeshiva had urged him to come to the Purim shpiel, but he had declined. He was suffering. He felt shaken to the dark root of his soul. He spent his mornings in front of the mirror, touching his eyes, nose, forehead, mouth and skin, as if by probing his features he would arrive at the meaning of his face, come to the person who was at the core of him. He groped and probed but no answers had come. Only a question: Why could he never be brave? Why was he such a chicken?

A few times he actually had been brave in his life: once, when he had gone a different path from all his peers who had become lawyers, actuaries and Wall Street investors and chosen to be an artist. A second time when he chose to become a religious Jew. But now his art was just a job, with its own corruptions, like any other job. As for his Torah path—that, too, had undergone a certain corruption of the soul. His soul had first propelled him to a Torah life. But all he'd done was disregard his soul, cramming it to fit into a page of Talmud, not caring if it chafed or ached, as long as it stayed on the page. Even as a religious Jew, he was leading a false life.

He picked up some marbles from the glass jar on his night table and rolled them from hand to hand, listening to their clink. Here it was, the happiest, wildest day in the Jewish year, and he was at home, alone, depleted. A piece of paper lay coiled inside his pocket, mailed, no doubt, by one of the matchmakers—probably Mrs. Bartosky—with a name and number scribbled on it. If he called, then he was just a pawn, outmaneuvered by the matchmakers into doing what *they* thought was right for him. Yet he wanted to speak to her, even see her. He supposed a month of no dates would create a hunger for any female, but who could tell? Now and then he smiled at the thought of her. He still knew nothing about how to oil a relationship, how to make it work. He still hardly understood himself. But what the hell. He had been brave once for art, and once for Torah. Why not be brave for the sake of marriage?

He dialed. "Talya?" An image of her hunched shoulders rose in his mind, but he quickly dismissed the thought.

"Yes?"

"Hi. Remember me? Binyamin Harris."

"Sorry, no."

He swallowed a sigh. "The artist," he said. It was quiet on the other end. He slumped. She didn't know who he was. "We met once."

Two more beats. Then: "Ohhhhhhh. That's right." She let out a small laugh. "You're the guy who sneezed into my napkin."

That's what she remembered? Before the arrow of humiliation could enter his heart, he shrugged it away. "Yup," he said. He tapped his chest. "That's me." He paused. "So are you going out with anybody right now?"

She coughed. "Actually I am."

"I see." He chewed on his knuckle for a moment. He began again, "But if you weren't busy, would you consider going out with me?"

She said doubtfully, "I'd consider it."

Another exchange or two, and they both hung up. Or she hung

up, but he sat on the edge of his bed, holding the receiver against his chest. He took in some air and let it out slow until there was no air left. He didn't feel sad, he didn't feel happy, only strangely suspended, a churning, an inner percolating, something new struggling inside him to emerge. She was right to reject him, he thought. He wasn't quite a person, yet. No wonder even that woman Beth hadn't particularly cared for him (not that he'd cared for her), as if she had sensed he lacked integrity and weight. Just then a phone voice began to spout some indignant recorded message and he clicked it off. To hell with the rabbis and matchmakers, he thought, and anyone who'd think less of him. He began to dial. "Please," he said, "can I have the information number in Safed?" He hardly paid attention to the lilting voice of the female operator, only half-wondering if she was pretty or not, and said, "Holy Beggars Institute. I'm looking for a yeshiva in Safed. Could you find me the number?"

※　※　※

At Broken Souls, balloons and streamers swayed drunkenly across the ceiling of the recreation room and a live three-piece band played softly. Some tables were spread with fruit, cakes, hamentaschen and bottles of grape juice, seltzer and sweet black beer. Beth hardly recognized the place.

Costumed people surged around her: a snake charmer smoking a cigar, a man in a box dressed as a computer, someone in a frog costume hopping after a man in blue tights carrying a sword, a woman dressed as the Kotel, a beige sheet draped over her, green moss and crumpled notes stapled to the front and back, on her shoulder a dove. She called, her arms outstretched, "Friends and fellow worshipers, I invite you to pray to me"; a fat-bellied Mexican drinking juice from a cup; a lady in vivid purple from neck to toe, with a little green doily on her head; an old man in a wheelchair, a stern eye painted in the middle of his forehead, who smiled lasciviously at Beth; a woman with blue and pink swirls on her face, her body swathed in pastel scarves. Beth asked her what she was. "Primordial Mist," the woman said and drifted away. A man stood to the side in regular jeans and sweater with a brown scar going down the side of his face. Was it a costume or was the scar real? A masked animal tamer walked by, whipping his black strap and holding a stuffed toy lion. The mustache on the mask was pencil thin and dangerous-looking. Something in his manner reminded her of Akiva, and he was tall like him, too.

A witch in a long pointed hat walked to the center of the room, angling the broom in her arms as if it was a guitar, her fingers strumming the straw part. "Hevra! Hevra!" she called out, but when no one quieted, she aimed her broom, gun-like, at the crowd. Beth's eyes narrowed: It had to be Orna; the social worker's flamboyant gestures were unmistakable. "Welcome to our Purim party," said the witch, and the crowd shifted its gaze toward her. She pointed at the huge crepe lettering that stretched across one wall and read: " 'The wine comes in— the secret comes out'—straight from the Talmud. So drink up and be happy. Let's start some dancing!" She gestured theatrically toward the band and they struck up a spirited tune: "When the month of Adar enters, joy abounds!"

"So where's the wine?" Beth wondered out loud. The witch sidled up to her and peered into her eyes. "You're staff, right?" she whispered.

"Orna, come on, it's me, Beth."

The witch's eyebrows shot up. "Bet! You look—oo la la!" She pulled a bottle of Araq from her black robes. "Here is secret wine for me and you," said Orna in a low voice. "No mixing medication with alcohol—don't let the patients see." She winked at Beth as she hoisted her stockings. Beth peered into the bottle of Araq, took a swig, followed it with another two and shakily returned the bottle to Orna.

"That's some fire water," she gasped. She'd eaten nothing that day because of the Purim fast.

The witch nodded approvingly, and with a final adjustment of her loose robes, continued her zigzag through the crowd.

The Araq went through her in hot surges and her head felt instantly lighter. She saw Zahava hovering near the food table and realized she was the only person in the room who wasn't in costume. Beth teetered up to her. "And what are you supposed to be?" she asked Zahava, who was holding a banana.

"I'm a soul," Zahava said. She stood there, eating the banana, tears in her eyes.

Beth reached over and hugged her. "You *are* a soul, you are." They clasped each other. She felt the softness of Zahava's bones, her smallness, her ache, and prayed for her. Then she asked, "Do you know who I am?"

Zahava stared at her, her eyes narrowing. "I know you. You're the Evil Impulse." She paused. "And you're a big hairy washing machine."

"Will you dance with me in the circle?" Beth asked.

Zahava nodded and put the banana on the table.

They joined hands and danced the hora. Zahava moved with unusual zest and grace. Beth kicked off her heels. Another woman joined them, Primordial Mist. For a minute the three of them went around and around, alone, completely lost in the steps, their feet guiding them, their hearts swept up with the beat. Then other women began to appear and joined hands: a gypsy, Mata Hari, a lady in a Golda Meir mask, the woman in purple and others.

The music spun them round and round. Beth's steps felt light, sure, joyous, as if she were dancing before God. Never had she felt so free. After all, everyone was costumed, and who could tell the difference between the patients, the staff and the visitors? She ran to the middle of the circle, her arms swooping into the air. She made hand motions as if she were an exotic belly dancer. She twirled like a dreidel, calling out the lines to the music.

Over on the men's side a frog juggled clementines; the man in the computer box crouched low and, with a strained expression, danced the kezatzka; a clown put bulls' horns to his ears and charged an imaginary cape; while a circle of men danced around them. It seemed the lion tamer—Akiva!—was the leader. Whenever he glanced in her direction, Beth made sure to look away, and he looked often. Then she gazed at him long and hard. What did it matter? She was completely protected by her gorilla outfit, he would never know. She fluttered her fan at him, nibbled it, and coyly hid her eyes when he glanced at her. But soon she tired of this game. She went in search of her shoes, put them on, and went to the table for a drink. Orna floated by and Beth took another long swallow of the Araq hidden in the witch's robes.

"Ah, it iz Queen Kong!" said a voice behind her.

Beth turned and found herself staring into the eyes of a huge-bellied man in a Mexican mask and sombrero.

"Yes!" She laughed. "And you are a bandeeto!"

From the corner of her eye she saw the lion tamer approaching. Confused, she raised her hand as if to stop him. Her head was whirling. The purple lady came up to her from behind and placed a gloved hand on her silk caftan. "Come, my lady gorilla," she beckoned with her finger. Beth inclined her head toward the woman. "Tonight it's Purim. And do you know, my Bet, do you know someone could look right through your soul tonight like a piece of glass? Yes, this could happen!" The woman nodded.

Beth stared at her. "Tsippi!" she burst out. "You're here!"

"Yes!" Tsippi beamed. "And I brought my husband." She pointed to a white-haired older man who was wearing a Mickey Mouse mask dangling around his neck.

"Your husband," she repeated. Slowly she drew her eyes from the dancing man toward Tsippi. "And what are you supposed to be?"

"I am an eggplant," said the Makolet woman with dignity, touching the green doily on her head.

"An eggplant?" Beth tilted her head.

"Why not? Food is simple—it is what it is," said Tsippi with a cryptic look on her purple shadowed face. Then she moved into a circle of women performing a skipping dance.

"But iz that true?" said a voice at her side. Beth whirled around and found herself looking back into the Mexican's eyes. "Take for instance ze orange." He plucked a clementine from the table and held it in a pinch between his finger and thumb. "On the outside, there iz a peel which nobody can eat. You might think—no good! But the inside iz very tasty. Food iz *not* what it seems!"

"Yes, you have a point," said Beth. Her feet were hurting again and she removed her shoes. "But what about the peach? It tastes just fine till your tooth reaches the pit in the middle. There's that kind of fruit, too."

The Mexican laughed from behind his mask. "Very clever. Which iz better? To see the peel right away, and then afterward to taste the good fruit, or to eat the fruit right away and to get a sad surprise—the pit!"

Beth fingered her false eyelashes. She could see the lion tamer laughing with Mist. "Why this or why that?" she said with a shrug. Her eyes wandered over the tables. She slowly withdrew her glove, finger by finger, and walked toward a bowl of blueberries. "This is the way—no peel, no pit." She took one in her palm, blessed it, then pushed the blueberry through the mouth opening in her mask. "And no residue."

"Ah." The Mexican stroked his fake black mustache. "You are almost a very wise woman." He paused. "You see, my friend, we need the shells and the pits. Imagine such a thing—an apple with no peel? Terrible. Why, soon the whole apple would turn brown and ugly. We must have the peel!" He said this earnestly, his hand on his heart.

"That's what *you* prefer," Beth said, replacing the glove on her hand. "But I prefer without pits or peels. Come to think of it, I like blueberries best, and strawberries and figs. That's what I like."

216

"Then, my dear lady, I will bring you figs, whatever you want. Come with me and I will show you the treasures of the Jerusalem Forest." He swooped off his sombrero, and bent low, toreador style, his arm pointed straight at the door.

"What?" said Beth. "Where?" Who was this man? She felt dizzy. Her eye caught on Dina, talking animatedly to the man with the scar on his face, and Primordial Mist laughingly pressing a stuffed toy lion into Akiva's arms. Apparently, they were an item. The sight of them together pierced her. Even Zahava seemed to have found someone. She was poking a broom, fencing style, at the man with blue tights and a sword dangling from his left hand. Beth took her shawl, put on her shoes and followed the Mexican through the glass exit doors.

He took her to a patio just behind the institute that opened onto a soft plain of grass flanked by three walls of trees. From inside, a dish crashed, followed by a high-pitched yelp of laughter. Then it was quiet, except for the low buzz of voices and music playing indistinctly from the building. She felt safe out here, close enough to the institute to call out if necessary. Not that she thought it might be necessary. But what if this Mexican were a deranged patient? Once, at Broken Souls, she had been engaged in amiable conversation with a refined-looking gentleman, when he suddenly turned furious and maniacal, coming toward her with clenched hands and demanding, "Give me chocolate!" The Mexican seemed harmless though, and definitely sane. The dark foliage from the Jerusalem Forest all around them made it hard to distinguish one tree from the other, but he seemed able to identify many of them.

"Here iz the fig tree!" He pointed. He moved nimbly among the foliage even though he had some weight on him. Next to his roly-poly figure, she felt like a tall weed, or maybe a flower.

"Maybe we shouldn't take," he said with regret, his hand on the thin tree trunk. "It doesn't belong to us."

"But it's the Sabbatical year," Beth pointed out. "These trees are permitted to everyone—that's the law."

His eyes shone from behind the mask. "Ah, Queen Kong iz a scholar, too."

Beth smiled. His eyes seemed nice—gentle and lively. She gave the trees a careless wave. "Better leave them on the tree. I doubt those figs are edible."

She turned to him, but there was only night air at her side. The Mexican had vanished. A few seconds later he appeared from behind an olive tree. "Excuse me," he said, ducking his head. "I had an itch." His mask seemed to bear a sheepish look. "Iz not polite to scratch in front of a lady."

She swung her arms as they passed through the slightly windy, yet pleasant night air. The trees rolled and swayed like dark green waves around them. The moon was almost full. Clouds made their way across the sky, then stretched out and dissolved. She seemed struck by the night. Everything hit her with a vivid clarity. Spring was coming. She could smell it in the forest. "Oh," she said aloud, "I wish, I wish . . ."

"What do you wish?" said the Mexican. "Tell me."

She burst out laughing. "Forgive me," she said, covering her mouth. "I'm just laughing because your tone is so sweet and serious, and your mask looks so cartoon-like, you know, like those villains that are always tying down some damsel to the railroad tracks. Forgive me."

"Ah, but if you could see yourself," he said, "apologizing with your two hands on your cheeks, and that crazy gorilla mask on your face."

They both chuckled.

She swung her arms again.

"So tell me, please, what do you wish?"

"I just wish I could forget myself." She spread out her arms in a wide-sweeping arc, embracing air.

"Ah, yes," he said.

"I wish," she said suddenly, "that there was a bathroom right here." She tapped her spiked heel into the ground. "So I wouldn't have to move. I could just stay here and look at the trees. But I'm sorry, bandito, I must go. I must go to the bathroom."

"Please don't leave!" He leaned forward, his arms outstretched.

She giggled in spite of herself. "Stop looking so tragic." She drew her shawl around her. "Oh, all right, I won't go. I was just joking anyway," she added. She bent and removed her high heels. What a night it was, what a crazy, beautiful night. She never went to the Jerusalem Forest at night—it was too dangerous—but now, here, under these circumstances, it seemed fine, no—a wonderful thing to do. Why, even the obese Mexican was beginning to look dashing. He stood with his thumbs hooked into his back pockets.

He had become quiet. She heard a soft breath leave him, a sigh that made her think there was a real person and not a cartoon character behind his mask. "Do you really want to forget yourself?" he asked her.

She nodded.

"Then first you must remember yourself." He pointed to her. "Turn," he told Beth.

"How's that?"

"Just turn, my lady friend, keep turning and turning till you can't turn anymore, till you fall to the ground. Don't worry, I will do the same thing." He took off his coat and spread it flat on the grass. "This iz for you, my lady, so when you lie on the ground you will not get too cold or your dress dirty."

What a bandito, she thought.

Then he spread out his arms and began to twirl in the grass.

Beth stood transfixed for a moment, then walked to the middle of a soft flat area of grass and planted her feet into the plunchy ground until she felt rooted. She spread out her arms, put one foot over the other, then again, and again, till she got into a steady rhythm of movement, a spin of motion, till it wasn't her legs telling her to move but her legs thinking and moving on their own, they knew, and she was turning, whirling, the wind whipping around her face and throat, the world black green and a random white speck of face. The face dissolved and all was black green and turning, the ground rising under her treading feet. She fell to the ground. She closed her eyes.

"What do you see, my lady?" the Mexican softly called.

She breathed in and out. "I don't see anything," she said. "I feel strange things. I feel the world vibrating."

"Do you like it?"

The earth was humming underneath her. She felt relaxed and alive, flat on the ground. "Yes, I like it."

"Why?" he asked.

She smiled in the dark, her eyes still closed. "It reminds me of a big vibrating chair that we used to have in our living room. I loved that chair."

"Tell me, please, did you spend much time on this special chair?"

She rubbed her eyes, trying to muffle the clear, practical tone of his words. "Oh yes," she said.

"Tell me."

The earth's humming began to recede under the insistence of his words. Beth blew out air and watched it disappear into the night. "It was a big, beige chair. When I was a young girl, I used to go traveling on it. I'd pretend it was a rocket taking off for some faraway orbit: Happy Land, I used to call it. I'd press all the buttons and the neck vibrator and the footrest and backrest, and soon I was buzzing all over. Usually Happy Land itself wasn't as interesting as the trip up there. So I didn't stay too long."

The sky let out a rumble. She turned over onto her stomach, raised her head and peered into the sky. She pressed her face into the cold ground, and blades of grass grazed her neck. "After my mother died I used to spend a lot of time on that chair. And when my father died, and most of the house got sold, I held on to that chair, but eventually it broke. You know," she lifted her head from the ground, "I used to think the whole world was vibrating, and then I realized it was just my house, and then after my father died, I saw it was him, just him. That's all." She plucked a blade of grass and stared at it. "When I came to Israel, some of that reverberating feeling returned."

"What do you mean—reverberating? I am not so sure what you mean. Iz it magic you want?"

She was silent. "It's more like an echo, I think," she said finally. "It's telling somebody a thought and he keeps what you say inside him and you just know it echoes there and echoes and echoes, never getting lost, going on forever."

"You want some eternity."

"Yes." She turned over on her back and lay on the ground, dazed, peaceful. She gazed at the billowy clouds. After a few minutes a light rain began to fall. The Mexican got to his knees and made his way over to her. Silently, he handed her his sombrero.

Thunder shook the grounds. They both lurched toward a bush. There they crouched and watched the fine spray of rain, each drop distinct yet misty in the light cast by the patio. A shadow flickered there and disappeared. The trees made a sighing sound. They sat in complete silence. "Who are you?" Beth asked.

He said nothing. He looked out at the rain, his palm held outward to catch a drop. Then he opened his shirt and began to pull out pillowcases, napkins, stuffing of all kinds. By the time he finished, he was not a fat man at all, only broad. "Don't you know who I am?" he said in an altered voice, the white material laying in drifts all around him.

"No," said Beth, but she trembled.

The quiet between them was heavy like a blanket. "I know who *you* are," he said finally. "I know your voice, the way it has of hesitating, then going up and down, that makes me kind of want to follow it and see where it will go; I know your walk—the slow, light steps you take even in those crazy shoes, it's you all over; and the tight way you hold your shoulders, but sometimes you relax and they look soft, touchable—how could I not know?" He picked up the stuffing and let it fall through his fingers. "I know you, Beth, I've known you for a hundred years."

Beth froze, utterly still.

"Don't—don't be embarrassed," he said, his voice close by. "I would have revealed myself sooner, but I just didn't want to wreck things. It was so lovely between us just now . . ." His voice trailed off.

She looked down at her hands, her feet, in disbelief. She felt a great commotion inside her. It was him. But how could it be? Then who was the lion tamer? "I—oh!" She felt horribly fragile and exposed, like a shack with the roof blown off. She clenched her body into a tight ball, her knees to her chest, her head buried.

"Please, Beth," he said miserably, "don't turn away, don't turn away from me."

She listened from her huddled position.

"Take off your mask," he said softly. He moved closer. "Let me see you without your mask, let me see you proud and beautiful, let me see you as the beautiful woman you are." He spoke in low, beseeching tones, each word falling like a stroke on her eyes, nose, chin and forehead. "Let me see you!"

She felt herself loosening from her own tight grip. With taut fingers, she flung off her mask. Her eyes shut tightly, she held her face to the sky. The rain fell onto her forehead and neck.

She felt something soft grazing her cheek. She opened her eyes. There was Akiva, on his knees, offering her a soggy leaf plucked from a tree, showing her a simple, humble face. His mask lay on the ground near the bushes. She picked up the mask and brought it to her lips. Akiva's head made a quick back and forth motion.

A shard of lightning split the sky, then seconds later thunder came, rolling soft and low.

Beth turned her eyes toward his. "God just took our picture."

"Yes." His eyes looked at hers and smiled.

She pulled a hunk of grass from the ground and let it fly. "We should start our own religion!"

Akiva flung his head back and whooped, and his hand shot into the air. He summersaulted down a small hill. Beth rolled on the wet grass, her silky caftan ruined, giddy with laughter. Then she stopped, and felt the slow beat of her heart. There was a yearning inside her, a fluttering that could not be contained. Her hands ached to touch him. She buried her fists under her arms.

"Maybe we should go back to the party," she said in a quiet voice.

Akiva looked at her from the ground, startled. Then comprehension spread over his face. He nodded.

Wordlessly, they reached for their masks, but Akiva reached hers first. His finger tenderly traced the outlines of its lips before he reluctantly handed it to her. They gathered the stuffing that lay scattered over the lawn, put on their masks and the two left the Jerusalem Forest and went toward the patio, toward the brightly lit room filled with music and voices.

※   ※   ※

Judy surveyed her guests around the dining room table, with its middle leaf added especially for the occasion of the afternoon Purim meal. The men wore Shabbat suits and black hats; the wives were in their wigs or fancier Shabbat hats—not a single guest in costume, she noted, and she felt foolish in her gold glitter wig. But she was the hostess. She could do what she wanted. The children—at least they had dressed up—had collected on the floor and were making piles of all the candy and food they had amassed from their shaloch manos Purim baskets: a pile for baked goods, a separate pile for grape juice and wine bottles, a pile for fruit, acceptable candy and candy whose kosher standard was not a hundred percent reliable. Her second daughter was acting as referee, using her good sense to handle the distribution of the more spectacular tidbits.

Dovid's face and neck were flushed. He had been drinking since ten o'clock and all morning had been making loud spiritual declarations to whoever would listen. Now, he had settled down. An enormous Belzer Hassid lay snoring under the table, and every now and then Judy's foot bumped his knee or shoulder. Avi Feld, Dovid's chevrutah, a thin, precise South African man with searing brown eyes, sat floppily in his chair, one arm slung along the back. He had been drinking, too. All the men had, except for Binyamin Harris. Binyamin sat quietly at the far end of the table. He had said little throughout the meal, and when he did speak, it was in a low, subdued voice. Just this morning she'd seen him in the street holding a shaloch manos basket, and on the spur of the moment she'd invited him to the Purim meal. He had seemed flustered. "I—I just want you to know," he said, "that I didn't really mean—" he broke off. "That I've had a change of—"

"Say no more." She emptied her face of any memory of their last conversation. "My kids have been asking for you. Really, come." They talked for a few minutes, and he confided that he hoped to leave his present yeshiva and go to a mystical place up in Safed, something odd-sounding, with the word "beggars" in it. He told her he'd gotten her note and called up Talya for a date, but she had declined. "Maybe it's for the best. I'd like to settle myself in that new yeshiva before I start dating again." He seemed relaxed and more approachable. But looking at him now, across the table, she could still sense his chagrin about their last phone conversation.

Chaya Feld, six months pregnant with a high color in her cheeks, lifted the back of her ponytail wig and swatted at her neck with a Spanish fan, her daughter's. "It's a mother's nightmare, this holiday," she was telling the other women. "The men are getting bombed, the kids are fritzed out on sugar, and who do they expect to hold it all together?"

The other women nodded. "Last year," Leah, a woman in an auburn wig, said, "Reuven went around kissing everybody at yeshiva, and then came home and vomited all over a basket of fresh laundry."

Judy passed around little shot glasses of Kahlúa, Amaretto and Sabra chocolate liqueur to the women. Half-empty bottles of Chivas Regal and Johnnie Walker clustered together like bowling pins. "Here, have something sweet." A few of the women took small sips.

Chaya Feld held out her palm plaintively. "Why do they have to be so stringent about the mitzvah of getting drunk?"

Dina from the Beit Shifra Yeshiva sat listening, her fist wedged under her chin. She was wearing her overly earnest expression, a look Judy had come to recognize meant she was uncomfortable, possibly because she was the only unmarried woman at the table. "The actual requirement," she said now, "is to drink to the point where one can't tell the difference between Haman the wicked and Mordechai the righteous." She removed a fleck of dust from her glasses and carefully smoothed a long, brown lock of hair behind her ear. "Technically speaking, according to certain authorities," she went on, "one could fulfill the mitzvah simply by falling asleep." She nodded, considered what she'd said, and nodded again. The women looked at each other, shrugging slightly, and Judy's heart contracted a little for her. She had hoped Dina would endear herself to the people at the table. Maybe they might know someone for her. But just now she seemed priggish.

Avi Feld was spouting forth on some topic, and Judy craned her ear, hoping to catch some Torah. ". . . so it's just possible then, that plants do have free choice, albeit on a different level than humans."

Dovid tapped his fork on the edge of the table. "Sure. Sure. A pansy in a quandary. Should I shed my petals or shouldn't I? Really, Avi. You're pushing it, even if it is Purim and your Torah is vodka-inspired."

"Don't be daft," said Avi, leaning over his chair to take a chocolate Crembo from the children's pile. "You're muddling my words.

I'm merely suggesting there may be an entire dimension to plants that we can't even conceive." He peeled off the colored foil from the Crembo and stuffed the creme wafer into his mouth. "Anyway," he said in a muffled voice, "I have a bias toward plants, I must tell you. I could swear they have souls." His clouded eyes glittered for a moment. "More soul than many people I know."

"Maybe Avi has a point," said Judy. She placed a platter of olives, pickled radishes and green pickled tomatoes on the table. "What about the first tree, the tree that refused to make its bark taste the same as the fruit? According to Rashi, the tree disobeyed God's explicit command, and if that doesn't imply free choice what does?" She had been boning up in that area of the Torah because of the Eve theory she was working on. Of course, a theory was only as good as the textual support you found for it; otherwise it was just pie in the sky. And to her pure amazement she had come across an ancient, little-known book called Avodas Hakodesh, by Rabeinu Meir Ibn Gabbai, which provided an excellent basis for her theory. She had told her thought to Naomi Safran who'd suggested she submit it to a Torah journal. To think she'd had a hand in revealing an aspect of God's Torah! Her pleasure was visceral.

Right now she heard grunts and acknowledgments around the table. Avi beamed. "A fine proof," he told her, lifting his shot glass.

"Cute," said Dovid. "Very cute." Judy gave him a look. Was he going to try to take her down a peg or two? She supposed he wasn't used to sharing the Torah limelight with her. But hadn't he encouraged her on this Torah path from the outset?

"I know that Rashi," said Leah. "I learned it in junior high school. I remember it clear as day."

"So why didn't you say it?" Chaya countered.

Leah shrugged and chose a pickle from the platter. "I didn't think the question was a matter of real debate."

"*I* have a question," said Binyamin. His cheeks were pink, almost like a girl's, and his voice was louder than usual. "A theological brain-teaser." Avi stopped making the airplane he was fashioning out of a paper napkin and everyone at the table turned toward Binyamin. He touched his hat, which was slightly large for his head. Someone should take ba'al teshuvas shopping when they first become religious, Judy thought. She'd never met one who didn't look vaguely ridiculous in a hat. "Can God create a rock so big that even He can't lift it?"

"Oh no." Avi aimed the airplane at Binyamin's hat, but it looped around into a chummus dip. "High school, dear fellow, high school."

Binyamin looked stricken. "You mean you already know the question?" A glance around the table confirmed that indeed, the question was not startlingly original or new. "Well, I—" he blushed. "Someone just asked me this question and I can't stop thinking about it."

Chaya said agreeably, "I, for one, never heard it. It sounds intriguing."

"Junior high school," Dina stated. "That's when I first heard it. Still," she said with a mollifying glance in Binyamin's direction, "I never heard a decent answer."

Binyamin still looked flustered. "So what is the answer, I'd like to know. I had no idea the question was such an obvious one."

"It's not that the question is so obvious." Dovid had his head propped in his palm and was looking out tiredly, his eyes hooded, drained from his morning drinking bout. "It's just not a real question."

"Oh really?" Binyamin's ears reddened. His hand again reached toward his hat brim.

"No. It's a set-up. And the question itself doesn't really tell you anything new or interesting about God."

"A set-up," Binyamin repeated. "Maybe that's what all questions are that have no answer."

It had become quiet at the table, and for a minute or two the children's conversation dominated everyone's attention. They were arguing over who would get the giant rainbow lollipop the size of a grape-fruit. Judy felt hostess pressure weighing on her, the need to make the guests agreeable or interesting to each other, or at least to make the conversation reach a climax, amount to something. "Well," she said, "let's analyze it." Dovid gave her an amused, sideways glance. Dina hunched forward in her seat, and Leah was carefully regarding her. Judy went on. "Think about it. Can God create a rock that He can't lift? Of course the question goes around in circles, a conundrum. If He can't do it, then obviously He's imperfect and not all-powerful, not what God's cracked up to be, and if He can do it, make a rock He can't lift, then again He has conferred inability on Himself." She spread out her fingers on the table. "So that's the problem, correct?"

Avi Feld flew another origami airplane in her direction. "Correct, correct," he sang out.

Judy picked up a long-stemmed wine glass and touched its rim. "No, God can't create such a rock, just as God can't make Himself ill or weak or immoral. But His very inability to become ill is His perfec-tion. That so called 'inability' is part of His perfection, His very power, what makes Him God." She set the wine glass down carefully.

Binyamin stared at her. "Explain that."

Judy blushed, conscious of everyone regarding her. "We confuse capacity with something positive," she said. "We assume if a person is capable of things, then it implies a certain power or ability. But what would you say about a God that 'is capable of' getting sick, stealing, breaking out in acne? Would such a God interest you?" She pointed her finger around the table and it landed on Chaya, who, startled, put a hand on her pregnant stomach. "He 'can do' these things, but does that add to God's attributes or diminish our perception of Him? If God could make such a rock, He'd be an anthropomorphized God who I wouldn't bother with anymore. But the 'can' part fools you into thinking it's something any respectable God should be capable of or interested in accomplishing."

Avi shifted his chair to better face her. "So you're saying 'can' and 'can't' are human constructs. They don't apply to the Divine, just to little folks like ourselves. Human beings." Judy thought a moment and nodded.

"In essence," Binyamin took up the thread, "it's a false question masquerading as a real one. Along the lines of what your husband said."

Judy tilted her head. "Well no, I wouldn't say that, exactly. I wouldn't say it's a false question. It challenged me to think about God differently. For instance, are there any legitimate limits to God's power?" She looked around the table. Dovid was staring quizzically at her. Everyone was staring—not only her husband, but her friends, her children, someone from the Beit Medrash, a bachelor she had set up, all the people who knew her in a different capacity. "I mean, when you think about it, any definition of God is going to pose a limit."

"Perhaps that's why Maimonides liked to describe God in terms of what He isn't, and not what He is," Avi Feld commented.

Binyamin brushed aside his remark. "Sounds like the way I date," he murmured. "I know who she isn't, not who she is." The guests chuckled, and Judy smiled. "So, Mrs. Bartosky, what you're saying—"

" 'Judy' is fine," she interjected.

"What you're saying," he continued, flushing slightly, "sounds to me like it's a matter of phraseology. The whole rock question just exists in language. Is that what you're saying?"

Judy considered. "Oh, I don't know. Maybe that's an alternative approach to your conundrum. Language poses the question, but language can't answer the question. The answer might not exist in language. The answer is there, but not in words."

Dovid had pulled himself out of his slouching position and was looking at her rather meditatively. "I'm enjoying this," he said. "I'm enjoying you." He took a fork and banged it lightly against a glass pitcher. "Here, here. Bravo, Judy, well done." He raised a glass toward her. "To my wife, the scholar."

Judy ducked her head. She saw Dina beaming at her. "Wow. Toasted twice in less than ten minutes," she mocked, as if it was no big deal. But she could feel each cell vibrating with pleasure and well-being. Not so much for being publicly acknowledged, but for her ability to comfortably share what she knew, for the keen joy of claiming her mind and along with it, her soul.

Binyamin was nodding to himself. "I like the way you discussed it. It satisfies." He removed his hat, revealing an abundance of silvery brown, wavy hair. He looked unusually winsome and sweet at that moment, and Judy noticed all eyes turning to him, their minds clicking with potential women. Even *she* had just thought of someone for him—a divorced woman with two children, gorgeous, funny and no-nonsense—but first she'd let him go off and settle in that new yeshiva up in Safed. He still had some work to do. Anyway, with men, there was always time.

"But where is it written?" said Leah, her expression aggrieved, as if something had been stolen from her. "What's the source for that?"

Judy lifted a brow. "The source?" she said. "A clear and inquiring mind."

Chapter Thirteen

AFTER WORK BETH MADE HER WAY TO BEIT SHIFRA'S. JUST AS she opened the door to the Beit Medrash, she felt her stomach bottoming out. She was frightened. She suddenly saw herself doing something ridiculous and humiliating in front of all the students, maybe lifting her dress high above her head, and screaming, "Do you love fish? I love God!" That should finish her.

It was late afternoon, and the sun slanted through the windows, throwing an intimate light on the whitewashed walls and the students in various tangled poses of study. Beth observed for a minute. She knew no one. She walked to the blackboard which listed the classes and sources, and purely out of habit wrote down the sources for Naomi Safran's class. She didn't even know if she'd stay, yet she went over to a gray metal bookshelf that extended the length of the entire wall and reached high to get a fat, blue book. Someone's arm reached behind her, higher, and got to the book first. She stepped back, startled, and turned around to tell off the student. Then she sputtered, "Judy! It's you!" and Judy handed over the book, smiling.

"I thought you were going to strain yourself," she said. "You really should use the step stool."

"The bookcase must be new," Beth said, kneading the back of her neck. "I don't remember having to reach so high."

"So you're going to start learning again?" Judy gazed at her with such anticipation that she shrank back in faint alarm.

"Just passing through. Seeing if anything's changed here."

"And has it? Aside from the bookcase?"

"Oh . . ." Beth's eyes swung around, and she pointed at a parchment-like wall hanging, and on it the words—"If you believe you can destroy, believe, believe that you can fix." "That poster," she said, "and the people. All the Americans from last year went back home. It's a completely different crew. I see hair clips are in this year." Beth rubbed the spine of the blue book. "Well, at least the books stayed the same. Good old books."

"Come, I want you to meet my chevrutah before she goes," Judy said, and gave a lopsided frown. "It's really too bad Lauren's leaving." They wound their way through scattered chairs, small tables, lecterns and fallen knapsacks.

"That's what they all do," Beth said philosophically, as they squeezed between two tables, narrowly avoiding a Styrofoam cup of coffee set on a table's edge. "The college girls come, they study, they love Israel, and then it's the end of the year, they cry at the airport, and they never come back. It's like camp to them."

"Oh Beth, don't be cynical. Not everyone's cut out for Aliyah, you know. We're the lucky ones." They continued walking toward a table at the outskirts, adjacent to one of the classrooms.

"That's right. We get to contend with the high cost of living, neighbors who want to exterminate you, bad toilet paper. How did the Sages put it?" Beth stepped over someone's jacket that lay on the floor and, as an afterthought, picked it up and draped it over a chair. " 'Three things are acquired only through great suffering: Torah, the land of Israel, and—' " she scratched the side of her nose, "the third I forget. A husband, maybe."

"No, no, it's the World To Come," Judy reminded her. She looked around the room, hands on hips. She pouted. "Oh. It looks like Lauren already left."

They stopped at a table, and nearby Beth could hear the rhythm of voices of a class in session. Someone was asking a question, and the teacher—she recognized the Chicago-accented voice of Naomi Safran—was offering an answer. The student didn't like the answer. She asked the question again, slightly altering it, her voice louder, and again the teacher answered. After the student asked the same question a third time, her voice edged with grievance, Naomi said, composedly, "I see I haven't answered your question to your satisfaction. Let's move on." There was a muffled titter in the class, and then someone read out another verse. Beth smiled. She liked how Naomi didn't bend herself out of shape or consider herself personally responsible to satisfy the student. Other teachers would have taken on that burden. *She* would have, if she'd been standing in front of the class. She liked that line: "I guess I haven't answered your question to your liking. Now let's move on." Maybe she'd have a chance to use it someday.

Judy had taken a seat at the table, and she patted the place across from her. "Put your books down." She glanced swiftly around the Beit Medrash. "We already said goodbye, but I didn't think Lauren would be leaving quite that fast. I'd love for you to meet her."

Beth slouched into a chair and rubbed her shoulders. She'd forgotten how heavy Torah books could be. "Don't worry, I'm sure she'll come by. If not, we can drop by her apartment."

Judy peered into a red notebook and flipped the pages. "What class are these books for? Naomi Safran's?"

Beth nodded, and her stomach tightened. Was Judy now going to ask her to be her new chevrutah? Now that Lauren was gone? It seemed too conscious, like being asked to go steady on the rebound.

Judy put her hands flat on the table. "So let's begin. I think we have all the books we need."

And Beth, without analyzing if she was truly ready—for anything—opened the book and began to read out loud.

One night, after they'd been dating for about six weeks, Beth and Akiva sat in the Jewish Quarter Cafe. They had placed their chairs side by side so neither would be deprived of the view, and Akiva asked, "Do you think I could make you happy?"

Beth turned to him and said, indifferently, as if she might be assessing the weather, "Yes, I think so." The orange lights of the Dome Mosque hit her eyes. Still looking ahead, she asked, "Do you think I could make you happy?"

"Yes."

They both sat slumped in their chairs.

After a minute, Akiva sat up dazedly. He looked at her and his face had a wild, white-water rafting look.

"What is it?" She touched the arm of his chair.

"I can't believe it." He shook his head and chuckled.

"Believe what? Tell me."

He took a mighty breath. "I think I just asked you to marry me, and I think you just said yes."

Beth squinted at him. Her brain fogged. She felt a great commotion inside her head, the gray and white materials inside her scrambling and unscrambling, and then there came a clearing, and she thought: Why not? All her grandiose seeking after all these years, and this was what it boiled down to: Why not. "Really?" she said, and then she nodded her assent, a quick dip of the chin.

And that's how she found herself going from hat stores to scarf shops, stocking up on headcoverings. Could it really be happening to her, she who had gone so long with nothing over her head? Hoods and umbrellas never counted. She was finally joining the ranks of the covered. She bought a magenta silk scarf with tassels and a short-brimmed hat that made her feel like an actress from the forties. She had never favored wigs. She ran her fingers through her fine brown hair. After the chuppah, no man would see it anymore. Except for Akiva. Then he would see the rest of her, too. If she thought about the wedding too much, she got squeamish. A wedding was her private desire made public, common knowledge. Oh, so that's the one she wants. That's the one she'll bed with. What was it anyone's business? But that was the way of the world. After the wedding, everyone would know her desire. The thought of a little privacy in the form of a scarf comforted her.

Beth wandered into the Makolet one afternoon, her arms filled with shopping—not only scarves and hats but pretty bras, panties, slips and nightgowns. In a fit she had thrown out all her faded and frayed underwear, dumped her stretched-out bras turned gray over the years, and even somewhat sadly gotten rid of her grandmother's gauzy striped nightgown, the only relic she had of her father's mother. It had made her feel close to her bubby when she wore it to sleep, but she wrapped it in soft paper and threw it out. She gripped her purchases to her chest. So now she had nice underwear for every day of the week, not just Shabbat. She felt wealthy.

The Makolet was empty except for Tsippi, bent over a wood-rimmed tray of rice. A small lamp with a strong bulb shone onto the tray. Her fingers were fluttering over the grains, flattening them, picking out the stony and discolored ones.

"Hello, Bet!" she said, raising her eyes and beaming at her. Beth could feel the warmth in the old woman's gaze. Ever since she had become engaged to Akiva, she'd been showered with acceptance, encouragement and outright love, the kind of warmth she had never experienced. The attention had a way of depressing her. All the approval she was getting now made her realize the love everyone must have been withholding from her all these years. More than that—they must have been hiding from her enormous amounts of irritation, maybe even contempt. She looked back over the years and situations that had puzzled her, reactions that had left her feeling empty, misunderstood, and she now had a new perspective about their frustration and annoyance with her. She suddenly felt sad for herself, all the sadness she had been oblivious to in the past, and sad for other single women, too, to be the bearer of so many people's contempt. Tsippi was still smiling at her now, and Beth, despite these misgivings, let the warmth penetrate her. She couldn't help herself. She was not immune to love.

Beth roamed down the aisles and returned with some celery knobs and daikon and turnip and burdock, homely vegetables that Akiva had introduced her to; she joined Tsippi at the cart table, rolling up her sleeves to help with the rice checking. Beth was better at removing the stones and the old, defective grains while Tsippi was good at detecting the hidden bugs and worms. A contentment settled upon Beth as she sat with Tsippi around the lamp, poking among the grains. Here it was rich, like butternut squash. She almost forgot the panic attack she'd had that morning as she lay in bed, going over all the little things that irritated her about Akiva. His beard needed better grooming. When he ate, he held his fork crudely, like a drumstick in his fist. He sang off-key. He began many sentences with "By the same token." Of course she could live with these pesky annoyances, but at the heart of these observations was a question: Was he the one God had planned for her from eternity?

Beth adjusted the light so it shone more directly on the rice platter. She said, "Tsippi, could you tell me something? How did you know your husband was the right one for you? Your besherte and all that?"

"I had a certain feeling," she began. She told Beth about her rescue efforts when she was a young woman in the camps, about going into the barracks late at night, searching for a pulse among all the bodies, reviving them if she could, and in the end reviving the body of the man who, after the war, became her husband. When she saw him again she recognized the little mushroom birthmark on his neck.

"And after all that, can I still say I knew?" Again, Tsippi poured more rice onto the platter and shook it gently from side to side until the grains evened out. "I didn't." Beth sucked in her breath, and Tsippi looked at her. "Well, if he's not for you? Believe me, you know right away. And if he is for you? You can marry him, you can have children with him, you can spend your life with him, and still, you never know."

They continued checking among the grains. Beth smiled. She liked the thought—this not knowing. Did she truly know that Akiva was the one for her? Did she know with complete certainty that God existed? Did she know without a doubt that the Torah was the absolute truth? No certainties, but she had a feeling, many feelings, an accumulation of experiences, each placed on a scale, another experience, another and another, the scale dropping lower and lower till it touched the ground of belief. Separately, the feelings proved nothing, but taken altogether they assumed a power. That was enough for her to live a life.

At home she slid off her shoes and dropped her shopping packages on the sofa. A scarf slithered out of one of the bags, and Beth picked it up, holding the boldly colored kerchief by its tips. When was the last time she'd bothered to try one on, when did she last have hope that one day she'd be wearing one of these things? She couldn't even say. She draped the scarf over her head, then criss-crossed the loops behind her neck and tied a knot. An expanse of material hung over the knot and she tucked that flap under the knot, so that the back had a little swell to it. That was the standard scarf look. Now she would look just like everyone else, now she would blend in, neatly classified and assured of her proper place in the social-religious scheme of things.

She went to the mirror in the hallway. Every strand of hair was covered. She saw a few ancient acne-pockmarks on her cheekbones.

She'd forgotten about those. No hair to camouflage the thickening around her neck, no bangs to soften the furrows and creases in her forehead. She had aged. Even she could see that. And her eyes looked sad. Too many injuries reflected in them: pain in the inner corners, fear in the fluttering lids, and in the dark orbs contradiction and struggle. It was too much. Everything was revealed. Anybody who'd look at her would . . . would know something about her, something more than she was willing to share about herself. With a scarf she was more exposed than ever. And here, she'd thought it would help her blend in.

The scarf was slipping off, and she realized she'd have to make a double knot to better secure it. Instead she flipped out some bangs from under the scarf. There. She smiled a little at her reflection. The bangs on her forehead softened things a bit. They camouflaged the anxiety, hid the furrows, they made her face manageable, a thing to be presented to the world. True, the really pious made sure to tuck every strand of hair under their scarves, and maybe she would some day. But to cover everything from the outset—she didn't think she could bear that degree of revelation.

Chapter Fourteen

AKIVA WALKED ALONG BAR-NACHMANI STREET TOWARD THE health-food store, whistling a Shlomo Carlebach tune. Four days to go, four more days to the chuppah. A skinny bald man walked by and frowned at him, but kept walking. Akiva stared at the retreating man. His pelvis suddenly felt weak, as if someone had unloaded five blocks of cement onto his midsection. "Dr. Sorscher," he stammered, then louder, "Dr. Sorscher, it's me, Akiva." The man craned his neck back for a moment, frowned again, then disappeared into Ibn Ezra Street. Akiva leaned against the wall of the Laundromat. The guy sure had looked like Dr. Sorscher, he thought. He dug his thumbs into the top of his spine to work out the tension and rolled his shoulders a few times. This was the second time he had seen Dr. Sorscher's look-alike. It spooked him.

He tried whistling again, but his mouth felt out of whack. Dr. Sorscher, he thought, the doctor with the pamphaldamine plan. On his first date with Beth, he'd mentioned the pamphaldamine drug, but he hadn't exactly explained what he meant by its awful side effects. Since getting engaged, he'd thought of telling her about the drug a number of times, but something always had come up. Somehow the subject of impotence had seemed too raw, certainly too raw for a woman who had yet to experience the potency of a man. Still, wasn't it only right that she should know everything about him? Especially since their wedding was only four days away? Truthfully, the whole subject made him anxious, and so he had taken the coward's way out and dismissed it. Dr. Sorscher's look-alike brought it into bright light.

Just outside the health-food store, Akiva looked through the glass windows and watched Sami, the Yemenite assistant, dark and fawnlike, prepare the tofu marinade. His dexterous fingers chopped the garlic and ginger. He shot tamari sauce into a pan with abandon. Akiva put his hand on the doorknob of the health store and felt a soft breathing at the back of his neck. He touched his neck and spun around. Nothing. Just a hot wind. A question fluttered around him, hovering like a dream. Just then a decision hit him full in the chest: He would tell Beth about the doctor's recommendation, he would tell her everything. No blips or barriers between them, just one clean expanse stretching from his innermost parts to hers. This was his wedding present to both of them. He would tell her now, immediately. No more delays. He hoped she would accept his procrastinating.

He turned into a little phone booth between a Laundromat and Teva Natural Foods. Before he dropped the asimone token, he yanked off a sprig of rosemary from a nearby bush and brought it to his nose. He stood there breathing in the scent, thinking and breathing. The heat of the day was beginning to roll in. He could feel the sun darkening his face. Finally, he released the token. "Beth?"

"Keevers!" said a slow, warm voice.

A wave of joy lifted him for two heartbeats. It had been maybe twelve hours since her voice had last revived him. Then dread fell. Maybe it would be wiser to tell her after the wedding. Lately, they'd been a little testy around each other. He supposed it was the sexual tension between them or maybe just pre-wedding jitters. "Is everything all right at work?" he asked. He knew she was unhappy there, was revving up to leave the job and her oily, petty-minded boss.

"The same. I'm not thinking about it now." He could hear the shrug over the phone. "It's just—" She gave an awkward laugh. "I had a strange dream last night."

"What was it?"

"In my dream you said you no longer had passionate feelings for me. Something like 'Yes, what we have is good—for a first marriage.' "

"I said that? That's crazy. I wouldn't say that."

"It's a dream," she reminded him. "Anyway, as long as you were being so honest, I confided I had widow fantasies. Sure I'd miss you if you died, but I was already looking forward to the next husband, the next marriage, and then you said—"

"Beth, why are you telling me this? We're not even married yet!" He rubbed his brows. They were taut. "This is a terrible dream. Do you mind if we talk about it some other time?"

"But it had a good ending," she protested. "Okay, forget it. What's on your mind?"

He stood there, wondering how he would say it. He watched a tall woman in sunglasses stride up to the health-food store. Something in the phone silence sounded strained. He made his voice gentle. "Beth, I'm sorry I interrupted your dream. You know I'd normally want to hear the details. But I'm a little anxious about something." He cleared moisture from his throat.

"All right, Keevers, tell me."

"I don't know if you remember a drug I told you about, the one I tried for my spasms?"

"I remember," she said after a pause. "It gave you awful side effects. Pamdalphamine."

"Pamphaldamine," he corrected, nonetheless amazed at her recall. "Well, there was more to it than I said." He told her about the doctor's recommendation and the additional side effect of impotence the drug might bring. When he finished speaking, he felt a trickle of nausea and had to lean against the outside of the phone booth. Seconds later, a surge of relief shot through him, surprising him with its warmth, and he knew he had made the right decision. "I would have told you then," he added, "but I was too embarrassed, I guess, to even bring up the idea of impotence."

Wind chimes ushered a slew of women into the health-food store. He watched them file in as he waited for Beth's reply. "Reminds me of an old man I knew in Canada," he went on. "In his eighties, dying. There was an operation that could've saved his life but would've left him impotent. He refused it, wouldn't consider it. In his eighties, can you believe it?" He crumpled the rosemary sprig between his thumb and forefinger. "Are you there, Beth?"

"Uh huh," she said. "I'm here. I'm just trying to absorb what you said."

The faintest of spasms rolled off his shoulders.

Beth coughed. "You mean the doctor could've adjusted the medication? No more sweating or nausea? No yellow eyes?"

"That's right. But there was the impotence to consider."

"Akiva, I—" she faltered, "I don't really understand. You mean that the spasms could be gone," he heard a snapping sound, "just like that? You don't have to be suffering every day?"

"I don't really suffer, Beth. You've spent enough time with me to know it's really not so bad." He wiped his hands against his shirt. The sun was getting to him. "Anyway, don't forget the impotence factor. That was what decided it."

"But we're only talking about a possibility of impotence, right? And it's reversible, too?" She spoke in a wondering voice.

"Twenty percent is not insignificant. And easy for the doctors to say it's reversible—it's not their body." He felt an edge creeping into his voice. If only a wind would come along, that cooling soothing Jerusalem wind.

"But what about my suffering?" he heard her say. "You're telling me I went through all that mental torment for nothing? You remember how hard it was for me to accept this? All you needed to do was swallow a pill, and you never told me?" Her breath came out in shallow spurts.

He stared at the receiver. "Beth, you're taking this wrong. I agree, I should have been more up front with you—I know that, and for that I apologize. But I'm telling you now. I couldn't tell you then. I wasn't ready. Too proud, too macho, I don't know." He paused. "I was wrong, but does that make me unforgivable, an evil person? All I know is, I'm telling you now for the sake of our relationship, to bring us closer together. It's my offering to you."

He heard Beth let out a sigh so deep he could feel it inside his own rib cage. She sighed again, a regular one. "Forget it," she said. "What's past is past. You're telling me now, and that's what counts." Her voice was gentle. "We can go forward from here. We could even celebrate."

He smiled. This was what he loved about Beth, her sweet reasonableness. "That's how I hoped you'd take it," he said quietly.

"And if God forbid you should become impotent, you could always stop taking it, right? I wonder what it'll be like," she burbled on, "you without spasms. That's the only way I've ever known you. But now that you'll be taking the pill—"

Akiva's headed rotated sharply back and forth. He let out a hiccup. "What are you talking about? I'm not taking anything. I'm not taking any chance with impotence. What's wrong with you? Didn't I make myself clear?" His raised a hand and said: "Impotence!" A black-hatted yeshiva student dragging a duffel bag of laundry looked at him. Akiva lowered his fist.

"What?" She fell into a stunned silence. Then her voice rose sharply. "Why did you tell me this to begin with?"

He practically shouted into the phone. "You're mixing up everything, Beth. I just wanted to let you know, so it would be clean between us, a hundred percent truth, a deeper understanding of each other. I wanted to start our marriage from a higher place." He wiped the corners of his mouth. "Look, let's save this for later, okay?"

He got off the phone, his hands shaking. All of him was shaking. He breathed in through his nose, letting out the air slowly, trying to calm himself, ashamed of the violence of his feelings. He'd come that close to cursing her. He wanted to throttle her for her obtuseness. She had no idea what she was saying, what she was suggesting. And what if the impotence wasn't reversible? he thought. The doctors would say, Oops, sorry, we goofed. No one toyed with the core material of a man. Even a dying eighty-year-old knew well enough what to leave intact. He wondered how the woman he was going to marry could know so little about men.

He walked toward the health-food store, drawing his sleeve across his forehead. He didn't know what to make of the situation. He had watched Beth struggle with his asperclonus syndrome, and he'd seen her come to a deep understanding and acceptance of him. He thought she understood about his asperclonus, that it wasn't just a condition, his burden to bear, but something more—he had never put it into words. His twitches—they were a part of him. He loved what they gave him: a place on top of the mountain, a chance to get a glimpse of people from the point of view of God—no fancy clothes, no mannerisms, no beauty or defect to divert the eye, just plain souls. He had always known this about his spasms, and while he had never spelled it out, perhaps from some instinct of wanting to protect what was fleeting and sacred, he'd believed Beth had known it, too. At times he had even wondered if she made too big a deal about the spasms, was too drawn to them, hypnotized by the mystique they created, dazzled by the hidden places they could reach. He shook his head. How far from the truth that was! He stared down at his hands. How could it be, the woman he loved understood so little of him.

"Hey, Sami," he said as he opened the door to Teva Natural

Foods. But Sami wasn't behind the counter. A short man with a bulging neck and a blue kerchief tied around his head stared at him as he entered. Someone new, he thought, and he gave a little nod, but the thick-necked man looked down, away, into the cash register. Sami was in the back, he said, frying tofu and making sandwiches.

Akiva wandered through the store, picking up goldenseal tablets, rice cheese, spelt flour and organic apples. He was looking for something, though he couldn't quite remember. Then he saw the recipe for Melancholy Brew.

He went up to the counter. "I'll take an ounce of melissa and an ounce of licorice root, and some peppermint." He watched the man unscrew the jars and weigh the herbs. He noted his smooth cheeks and uncreviced forehead, the red raw lips—a younger man, Akiva now saw, younger than he had thought, in his early twenties. After tying them shut, he placed the bags of herbs on the counter.

Akiva pointed at the little vials of tincture sitting on shelves behind a glass door. "And also some of that motherwort."

The assistant slowly slid open the glass door. Akiva could've gotten the vial himself, but the fragile vials made him nervous. If he were to suddenly have a spasm, a thrash of his arm could destroy hundreds if not thousands of dollars in herbal medicines. Why take a chance? The assistant placed the vial on the counter with a little smack, and it stood slim and lonely next to the two bulging bags of herbs.

"Oh." Akiva smacked the edge of his forehead. "Did I ask for motherwort? I meant blessed thistle. Sorry."

The assistant fingered the hanging loop of his kerchief. Then he took the small bottle into his palm and again slid open the door, centimeter by centimeter, his hand damp against the glass. He found the blessed thistle, replaced it with the motherwort, then placed his hand on the glass and pushed to close it. His fingers trembled.

Akiva watched him, sensing the enormous strain this young man was experiencing, that somehow he had brought on. Akiva felt a low, pulling pressure in the space between his eyes. A muscle jumped in his palm. Keep still, he commanded his hand. Keep still, he ordered, but with a groan he already sensed his body gearing up for something big. He tried to clench his hand into a fist—sometimes that stopped a spasm—but his fingers spread out taut and stiff, and refused to bend. But his arm could move. He would move his arm away from the glass display of tinctures. His elbow remained locked but he swung his body around, away from the display, so that his arm followed, and his hand followed the arm, like a metal ball at the end of a chain. Splat! His hand had come down hard and flat on a bag of chamomile. The bag burst, spraying the counter, the tofu sandwiches, the red-lipped young assistant. Akiva stared at the flecks of green and yellow herb on his face. He let out his breath. The spasm had passed. But a moment later, his body spun into a frenzy. Something was shaking him, making every limb floppy and loose and without will, all of his inner organs unmoored. His mind went limp. His eyes and tongue wobbled inside him. He hiccuped in rapid succession. A purple light blinked in the back of his head, and then the purple light broke into tiny dots, bouncing and floating across the screen of his mind until the dots dissolved, and there he was, sprawled out on the hard, cold tiles of Teva Natural Food Stores. He lay there, his hands spread on the floor. He pressed down on the outer corners of his brows, going inward till he reached the points on either side of his nose. His vision gradually rearranged itself before his eyes. Sami was standing over him, looking down with a bland, motherly concern.

"That was a rough one, boss," Sami said. Reaching low, he pulled Akiva to a standing position. Akiva straightened his shirt and adjusted his collar. He took in the other customers, women of varying ages, and gave them the I'm-all-right-but-yep-that's-me smile he usually reserved for such episodes. Then his eyes fell on the young assistant crouched in a corner, his kerchief undone, his arm held up before him like a shield.

Akiva squinted and took a step toward the young man.

"Don't!" the young man cried. "Don't come close, don't hurt me, just don't hurt me!" His arms criss-crossed over his face.

Akiva's mouth fell. "What the—" He glanced at Sami, bewildered. "Look, I'm not going to hurt you. I just have a muscle that jumps now and then. Don't take it wrong." He walked toward him, an arm outstretched in a protective arc.

The young man howled. "Ayeee, ayyy, dooon't, dooon't come close, don't beat me up." He took his head into his hands and began to shake and quiver. "Dooon't hurt me."

Akiva stopped mid-stride.

A dark, lovely woman with a pointed chin gave him a severe look. "Just go away, let him be. He's frightened and you're only making it worse."

Akiva laid his fingers on his chest. "But I—"

Another woman shouted, "Pick on someone your own size, you big bull."

"You got it all wrong, don't you see—" Akiva turned to Sami with a pleading look. "Tell them I'm okay."

"Something happened to this guy in the army," Sami said in a low voice. "Somebody did some job on him. He was up there in Lebanon. He's the owner's nephew."

Akiva thrust his fists despairingly into his pockets. "I think I—"

Sami put a hand on his shoulder. He whispered, "Better get some fresh air."

Akiva retrieved his knapsack and jerked the door shut behind him as he left the store, walking with hard, flat steps. The wrongness of the young man's accusations struck him with every step he took. His temples throbbed. The sun bore down intensely, frying his beard, making him feel ironed to the sidewalk. He turned on one of the streets, making his way to the library. He always went there to clear his head. He could've gone to the Kotel but the Western Wall wasn't beckoning to him just now. It wasn't prayer he wanted. He didn't need God's eyes on him, but something else. At the library, he flipped through magazines, used the bathroom and wandered over to the windmill across the street where he'd had his first date with Beth. If only he could see her, touch her, make sense of the craziness that had passed between them. If only they were married already. He needed her, he needed her to say, "Keevers, the man was disturbed, you'd never hurt anybody, that's not you." That's what he needed. A human eye, a wife's assessment, his wife-to-be. Somebody who knew him, who could tell him what he was, and what he wasn't.

Out on the street he saw a number fifteen bus, which would bring him to Beth's work. As he climbed the steep bus steps, his glance fell on a beefy, bald man behind the wheel. Akiva raised his lids. There sat Kojak, squat and proud, a fleshy arm extended, punching holes into the passengers' bus cards. Kojak, who had thrown him off the bus. This was the first time he'd seen him since then. Maybe Kojak had forgotten him. But what if he hadn't? He couldn't bear the thought of being thrown off the bus again, not today. He'd had his own card extended but now withdrew it hastily. Kojak looked up. His eyes opened wide and his handsome face registered recognition, then, for a brief instance, shame. "Nu," he said finally, "get on the bus." He motioned a stubby finger. "I remember you. I made a mistake. Somebody on the bus told me all about you." Akiva stood, holding his bus card, on the cusp of decision. Then the doors shut behind him and the bus gave a forward lurch as Kojak pressed on the gas. "Don't worry," he added gruffly. "You'll be okay on this bus. I'll make sure nothing bad will happen."

He wanted to reach forward and hug the driver, his former foe. Instead he held out his bus card, got a card punch in the shape of a moon and took a few steps into the crowded aisle where he grasped a pole for support.

Kojak hollered, "If you people in the middle don't move to the back and make room, I'm not driving this bus anywhere."

The crowd shifted, squashed into themselves, and three feet of aisle opened up. Kojak glanced again into the mirror. Then he called out, "You, the man with the red beard and the strange glasses. Get up, get out of your seat." A man with a red beard and glasses touched his throat, a frightened look on his face. "Yes, you! We have a sick person here who needs a seat."

Akiva shook his head, smiling. The man ruled his bus mightily. He looked around the bus for the sick person and then with a dread uncoiling inside him, saw Kojak gesturing him toward the empty seat. "See, I told you you'll be okay here," he said to Akiva.

Akiva blinked. He touched his chest. It's me, he thought, I'm the sick person. He closed his eyes tight, his face boarded up, like an old house. There he stood, clutching the pole, ignoring Kojak and the entreaties of the passengers to stop being foolish and take the seat. He didn't want to listen to these people. He was tired of looking at them. What was the point when no one saw him? He saw into everybody, but no one saw him. He felt a tickle of a sob in his throat, a terrible wave of self-pity about to carry him off in its tides, when suddenly he thought of God. God had no friends. He was always being misperceived, misunderstood, cast as a charlatan, or maligned as an extorter of prayers to gratify a monstrous ego, not a real entity but the projection of immature need. And the people who paid Him homage were worse with their sugar-coating, transforming God into a Hallmark card, a god who only rained goodness on the world, a god for the naive and vapid of soul. Somehow God survived the distortions and slurs, survived the stupid homage, too, and remained God. That was the miracle of His existence. But he didn't remain Akiva. There were nicks all over him, internal dents. Cast as something false, something that he wasn't, over and over, addict, invalid, attacker, saint—there was no joy in that. Abruptly he pulled the cord overhead.

The bus passed a cross-section, then came to a stop. Akiva fled the bus, Kojak and its passengers. He walked quickly, past a beggar with his head swathed in bandages, past a soldier in a mini-skirt, past a small parade of sheep led by an Arab youth. His pace quickened, then he broke loose into a run, running, till he turned into a large gray building, eucalyptus trees on either side. He climbed the stairs to Beth's office, two at a time, walked past her boss who was smiling at himself in a mirror, rapped loudly on her door, with its poster of Israeli desert thorns and its caption: 'I Never Promised You A Rose Garden,' then, unable to wait, flung open the door. She stood by the window, half-turned, sucking on a pen. Her eyes widened. "Akiva! I—"

"Beth—I had to speak with you." He poured out his day, the string of misperceptions, the kerchiefed clerk in the health store, the customers, the bus driver, the passengers, dredging up others, and lay them before her.

"Oh, Akiva, how awful." Her eyes commiserated. But why were her nostrils quivering? She looked like she was struggling to keep her face neutral, free of mirth.

Akiva stared at her.

Beth said, "Why are you looking at me that way?"

He said tensely, "Do you think I enjoy this?" His arm swept his body. "Being treated like a freak?"

She shrugged.

He clenched his fist. "You must think I like it."

"I don't know," she said, looking out the window. "I don't know what's going on anymore."

He felt whipped. He made an abrupt movement with his hand, dismissing the air between them. A glass mug fell off a table, and rose-colored liquid and glass sprayed across the floor. He stared at the glass pieces.

He heard Beth's voice. "Akiva, you're so angry at everyone who gets you all wrong. Actually, everyone should be angry at you. You're the one who spends all his time trying to trick people."

"Tricks? I'm a trickster?"

"You're no better than anyone."

He covered his eyes, his fingers digging deeper and deeper into his temples as if to contain everything. All along—in his heart of hearts—he'd thought he was a saint, hadn't he? He felt his mind go slack, stupid, struggling to push away the thought. Come on, he shook himself. You think you're God's special suffering servant, don't you? Granted an extra closeness, and all because of your holy spasms. A knife of self-loathing stabbed him. You think your spasms bring you closer to God, closer to people. How wrong you were, how mistaken.

She said softly, "No better, but no less lovable."

He clenched his body. He was deflating, he was just a beach ball with the air all punched out, filled with holes so no one could blow him up again. He raised his eyes toward Beth.

"So . . . that's why God put me here, just to be like everyone else?" But even as he said these words of half-complaint he knew the game was up, no more sympathy or encouragement, not from God, not from his wife-to-be, not even from himself. He felt himself contracting further and further before Beth's eyes, into some warm, helpless living thing, bringing him closer and closer to her, and all of him ached with the effort of it.

Chapter Fifteen

THE SUN SHONE SHARP AND BRIGHT IN THE SKY LIKE A YELLOW Frisbee. Beth sat on a huge wicker bridal chair which was plunked down in the middle of a soft, grassy plain, the same plain she had twirled on that Purim night with Akiva. The Jerusalem Forest flanked Beth on all three sides, and to her back was the Broken Souls building. Judy had done unusual and subtle things to her eyes and lips and had swept her hair up in an exotic bun, revealing the beautiful contours of her neck for the first time. Nearby the guitarist from "Rachel's Secrets" strummed Hassidic melodies under a fig tree.

Orna and Estrella walked among the guests with platters of cut vegetables, eggplant, chummus and tahini dip. Tsippi went from guest to guest collecting the names of those who wanted the bride to pray for them—it was known that a bride and groom's supplications under the canopy had extra impact in the heavens. For Beth and Akiva, today was their private Yom Kippur. Each had been fasting all day, and each would stand under the chuppah forgiven of all former sins. Except for a few of the male patients from Broken Souls, who were walking slowly around outside, most of the men were indoors with Akiva and the rabbis, who were huddling over the marriage documents. Akiva's father and older brother had made the trip from Canada, as well as his grandmother, a surprisingly robust woman of ninety-two.

Dina stayed at the bride's side, plucking at the gown's tulle skirt piece. "Well, it's really happening," she said for the fifth time. She squeezed Beth's arm. "You're not going to turn into one of those married women, are you? The ones who look at older singles in that awful way?"

"Which way?" said Beth.

"Like you're crippled or something."

"I'm afraid so," Beth said. Dina dropped her arm. "Just kidding. It's too late for me, anyway," she said in a low voice, still smiling at the guests milling around. "I'll always be a single woman in their eyes. At best, the woman who got married late."

Dina became silent as a neighbor of Beth's rushed over and poured blessings over her in Hebrew so rapid that the only distinguishable word was "seed," and then rushed away. "Single forever," Dina said in a doomed voice, after she left. "Why even bother getting married?"

"Oh, Dina, I don't really want to shake being single, not entirely at least. It's given me some things, you know."

"Like what?" Dina's lip curled.

"Oh, I don't know. Added edge in prayer, I think. Single people pray differently. We know we're really alone and that's the best way to stand before God. We can't afford to rely on a spouse's prayers in case ours aren't good enough."

Dina nodded, mulling this. "I'd rather have been a lousy davenner and married young." She gripped Beth's arm again. "You're really getting married!" It started out gleefully and ended in a kind of wail.

Someone let out a loud and jubilant sound. It was Estrella Abutbul, Beth saw, jangling her many bracelets, doing her Sephardic ululating.

Estrella gave a sheepish smile. "I saw a man coming toward us, the father of the groom, and I thought: the bedeken ceremony is starting, and no one is even singing!"

Beth smiled back. Her eyes roamed over the guests, seeking out any she had not yet personally greeted.

A few feet away Orna was talking to some staff at Broken Souls who had drifted over from inside.

"And then Professor Naveh—he's at Hebrew University, you know. Well, he got up and told a story about this rabbi he used to be friendly with in his youth." Ah, they had just come back from the peace rally, thought Beth. She would have liked to have gone, too. "Then," Orna continued, "when he got older and took off his yarmulka, he tried to avoid the rabbi whenever he saw him in the street. Finally the rabbi stopped him one day and said, 'Why are you always running away from me?' Professor Naveh admitted finally that he was embarrassed he wasn't wearing a kippah in front of the rabbi. The rabbi said, 'I'm a short man. My head only reaches your shoulders. I can't see what's on top of your head. I can only see your heart.' "

Doctor Carmi, who had sauntered over, took up the narration. "And then everyone joined hands and danced the hora and there was peace in Jerusalem."

Orna pointed a scolding finger. "Really, Doctor Carmi. It was quite moving, even for a secular sabra like me."

One of the medics at Broken Souls said, "I like the part when that other speaker stood up and said—'How quick we are to judge. How we'd like to think behind every Hassid or Hareidi is a primitive-thinking backward person who wants to control our lives, and the religious think behind every secular person is an adulterer on drugs. We have to get to know each other.' " He reached over and teased an earring dangling from Orna's right lobe. "Is that an Eilat stone?"

Orna yawned and flicked away his hand.

Doctor Carmi drank something and set the paper cup down on a small table. "Give me a break. Do you really think that getting religious and secular kids together to decorate those bombed-out bus shelters is going to fix anything? Calling them sukkot of peace?" He gave a weary roll of the eye.

"It makes people feel hopeful. And what's wrong with that?" said Orna.

Dina called out, "They're coming, I hear them!"

The guests craned their necks, and the people by the drinks rushed over to the bride's section. Estrella ululated, and the other Sephardic neighbors joined in, tongues vibrating, deep gurgling howls emanating from their throats.

The sound of singing and stomping feet came closer and closer. "May you rejoice in your beloved as Adam and Eve rejoiced in the Garden of Eden," they sang. The men crossed the patio and moved rhythmically onto the lawn. Mutti was clapping his hands, his eyes open, with only the whites to be seen, his face in ecstasy. Yisrael held up a stick with shiny, colored streamers flying in every direction. Dr. Carmi shuffled along the fringe of the crowd and then he, too, became swept up with the throng of dancing men. The Sephardic women let out another chorus of high-pitched bleating sounds. The other women clapped their hands and looked out with great anticipation, as if they, too, were becoming brides.

The men made their way to the center of the grass mound, in between the two extended lines of women. The crowd parted and Akiva appeared. He wore a trim black suit and his face looked scrubbed and very clean. He walked toward Beth, his steps slow and dreamy.

At last he stood before her. He had arrived. She looked at him. He looked at her. Now what? He was supposed to take the gauzy material of her bridal veil and gently bring it to rest over her face. Instead he just stood there, his hands at either side, staring at her. The singing died down. It was absolutely still and quiet except for the slight swaying of the trees.

It was a simple look he gave her. Here I am. Here you are. Beth nodded. His muscles clenched in his face and shoulders. His entire body jerked and quivered, followed by a soft hiccup.

The guests stirred uneasily.

With a delicate and sinuous movement of his hands, Akiva pulled the veil over her eyes, while she looked at him, smiling and smiling. There was a rush of motion: The men withdrew, dancing and singing in a more subdued manner, taking Akiva and shuffling away with him as he looked over his shoulder at Beth.

She sat in her gauzy veil, the folds falling lightly on her face and shoulders all the way to her lap. A breeze blew and fluttered it, and she held it down with her hand. Through the fine criss-cross of white, everyone looked exceptionally beautiful. And there were the trees surrounding the guests, the trees nodding and bobbing like favorite uncles, aunts and cousins, the large, extended family she'd never had. And in the distance the Jerusalem hills. She thought of all the times she had eaten in her apartment alone, looking hungrily out at the Jerusalem Forest as if some secret were buried in its rangy hills, in the sunsets, in the evening skies, some God secret that would explain all the things she had wondered about as a child, things she still thought about now. Sometimes when she looked up at a Jerusalem evening sky, it stretched out like some vast exquisite umbrella, the umbrella of Torah under which the whole world huddled. But some part of her always wondered if yet another umbrella was held even higher, above the Torah umbrella, extending farther, explaining even more. Maybe there was another Torah hidden somewhere, the Torah of God's thoughts, before God had to think practically and create a world for people to live in, the Torah that preceded creation. It was that umbrella she wondered about when she felt her heart sucked up in the vastness of a Jerusalem sky. She wondered about these things, and she never wanted to stop wondering. A man's love wouldn't change that. Not a man's love and not the approval of all the people of Jerusalem.

She peered out through the gauzy material and saw the women running from one to the other, whispering in urgent tones. Someone was supposed to place two hands on her head and bless her and then escort her to the chuppah, an act that had always been the privilege of the bride's mother or father. Who would bless her now? She wiped at her eyes with her sleeve. She saw Estrella look at Tsippi, making a motion for her to step forward. Tsippi shook her head slightly, pointing to Akiva's grandmother, that the honor belonged to her. Judy cast the grandmother a meaningful look. The old woman hesitated, then took an awkward step toward the bridal chair, then stopped in confusion.

Beth looked across the lawn at a white tallis draped over four poles and, underneath, Akiva standing, waiting for her. She bent forward, her arms locked around her waist, her head almost touching her knees. A weepy tremor took hold of her, then another, and then she shook herself, snapping out of it. Suddenly she knew who was going to bless her, and she lifted her head. Judy reached under the veil and wiped a smudge of mascara that had stained her cheek. Beth smiled and shrugged away her hand. She gingerly removed the veil's clasp from her hair.

"Bet! What are you doing?" Estrella asked. The women drew closer.

Beth put a finger to her lips. With a duck below her chair, she pulled out the beaded cosmetic bag and fished around inside. Ah! There it was. She drew out a bristle brush and with her other hand she undid the bun at the nape of her neck. Her hair lay in brown twirls against her shoulders, a strand here, a lock there, and she lifted the brush and slowly pulled it through her hair. She began brushing hard. She brushed it shiny, till the strands crackled, till she felt a glow about her head, like a blessing, like the gentlest touch of a hand.

She placed the veil back on her hair, rearranging the folds over her face. Then she stood and stared out at all the friendly, solemn eyes that were turned toward her. They're happy for me, she thought, they've been rooting for me all these years, with their annoyance and their advice and their love.

"Hold my hands!" Beth called loudly.

Immediately, two lines of women formed from where she stood, their arms interlocking, their hands clasped. Zahava, at her left, held on to her hand, and Orna held hers, and she in turn gave her hand to Estrella, who reached out to Judy, who held Miri. Beth extended her arm to Akiva's grandmother at her right, who grasped Tsippi's hand, who held Naomi's, who in turn held Dina's, on and on, till all the guests were joined, making a huge capital **V** of women.

Beth swung her arms, and a wave of arms rocked with her.

"Don't let go!" she cried to the women. "You're all coming with me!" Hands tightened. Cheeks flushed. She drew in a breath. As one, the women stepped forward.